James,

# Murder Gone Missing

# A Southern California Mystery

*Every good wish,*

*Lida,*

*Sideris*

Copyright Page

Murder Gone Missing
A Southern California Mystery

First Edition | February 2018

Level Best Books
www.levelbestbooks.com

Trade Paperback ISBN: 978-1-947915-04-6
Also Available in e-book

Printed in the United States of America

To MomV who encouraged me to write a mystery she'd like to read.

## CHAPTER 1

## NIGHT MOVES

I cut the headlights and turned onto Lunada Bay Road. Fog crept around the hilly street, clasping hands with the darkness. I could barely see more than a few feet ahead.

I eased my foot off the accelerator and parked two houses away from my target. I slipped into sneakers stored in the backseat of my car. Handy for walks on the Hermosa Beach Strand, undercover work, and kicking in doors, which I had yet to do, but there was always hope. I still wore my black pants and matching silk blouse from my day at the office. It would be easy to disappear into the night. There were six houses on the quiet cul de sac and not a streetlamp in sight.

A cool breeze whipped my hair across my face as I tiptoed across the short cement driveway. I'd waltz in and out of the place in less than ten minutes. The sliding glass door in the family room never latched quite right and hadn't since I graduated high school nearly a decade ago. The slider sat on a small balcony, just low enough for an amateur gymnast like myself to climb up and over. The master bedroom was at the opposite end of the Spanish style home, so the chances of being caught were nil. Plus, the occupant took her beauty sleep seriously.

I edged toward the side of the garage and unlatched the tall wooden gate leading to a trash area concealed by six-foot high stucco walls. In slow motion, I up-ended a plastic receptacle, climbed atop, and pulled myself onto the wall. I straightened, balancing like a tightrope walker, and leapt onto the side balcony, toes between slats, holding onto the wooden rail for dear life. My moves were awkward, but they got me there. I hoisted myself over the balustrade and landed in a huddle. I stood and grabbed the slider handle. I pulled it up and toward me, but the door wouldn't budge.

"Arggggh."

There was a trick to this, but what was it? Jiggling the handle? Pulling it down first? My ears perked. I crouched down low.

A light tapping sound, faint at first, grew louder. Closer. Footsteps. Someone was on the driveway. My mind fumbled over excuses for being on the balcony this time of night, but I didn't need any. The taps faded. Before I could stand, they grew loud again. And faster. They stopped closeby. I held my breath.

The gate to the trash enclosure creaked open. Months had gone by without my doing anything remotely resembling PI work…until tonight. What were the odds a burglar would strike and use my means of entry?

I heard mumblings, and a male voice spitting out a rush of words.

"Pick up, pick up. Where are you?" A whisper rattled my side of the night.

Who was he calling? A cohort? I lifted my eyes. I spied the intruder's head and shoulders in the enclosure. Dark waves of hair bristled in random directions. The light of his smart phone made his profile glow. I recognized the ski-slopey nose and jumped to my feet. "Michael," I whispered.

He turned abruptly, dropped his phone, and stumbled, sending a trashcan crashing to the ground. The light turned on in the house next door. A window slid open. Michael ducked and so did I. A moment later, meows howled from the trash area, breaking the silence. I stifled a snicker. Michael did a fine impression of a soulful cat. Throaty meows grew louder, followed by a final meow at a higher pitch. The window slammed shut and the room went dark. We got to our feet at the same time.

"Don't you want to finish your song?" I asked.

"I can't remember the rest of the words." He stared at me, hazel eyes open wide. His breath escaped in short bursts. "I've been calling you all day, Corrie. Why are you sneaking around your mom's house?"

"I could ask you the same." In my case, it kept my breaking and entering skills from getting rusty. And she had something I needed. Something she didn't need to know about. "What are you doing here?"

"Looking for you. Everywhere. I went to your place. Called your office. Your cell. You didn't answer."

"It's on mute," I said.

We spoke in fast whispers, playing catch-up to make sense of this odd rendezvous. Michael and I had been best friends since junior high.

We'd spent a lot of quality time together lately, solving a homicide, but I hadn't heard from him in days.

"Don't you ever keep the ringer on? What if there's an emergency? Like now."

"You okay?" I asked him.

He turned and eased out of the enclosure. He shut the gate and tiptoed closer, until he stood below the balcony, head tilted back. "I am not okay," he whispered, moonlight in his hair. "I'm terrible." Beads of sweat splashed across his forehead. "I'm worse than terrible."

"Hold on." I threw a leg over the balustrade and dropped to the ground. At six feet, he had a few inches on me. His face was pale, his mouth hung open, and his gray dress shirt clung to his skin. I'd never seen him so distressed. "Wait a minute. This is serious. Talk to me."

"I'm not sure what happened. I marched into his office to tell him he was wrong." Michael spoke at an unnaturally high pitch. "He *was* wrong." His next words shot out in a stream. "It shouldn't have happened. I really messed things up. We gotta go." He grabbed my hand and turned to leave, but I stood firm. I looked up at the neighbor's window next door. No sign of life.

"Go where?" I asked. "Is there a problem at school?" Michael was co-associate dean at a small private tech college in Los Angeles.

"I'll say there is. Today, President MacTavish asked to see me. To tell me I was demoted. Without explanation. To junior faculty advisor. Effective immediately. I was stunned and...mad. I wanted to punch him in his...in his..."

"Why would he demote you out of the blue?" I inched toward the street, Michael by my side.

"Ever since I started this job, he's had it out for me. Of course, he has it out for everyone. He told me I was a weak, pathetic excuse of an associate dean who should never have gotten the job in the first place."

"How awful."

"I stormed off and wrote a letter of resignation. It was a good one, too. I poured out all my feelings. The demotion made zero sense...it wasn't right, Corrie."

"It sure wasn't. Not with your know-how and credentials." Michael had been a computer science professor at a big-name private tech college on the East Coast before taking this job.

"My demotion makes Alyce sole associate dean, and leaves me out in the cold."

Michael had mentioned Alyce before, and never in a flattering way. "She's your co-dean?"

"*Was* my co-dean. I can't believe it. I went back to Mac's office later. He was sitting at his desk when I went in. I told him how I felt. Got everything off my chest." Michael squeezed shut his eyes and flipped them open. "But then I had to call a timeout."

We'd reached the street. "He refused to talk to you?"

"You could say that. He was dead."

## Chapter 2

## Night Terrors

I was witnessing a different Michael tonight. Gone was the good-natured guy who didn't have a violent bone in his slim but athletically toned body. Before me stood a man who might consider using force on a case-by-case basis. Had I been a bad influence on him? A mild breeze rustled the fronds on a nearby palm tree. The chilly night yawned and moaned around us. Or maybe the moan came from me.

"Oh, dear goodness. I'm so sorry," I said. "Let's go inside Mom's and sit down. We'll use the front door this time."

"No, we can't. We've gotta go back to the crime scene."

"What crime scene? He was an old guy, wasn't he? He probably died of a heart attack."

"Trust me. He didn't die of natural causes."

"What? How do you know?"

He gulped. "I'll explain on the way." He darted toward his car. "Hold on." Michael stopped and turned to me. "I interrupted you. What were you doing?"

"Nothing that can't wait."

"You weren't going to—"

"Course not." I turned and headed to the road, Michael at my heels. Truth is, I *was* going to. Break into Mom's house, that is. She'd left me no choice. It's what any red blooded, fashion conscious, newly minted lawyer would do when she worked in a movie studio and had nothing to wear. Mom was the senior buyer of designer collections at Saks Fifth Avenue. She'd attached a padlock on her closet door after I'd borrowed a few items and returned one with a small stain...and another with a rip in a seam. My work required a high-end wardrobe. Competence and clothes were valued equally in the entertainment industry. The last time I was at Mom's, the padlock had gone missing. But so had her choice wardrobe pieces. Tonight's plan was to sneak in, locate the new hiding spot, and borrow an item or two. I'd return them before she noticed. And we'd live happily ever after.

"Let's take my car." Michael's hand dug into his pockets. A thin black wallet tumbled out, followed by the clang of the car key.

I grabbed the key. "I'll drive."

Within minutes, I'd angled behind the wheel of Michael's BMW and aimed toward the 405 freeway. He was in no shape to drive. Even in his normal state, he motored like a geriatric on sedatives. Plus, I loved driving his M3. It was an older model, but it chewed up the asphalt and spit it out behind us.

"Tell me what happened." I sped through a red light. I'd slowed and checked the intersection before hurling through, but Michael bolted upright, his shoulders shot up to his ears. One hand gripped the top of the dash, the other the parking brake. "Let go of the brake, Michael." I uncurled his fingers, but he held on to my hand. "Talk to me."

He sucked in a breath. "I spent hours trying to cool down and finally went back to Mac's office. To give him my resignation letter. It was mostly dark when I got there. I couldn't find the light switch. That's what anger does to a person, makes a simple task impossible. I thought about turning on the lamp. But I didn't know if he'd get mad—"

"Focus."

"Right. I could barely see his silhouette sitting in the chair behind his desk. A light was on outside his window. He was leaning off to one side like he was reaching down for something on the floor. I told him what he did was unacceptable. I was so beside myself, I nearly knocked over this ugly orange lamp—"

"Harmless move."

"It gets worse." Michael leaned forward, one eye on me, and the other on the lumbering freeway traffic. "I walked toward him. Instead of handing him my letter of resignation, I crumpled and threw it at him. To show him I meant business. It landed in his lap. I expected him to explode, but he didn't flinch. He just kept right on leaning. I told him the demotion was uncalled for. That he could take my letter and shove it up his beef jerky butt. He didn't say a word. That wasn't like him. He was always blowing hot air. So I moved closer. That's when I saw it. Gleaming."

"What gleamed?"

"The knife in his back."

"What? Are you sure? Did you call the police?"

"No."

"How could you not call the cops?"

He swallowed his Adam's apple and turned to face me. "I panicked. I backed away and bumped into the desk. I thought someone was standing behind me, so I jumped. The next thing I knew, I landed in Mac's lap. I scrambled out, knocking over a table and a plant on the way. I kept running 'til I got to my car."

"Are you sure he was dead?"

Michael gulped. "His hand was so cold. He was staring out. Not blinking..." He covered his eyes with a hand. "Corrie, there's a killer on the loose. And I didn't call the cops." He grabbed his phone. "Because..."

"Yes?"

"Of the resignation letter."

"Nothing wrong with resigning."

Michael gulped. "It said more than 'I resign.'"

"It said you were leaving the school?"

He shook his head.

"That he was a demented old fool?"

The next words spilled out, "I said I'd kill to keep my job." Michael groaned and held his head in his hands.

"Oh, no." I eased off the freeway and pulled onto the shoulder of the road. I turned toward Michael. His handsome face had given way to despair. "For such a smart guy, that was a dumb thing to do."

"How was I supposed to know he'd get himself stabbed in the back? That's when I called you."

"Did you call James?"

James Zachary was Michael's other best friend. He was also the hottest assistant district attorney in Orange County, and maybe any county or even any continent, for that matter. James had helped me big-time with the homicide at the studio where I worked. The fact that Michael and James had both been part of that mix left me...with mixed feelings.

"A DA's the last person I'd want to call after messing with a crime scene. Besides, you're the daughter of the world's greatest PI."

My father had been gone nearly a year. A father I'd hardly known outside of time spent together trailing suspects, testing my crime scene knowledge, or target practicing at his indoor shooting range. "A PI who's no longer around."

"I didn't mean—"

"Did anyone see you go into the president's office?" I asked.

"No, well...maybe. I don't know."

"Before we call the cops, we need to get your letter. And clean things up. Not necessarily in that order. We'll call afterward."

Fifty traffic-infested minutes later, we motored into the faculty lot of Los Angeles Technical University--LA Tech to the homies--where scientific, engineering, and technical overachievers gathered to shine. Michael had an undergrad degree from Princeton and a PhD from Stanford in computer science. He'd landed this gig about the same time I'd landed mine. Almost four months ago. It had been a roller coaster ride for us both ever since.

I parked in the first floor of a multi-level parking structure and turned to Michael. "Ready?"

He nodded and slipped on a jacket. We stepped out into the cool night. Cars whizzed past on Los Angeles Boulevard. The odor of escaping exhaust mingled with the scent of kitty litter, courtesy of droppings from a towering Jacaranda tree. A cloud of purple flowers haloed its branches; sticky petals and crushed brown pods lay pasted onto the concrete sidewalk. I shivered, but not for long. Michael eased my arms into a blue sweatshirt. The gold lettering across the front paid tribute to my alma mater, UCLA. He zipped me up.

"Thank you," I said. Even in his flustered state, he was thoughtful.

"Thank James. It's his sweatshirt. He threw it in my trunk after our last video game extravaganza. I forgot about it. Until now. But Corrie?" Michael squeezed my shoulders and managed a small smile. "Thank you."

"I haven't done anything yet."

"But you always do. And you dropped breaking into your mom's to help me." We walked side by side.

"That's what best friends do," I said. "More than best friends do that kind of stuff, too." Uh-oh. I was overcomplicating things. "Glad to help."

"This way," Michael said. He headed toward the street.

The campus sat nestled between stately manor homes and the looming shadow of the San Gabriel Mountains, ten minutes from downtown L.A. I tossed a look behind me to memorize where we'd parked in case we needed a fast exit. The structure's rooftop was a dead ringer for an airport hangar. That's what I told Michael.

"Those are solar panels." He dragged his sneakers. "Did you have to say *dead*?" His brows crumpled together, carving twin worry lines between them. "I can't go back in there."

"Don't go all Cowardly Lion on me. Be the king of beasts. If you're caught in a trap, gnaw off your paw and keep moving."

Michael straightened his shoulders. "You're right. I'll start gnawing."

"Inhale confidence. Exhale fear."

We dropped all talk and crossed the street, turning onto a garden path, past time-honored, white washed buildings housing classrooms and labs. The campus was tiny compared to UCLA's sprawling four hundred acres. I'd heard the student population at LA Tech hovered around two thousand. No chance of getting lost in the crowd.

We tramped across a dry patch of lawn and through a stark arcade. Michael paused by a pillar and pointed to a short flight of stairs leading to the Hall of Administration.

"He's in there," Michael said.

The entry was guarded by black iron gates flanked by stone columns. Elaborate shell and floral volutes topped the columns. The building belonged in the Getty Villa not a college campus.

"Are those gates locked?" I asked.

Michael's mouth nearly touched my ear, spreading goose bumps beneath my sweatshirt. "See that small black box on one side? That's a security door reader. I can swipe us in, but let's go stealth instead. We don't want to chance being seen. Come on."

I tailed his crouching figure across the lawn. We'd barely turned the corner of the Admin Hall when the front gate swung open. I paused mid-flight. A woman skipped down the concrete steps, smooth blonde hair flying behind her. She wore a short black dress that hugged her waist and flared at the hips. A bank of clouds shielded the moon, but enough light shone for me to see her angular face had a masculine touch. Long stork-like legs ended in a pair of ballet flats. What was she running from? Or to?

"Psst! Over here!" Michael surfaced from the shadows in a darkened edge of the building.

I joined him.

"That was her," he whispered.

"Who?"

"Alyce Scerbo. My co-associate dean." He was breathing in short bursts again. "What if she went in to see MacTavish?"

"Why would she?"

"To discuss her new role—"

"At eleven o'clock at night? No. Listen, I need you to be cool. I need you to be awesome."

"Right. I'm fine. But what if she called the police?"

"She was in a casual rush, not the hyperventilating kind of rush when one finds her boss murdered. And if she did call the cops, she'd likely wait for them, not take off."

Michael chewed on my explanation. His frantic blinking slowed. "You're right."

"Now, can you focus?"

"Yes, I can. Corrie, I'm so thankful you're here with me, and that we're going to do our best to stick to the rules 'cause you know I'm not a good law-breaker, even if that's what you do really well, and I sure could use a beer. Preferably on tap, but I'd even take a root beer if there was one."

"Wow. That was really…specific."

"Let's get this over with."

Michael hustled around the perimeter of the Hall. He put on the brakes near a row of neatly trimmed bushes. I followed suit, stepping between the shrubs and onto a strip of dirt beside the structure. Michael knelt beneath a narrow set of double windows with a ledge perfect for cooling fresh baked pies. I could have used a piece of pie. Apple or coconut cream—

"I've got a plan," he said. "The windows—"

"Smashing windows to break in will get us an audience. We don't want that. But we could use James' sweatshirt to stifle the noise—"

"These office windows are mine. They're unlocked. I climbed out this way so no one would see me leave."

"Good call. But don't they open from the inside? How're we getting in?"

"Part of my plan." Michael stood and plucked out a smallish, plastic protractor from the inner sanctum of his jacket. He slid it between the vertical slot of the windows and jiggled.

I looked over my shoulder. The flicker of a high intensity beam broke through the darkness, accompanied by the shuffle of soft rubber soles. The shuffle was uneven, like the walker dragged a shoe along the pavement. The powerful light could mean only one thing. "Hurry, Michael. A flashlight's headed this way."

"What?"

"Campus security on patrol, coming right at us."

"Oh my–"

That's when I heard the protractor snap.

"Abort. Hit the dirt." I grabbed Michael and yanked him down, all six feet of him. We lay on our stomachs behind the bushes bordering the building, his feet near my head. I rested my chin against my fist and waited.

The odd shuffling grew louder. I tracked the beam of light in my vision until it stopped, near enough for me to hear coarse breathing. And sniffing. Damn my perfume. If I could smell the smoky vanilla and citrus, so could he. He shifted off the concrete and onto the grass. A twig cracked beneath his feet. The light shone close to my shoes.

A rapid tap, tap, tap of heels tripped into the scene. "Hey!" a raspy female voice called. "I need to get into the Admin Hall."

"Is this an emergency?" the guard asked.

"Yes."

"A matter of life or death?"

"It is important. It could be a mind-changer. I need to deliver this letter to the president. Tonight."

"Come back during the week. The building opens at seven."

"I need to do it now." Her heels pranced closer to the security detail. The heavy scent of gardenias wafted toward me. "The co-associate dean of the computer science department was fired today."

I heard a snort from Michael. I jerked his pant leg to remind him to stay silent.

"It was so wrong." Her tone went up a notch. "Michael Parris has helped me and many other students. This letter explains why the president needs to retract the termination. I've been in the library for hours composing it."

"Not tonight. It's late. And I'm on an assignment. Besides, President MacTavish is not in right now. You'll have to wait."

She swore. "That is cold. Well, how about walking me to my dorm? Or do I have to wait for that, too? I do not do well on moonless nights."

"What are you, a werewolf?" the security guard asked with a snicker.

"Forget it." She stomped off.

"Hold on." The light switched direction, and the security detail shuffled after her with his lopsided gait.

I waited until the hum of nearby traffic was the only sound and jumped to my feet. "Bullet dodged." I brushed the dirt and leaves from my front side. "You can get up now. Michael?"

He slowly rose to a kneeling position and turned to sit on his bottom. "Great. She thinks I was fired."

"Was she someone you know?"

"Her voice was familiar. I had a lunch meeting last week with members of student government. It might have been Loretta, the student body president." Michael got to his feet. "Even she knows the president was wrong. I don't know if I can go back in there."

"Yes, you can. We're sticking to your plan, remember?"

"The plan was to climb in through this window, sneak upstairs, grab my resignation-slash-hate note, clean up, and leave. But that was before I realized how complicated this is."

"Do you have the knife I gave you?"

A few months ago, we'd practiced throwing sharp objects to the dartboard hanging on my living room wall. Just for fun. Objects like knives and Japanese throwing stars, otherwise known as shuriken, my favorite weapon of choice. Michael couldn't get the shuriken down, but knife throwing was in his league. I gifted him with a three-inch blade to use in case of an emergency.

"Well?" I crossed my arms against my chest.

He reached inside his jacket and pulled out the knife.

"Why use a protractor to break in when you have that?"

Michael rose to his feet. "I was trying to open the window without leaving any marks. Otherwise, my office could be branded as the exit point for the real killer when it was me leaving."

The glow from dim lamplight illuminated twigs and leaves lodging in his thick, dark hair. Considering he wasn't the daughter of a famous private investigator, harbored an aversion to weaponry, and lacked a covert mind, he made perfect sense.

"Good point. Let me think." My fingertips brushed along the edge of the casement window. "The window isn't locked, but it pushes outward. We need something softer than metal to slide underneath, like your protractor before it snapped." I scanned the greenery around us. "Find me a twig."

"What kind of twig?"

"A sturdy one. With an equally sturdy prong."

Michael waded through the shrubs and onto the path. I shielded my knuckle with a rubbery leaf from a nearby magnolia tree, and pressed it against the window, hoping it would spring back. It didn't. I used the leaf to push against the edges of the window, to loosen things up. Still nothing.

"How about this?" He held out a twig about an eighth of an inch in diameter and three inches long. One stubby arm stuck outward.

I tried inserting the twig into the horizontal crack of the window, but the twig was too fat.

"Try this." Michael held out a slimmer one. His other hand held similar specimens.

I stuck the next twig under the window, prong sideways. I twisted it upward, so the prong lay against the window. I gave a firm pull. The window pushed out, nearly smacking me in the face.

My private investigator genes were thriving after all.

"Cool. That was so MacGyver-ish. Let me give you a hand, my lady."

He gave me a leg up and I slid in, thighs scraping against the rough sill. I landed on the hardwood floor. Michael followed close behind. The small space reeked of shoe polish and salsa. Michael polished his Oxfords weekly, and salsa was a favorite snack. An empty bag of chips sat in the trash basket. I spied paperclips on his desk. Paperclips were useful for all sorts of things: hiding bra straps, opening envelopes...and picking locks. I plucked up two of them and followed him out.

Michael took the lead down a shadowy corridor, up a staircase, and down another hallway. We stopped in front of a closed door, marked *Office of the President.*

"Open it," I said.

"I don't have a key."

"How did you get in before?"

"It was unlocked."

"Try it."

"You try."

"Your fingerprints are already on it. And you know your way around."

"I tripped my way around. Besides, I'm feeling traumatized all over again."

"Michael, you–"

Hearing the rattle of a cart echo at the far end of the corridor, we both reached for the doorknob. Our fingers fumbled and twisted together.

"Ow!" Michael mouthed after I slapped his wrist with my free hand. "It's locked."

I pulled out the paperclips. I'd never actually broken in this way, but I'd watched Dad and it looked fairly easy. I shaped one into a hook and straightened a portion of the other into a line.

Michael leaned against the wall, providing a barrier between the approaching cart and me. I inserted the clips into the keyhole, raking and slipping them in and out several times, pushing up and down. I turned the knob. No give. I raked again, quicker this time.

"Hurry."

"Am I not going fast enough for you?" I gritted my teeth and pulled out the clips. I reshaped them and inserted again. In, up, pull out, and we stumbled forward into the office. I closed the door behind us and pressed my back against it. Michael's sneakers were rooted to the dark wood floor in front of me. I surveyed the scene.

White acoustic tiles crowded the ceiling; fluorescent lights running near the center lit the tidy, wood-paneled office. Framed battle scenes stamped the walls. A massive bookcase lined the back section, housing thick volumes. On the wall next to the bookcase hung an old clock with roman numerals and a swinging pendulum. A large oriental carpet spread across the floor, providing the only splash of color.

"It wasn't like this when I left," Michael said.

"I don't see—"

"Oh, my God."

## CHAPTER 3

### MISSING IN INACTION

"He's gone." Michael stared at the empty leather chair behind the oversized desk. The chair swiveled slightly toward the window, as if the occupant leisurely stood and left to go home for the evening. "Mac's disappeared." Michael dashed around the room like a ball launched in a pinball machine. "This plant..." He pointed to a tall, ornamental fig roosting by a shuttered window. "I accidentally knocked against it, spilling potting soil on the floor. I thought of how mad Mac would be at the mess...if he wasn't dead." Michael gulped and pointed to a small side table. "That table was knocked over. It's all been cleaned up. Like it never happened."

I stepped forward and scanned the area around the chair. "A knife wound means bleeding. There should be signs of blood here."

Michael came up next to me. I think I heard his teeth chattering.

"Try to remember what this place looked like before you left," I said. "Was his desk clean or messy?" I surveyed the mostly barren desktop. Nothing but a pen and a photo of a dog with white curls and dark, soulful eyes.

"Mac was a neat freak. Everything had to be in its place or else."

"What was he wearing when you found him?" If I got Michael to focus, he might remember something important.

"A polka dot bow tie and dark blue suit. He looked normal. Except for the knife in his back."

"You're sure he was dead and not wounded?"

"Very sure. Besides, the icy skin and blank stare, he..." his voice trailed to a whisper.

"Yes?"

"Blood was dripping down the side of his mouth."

"Oh." I'd seen that before at a crime scene. A person might bleed from the mouth if a lung was punctured.

"And there was blood all over his chair."

I ran my hand against the smooth, black leather. It was clean. "What kind of knife?"

"One with a long, white handle. Like the kind you use to carve a turkey."

"Did you touch it?

"No. I would never. I can't believe he was…murdered. And that someone came back after I left and cleaned everything up. Who would do that?"

"You mean besides the killer?"

"I should call the police now, right? The murder trail's getting colder by the second."

"Give me a minute. This is not my first post-mortem, tampered-with crime scene." I felt certain the body snatcher had forgotten something. "Check the area around the desk."

Michael edged forward and eyed the floor. He knelt and ran his fingers along the grainy wood. I scrambled over to a pair of tall casement windows behind the desk and turned the crank mechanism. They creaked and opened outward to ninety degrees. I stuck my head out into the crisp night. A waist-high, black iron railing bordered a narrow balcony. There was barely enough room for me to fit. It looked like a fifteen-foot drop to the ground.

"The floor's clean," Michael said. "White glove test clean. Don't you think that's suspicious?"

I rejoined Michael. He crawled around the desk's border. "I do," I said. "Janitorial crews are notorious for minimal cleaning efforts. At best, they empty the trash and wipe easy-to-reach surface areas. Floor polishing is not in their repertoire. Especially a wood floor where dirt and dust are hardly visible."

"Not a stray staple or piece of lint in sight."

I searched beneath the desk. The floor had been wiped, if not polished. I squinted. Lounging against one desk leg lay a strand of long blonde hair. I picked it up.

He crawled over to me. "It's Alyce's."

"Or it could belong to another blonde. What do you know about Alyce?"

"We were hired at the same time to see who'd be better able to take over the computer science department after six months. We're supposed to work together, but she keeps bailing on projects and leaving me to finish. That's what I've been doing the past few days. Which means she had plenty of time on her backstabbing hands."

"A strand doesn't prove murder. It only means someone with blonde hair was in here. Keep looking." I slipped out of the sweatshirt and dropped it on the desk chair. On the floor next to the bookcase, I spied a pair of tan, suede Wallabees that looked like they'd been carved from a chunk of Parmesan cheese. Must be a favorite shoe of the elderly. I got back down on all fours next to Michael.

We crawled fruitlessly for the next five minutes. I'd never seen such cleanliness. I rose to my feet and peered into a wire mesh basket sitting beneath the desk. An empty sandwich wrapper and foam cup sat near the bottom. Lodged on its side, nestled between the scraps, lay a cigarette butt with a pink lipstick stain. I dropped the cigarette into the pocket of my purse and straightened. I picked up the framed portrait of the floppy-eared dog on Mac's desk. The little guy sat on a small oriental carpet, head slightly tilted, his face smothered in curly white hair. Near the desk sat two small chrome dog bowls. One was empty. The other held water.

"Was Mac a dog lover?" I asked.

Michael straightened up. "Dog lover? That man was a soul crusher and spirit mangler. That went for humans and animals." He stared at the photo. "Ah, isn't Leopold cute? He's new around here. A long-time donor dropped Leo off last week and put Mac in charge of him. The donor said Leo was an excellent judge of character and if he didn't take to Mac in two weeks, no million-dollar endowment. Leo went missing yesterday afternoon."

"Missing as in...?"

"He vanished. That's how my morning started. Mac asked what I knew about Leo," Michael said. "Then he accused me of hiding him. He said he didn't like my idea of a practical joke. But I didn't take Leo."

"Why would he blame you?"

"Maybe because Mac was a paranoid lunatic when he wasn't playing tyrannical school ruler."

"Any idea where Leo could be?"

"I didn't even know he was missing. Only proves he was insane. Mac, that is, not Leo. Wait, maybe he blamed me for Leo's disappearance. That would be just like him. Maybe that was the reason for my demotion. But that's ridiculous."

"It's an odd coincidence," I said and looked around the office. "There are no photos of your boss around here. What did he look like?"

"Picture Moby Dick with a mop of white hair, glasses, and an expression that looks like he's sucking a sour lemon."

"So he's a big guy." I stepped over to a window. "How would the killer get a large body out?"

"You think Mac's still here?" Michael's head turned toward a closet door pressed inside a wall. He padded over. His hand shot out, pausing mid-air, an inch from the knob.

"Go ahead." I moved behind him.

"What if he's—"

"There's only one way to find out."

Michael's hand whipped out and latched onto the knob. He gave it a quick turn and pulled it toward him. We leaned forward and peered into the dark space. Jackets, a black overcoat, and a graduation cap and gown occupied the confines. Three pairs of shoes rested on the floor.

"Nothing. That's good. But not really." He turned to me. "Because we still got nada."

I took his hand. "We'll get through this. You have no reason to be nervous."

"Who me? Nervous?"

"Your hand's a little moist."

"Finding Mac dead and knowing there's a killer on the loose...I'm terrified. More than a little."

"Let's keep our heads and we'll figure this out. See how calm I am?" I unclenched my teeth.

The old clock by the bookcase chose that moment to chime. I turned and kicked out, knocking over a chair.

Michael slammed the closet door and slid next to me. "Are we still calm?"

"Damn straight." I slowed my breath. "Okay, let's scram. Cool and calm, all the way."

A dull rattle came from the hallway, the sound we'd heard earlier. A cart creaked to a stop outside the door to the office. A pair of keys jangled in the lock. I swallowed. "Remember what I said about staying calm? Forget it."

# CHAPTER 4

## CLOSE QUARTERS

I stood in the dark, claustrophobic, musty smelling space, with no means of escape, next to a man I liked immensely and was possibly in love with, and waited for the janitor to make his entrance. Michael and I faced each other, chest-to-chest in Mac's closet, all cozy, except for the clothes hangers jabbing our sides and shoulders, and men's shoes wedged beneath our feet. But that didn't stop the small electric current running through my heart.

"He might destroy evidence," Michael whispered in my ear.

"What happened to the note?"

"Huh?"

"Your resignation letter. The one you tossed on his lap."

Michael opened his mouth and wheezed.

"Never mind," I whispered. "We'll deal with that later."

The office door clicked open. The cart rolled in, wheels rattling. My fingers tensed and relaxed.

"You're not exactly alone in here," Michael whispered when my fingertips grazed his vitals.

"Sorry." I was close to becoming unhinged. What happened to my simple night of breaking into Mom's house to borrow a few clothes?

We heard the rustle of plastic, and the slap of the metal wastebasket onto the floor. The janitor would be gone momentarily, right? He probably had one foot hanging out the door. I waited, palm pressed against the doorknob.

The cart rattled again. A screw must have come loose because the rattling grew louder.

"Corrie," Michael whispered into my ear. His breath was hot and moist. "He's coming closer."

My hand gripped the knob, my heartbeat topped the charts. Beads of sweat ran between my breasts.

The cart quieted at the same time the knob in my hand turned left and right. I pulled it toward me. Michael's damp grip slammed down on mine. The janitor was no quitter. Maybe the cleaning skills were slack, but the grip was firm. The door shuddered in protest as the tug of war grew stronger.

My hand slid off the knob, taking Michael's with it. Darkness rolled into light.

"What do you think you're doing?" I asked. That was the best I could do, given the circumstances. I stepped out into the open, Michael by my side.

A tall, husky man stood gaping. Wispy gray hair fanned the sides of his head and a clump of the same sat on his scalp. He wore a baggy blue polo shirt and jeans. Wide, dark eyes flicked between Michael and me.

"How…how did he know I was going to…is that why you're here?" he asked.

Emboldened by his stammering, I advanced. The thin odor of weakness escaped from this fellow, overpowering the smell of cleaning agents coming from his cart. If he thought he was in the wrong, and not the two of us who happened to be hiding in the closet where we shouldn't be, who was I to argue? "Yes."

"What does he expect?" the man asked. "After the way he treats everybody." He peered at Michael. "You're not going to tell him, are you? Look what he did to you."

"I…yes," Michael replied. "Or no, I mean. How can I possibly tell him after what he did to me? By the way, how do you know about that?"

"About your demotion? Big Mac held a press conference with the school paper this morning."

"Before telling me?" Michael stepped forward. "Was I the last to know?"

"Looks that way," he said.

I had to act fast before the janitor figured things out. "Since Big Mac is so abominable, we won't say anything to him about what you were going to do."

"That's a relief," the janitor said.

"What's your beef with him?" I asked.

"I took this job six years ago to meet the people who could get me into this school, without my actually having to apply."

"Like in *Good Will Hunting*?" Michael said. "You wanted a professor to take you under his wing?"

"Exactly. Sort of. If Matt Damon's character was nearing retirement, didn't drink so much, and had less hair, he could have been me. It's been my lifelong dream to get into this college. Two faculty members wrote letters on my behalf. They believe in my quantum negativity theory."

"But MacTavish didn't…" I prompted.

"He said I needed a high school diploma. So I got one. I aced night school. I was class valedictorian. Then he told me I needed two more letters of recommendation. I got those too. But Big Mac still wouldn't play ball. He said the admission rules couldn't be bent just because I worked here. Talk about academic elitism."

"That's low," Michael said. He put a hand on the guy's shoulder. "So you killed him?"

"Killed who?"

"He means figuratively," I said. "That's what we…students and faculty do. Big Mac is such a pain, we're always talking about creative ways of getting under his skin."

His face broke into a cheeky grin. "I like that."

"That's why you were trying to get into the closet. To…" I started.

"Plant the rats. That's right."

"What?" Michael and I asked in unison.

"Big Mac is a big fan of animal testing. It's just plain cruel. More than a hundred million mice and rats are killed every year in lab experiments. They're abused and terrorized." The janitor reached into a large paper bag nestled in the bottom of his supply cart and pulled out a thick plastic bag holding two large gray lumps. "Here are two victims I took from a lab. I'm going to stuff his coat pockets with them. To give Big Mac a taste of his own medicine. He puts on that old overcoat every morning when he goes to the faculty lounge. Nothing stinks more than dead rats at sunrise." He opened the bag a smidge. Michael and I turned our noses away from the dirty sock stink reeking from the plastic.

"Brilliant and corrupt at the same time," I said.

"Did you overhear me talking to myself when I was cleaning the faculty toilets last night?" he asked Michael. He took a step toward the closet and reached for the coat. "Is that how you knew I'd be here?"

Michael scratched his head. "Seems like I've heard you in there before. Was that you singing 'Ol Man River'?"

He grinned. "It was. I break out into song to get rid of the tedium. It helps. You sure you're not on his side?" He stuffed each pocket with a rat and turned back to us.

"Okay, look. Here are the facts," I said. "We're here to avenge Michael's demotion."

"What are you going to do?" The janitor turned our way and leaned forward, eyes glittering. His slinky smile befitted a court jester. "Spread jalapeno sauce on the back of his collar? Rig a bottle of laughing gas so it explodes on him? He could use some. Big Mac hasn't laughed a day in his life."

"We're going to slip wet seaweed into his Oxfords so that when he puts them on, he'll find a squishy surprise," I said.

Michael turned to me. "We were?" He looked at the janitor. "I mean, yes, we're going to stuff seaweed in his Oxfords. It's in my office. In seawater to keep it fresh."

The janitor pumped his fist. "His feet'll be slimed!"

"Did…I mean, does Big Mac have any friends?" I asked.

"Not here, he doesn't."

"How does he stay in power?"

"Students flock to this campus from around the globe because of the school's reputation. They don't have much contact with him. The Board of Directors needs Big Mac for his intimidation skills. He's really good at harassing donors into writing fat checks. I know. I clean the boardroom after meetings. And…" He leaned toward us. "I can hear every word when I polish the doorknob in the hallway."

"He treats everyone like dirt under his feet," Michael said.

"Sometimes I feel like a soup can tied to a rear bumper, left to clang the whole honeymoon drive," he said. "And then chucked in some God-forsaken dumpster. We're all dented soup cans to him."

"Man, I hate dents." Michael whipped out his wallet. He removed a business card and handed it to the guy. "You and me, we're in the same boat, or closet, so to speak. This is our little secret. Maybe we can help each other. Not that we need to, but if the occasion should arise..." Michael stretched out his arm.

"Ian Blotter." He shook Michael's hand. "Forever school janitor, if Big Mac has his way." He dug into a pocket and handed me his business card. "I always keep these handy. I do butlering on the side. Or it is buttling?"

"Maybe you can still get in," Michael said. "Mac may be in for a short—"

My elbow jammed against Michael's abdomen.

He coughed. "Ahem, a shock, he's in for a shock after your rat attack and our seaweed surprise. It might change things. People can change."

Ian threw a calloused hand at us. "Not him." He took his place behind his cart and shook his head. He wheeled his cart out of the office and into the dim corridor. "He'll be a dirty rat until the day he dies."

## CHAPTER 5

### MISSING SOME BODY

"So we broke into the president's office," I said. "And were busted. Ian's not going to squeal."

We'd nearly reached Palos Verdes with me behind the wheel again. I couldn't trust Michael to motor more than fifteen miles per hour. He was that preoccupied. We'd spent most of the ride coming up with theories about the missing body, none of which made sense. Now we turned to the topic of laws we'd broken.

"I can't believe Mac's dead. Not just dead. Murdered." Michael's voice went up a notch. "And missing. This is the part where I call the police. Something I should have done already."

"Wait. Just a bit." I shivered and rubbed a hand along the top of my opposite arm. "Let's think things through more carefully." Especially now that Ian had caught us in the office.

"How would I even explain tonight?" Michael asked. "An after-hours raid of the crime scene by the recently demoted ex-co-associate dean?"

"The killer brought the knife with him," I said. "Why?"

"I don't think he was thinking of carving a roast."

"Maybe it was meant to threaten Big Mac. To get him to do something."

"And Mac refused, which would be just like him. Maybe it was a robbery gone bad."

"After he stabbed Big Mac, the killer left the office—"

"He could have been hiding in there when I went back."

"Or he could have gone to enlist help to dispose of the body, and returned while you were out looking for me. That would explain the unlocked office door when you went in with the resignation letter."

"The letter! Holy smoke. Where is it?" Michael said.

"Whoever took the body must have it."

"That letter could put a noose around my neck."

"This isn't Dodge City," I said.

Michael turned to me. "Do you think Ian saw us breaking in?"

"He would have said something or given himself away. I noticed a pair of ear buds in the tray of his cart, plugged into his phone. He'd probably been listening to music or singing along, and not primed to keenly observe or hear."

"Good. I mean, good for us."

"Yet he didn't ask how we got in, either."

"Holy moly."

I pulled onto Mom's street and parked. "Any chance the killer could have escaped with Big Mac out the second story window?"

"No way to squeeze him through. Unless…you think he was chopped up? Would that take long? There was a lot of Mac to go around."

"Cleanup could take awhile with body parts."

"I won't ask how you know that." He looked down at his hands. "Mac wasn't a nice guy, but murder's a horrible thing. To think there's someone out there—"

"We'll find him."

I started my car and coasted down Mom's street. She was a deep sleeper, but still. I didn't want her to grill me about why I was parked there. She gave the third degree like a hardened police chief. Why did she always assume I was doing something she wouldn't approve of? I just couldn't figure her out.

I hightailed it back to my place, taking Coast Highway. Fifteen minutes later I'd pulled into my garage, gotten out, and waited for Michael outside my unit. I lived in a cozy little bootleg unit a few blocks from the golden sands of Hermosa Beach. If I listened really hard, I could hear the echo of crashing waves in the middle of the night. Like I could now. Michael pulled into my driveway moments later.

We skipped up the staircase to my doorstep. I rummaged through my handbag. My key was MIA.

"Drat. We might have to wait in the great outdoors a little longer than anticipated," I said.

"What do you mean?"

"Can't find my key. Wait." I still had paperclips. "Got a light?"

Michael lifted his smartphone, put it in flashlight mode, and bent over the doorknob. I'd barely shoved in a clip before a high beam illuminated my section of the duplex. We turned and shielded our eyes. A small figure stood on the porch of the back unit.

"What are you trying to do? Burn a hole through us?" Michael asked.

"Who's there?" A perky voice spoke up.

"Miss Trudy? It's me. Corrie."

The night went dark again.

"Who's she?" Michael whispered.

"The landlady."

"How come I've never seen her?"

"She travels a lot. She's a flight attendant," I said.

Twenty paces separated our units, but it took Miss Trudy a full minute to reach us. She stood beneath the top of my stairs and peered up. Her coppery hair was twisted in a jaunty knot at her crown. She still wore her navy uniform and crisp white blouse. Her face was a roadmap displaying the many routes she'd traveled. She didn't look a day under ninety.

"Did she fly with the Wright brothers?" Michael whispered.

"By golly, it is you," she said to me. "It's nearly one o'clock in the morning. You forget your key?"

"Yes, but—"

"I'm coming." She took her time climbing the six stairs to my doorstep. "Stand aside." She put out a hand and lifted a leg.

"Don't you have a spare?" Michael asked.

She dropped her foot and stared up at him. "What do you think this is? A tire store?" She puttered closer to the door and patted the area beneath the knob. "That's it. The sweet spot. Every door has one." She flicked Michael's chest with a back of her hand. "So does every man." She straightened and lifted a low-heeled wedge.

"Miss Trudy, wait." I stepped closer. "Mind if I try? I've always wanted to break down a door. It's on my bucket list."

She tapped Michael on the shoulder and said, "She's the spitting image of me when I was her age."

Michael and I swapped glances. Miss Trudy was blue-eyed, fair-skinned, and petite enough to buy clothes in the children's department if she'd a mind to. I, on the other hand, was five-foot-seven in my stocking feet, my hair was thick and dark, and I could never pull off her tidy hairstyle.

She stepped back and gave Michael the once-over. "You. Give it a whirl. Use your heel and aim below the knob."

"Okay." Michael focused, turned his body sideways, and put up his fists. He kicked out his leg and slammed the spot hard. The door busted open.

"You'll have to pay for that." Miss Trudy tottered away.

We gaped at the opening.

I stepped in and turned on a light. "You just picked up a useful life skill."

Michael stood aglow for a moment before bending over to examine the damage. "Some paint and wood filler will patch this up in a flash." He straightened to look at me. "If I hadn't stewed over the demotion for so long, I might've caught Mac's killer red-handed. Or even stopped it from happening."

"Or gotten yourself killed." I rubbed a hand along his arm. I was glad he was here, with me. I opened my mouth to tell him so, but this is what spilled out: "I'm beat. Want to spend the night?"

"Can I?" Michael stepped inside.

"Sure." I grabbed a blanket and pillow out of the hall closet and shut the door quickly to hide the jumble of towels, sheets, and quilts stuffed inside. No need to cause Michael more alarm. He walked on the tidy side of life. I walked toward the futon. "The futon's not all that comfortable."

"It's perfect. I'll fix up the door."

In ten minutes, Michael hauled up a toolkit from the trunk of his car and patched the damage. A small piece of bare wood lay exposed near the knob, but the lock worked fine. He patted his pockets. "Can I use your phone? Must have left mine in the car."

"Go ahead. It's charging in the kitchen. Be right back." I raced to my room, touched up my makeup, and tidied my hair. I brushed my teeth in lightening speed and hurried to the living room.

"Sorry, Corrie. I ruined your night." Michael sat on the futon.

"*Au contraire*. You stopped me from getting in trouble with my mom."

"Really?" Michael's face broke into the cheery smile I'd missed seeing the past few hours. "We're so…compatible. Must be 'cause you're my oldest friend."

"You've known James since kindergarten," I said. "You and I only met in sixth grade."

"You're my oldest girl friend." His face flushed. "I don't mean that kind, not that you're not that kind or couldn't be…" He cleared his throat. "What I mean is—"

A loud buzz interrupted our near moment of truth.

"Who's that?" Michael's eyes turned round, all blood fled from his face.

I held up a hand and took three long strides to the hall closet. A pocket pistol was stashed in a locked metal box on the top shelf. I unlocked the lid and grabbed it.

"In there." I pointed to my bedroom.

"What are you doing?" His gaze was fixed on the pistol.

"Playing it safe." I held the gun behind me and edged toward the door. I'd shadowed my father enough to still attract attention at odd times by odd people who thought I'd inherited Dad's keen sleuthing skills. Illegal weaponry, yes. Sleuthing skills, not so much. "Who is it?"

"It's me. Open up."

## CHAPTER 6

### THREE'S COMPANY

My grip tightened on the doorknob. I yanked it open. A broad-shouldered man in a white t-shirt and faded jeans stood on the porch. Tousled brown waves framed an absurdly handsome face, jungle green eyes bored right through mine. Two long-necked beers clinked between his fingers. He wore a ridiculous smile reserved for the idiot females that usually clung to him.

"Aren't you going to invite me in?" he asked.

I snapped out of my hot guy stupor and stepped aside.

James' gaze took a leisurely stroll over me. Goose bumps skidded up and down my arms.

"Why is it every time I come over, you've got a gun in your hand?"

"Hey, bro. You've been here before?" Michael asked, walking out of my bedroom.

James had followed me home one night to make sure no bad guys awaited my arrival. He took my safety seriously. More seriously than I did. I'd shown him my gun to prove I wouldn't be bad guy prey. Not easy prey, anyway.

"What are you doing here?" I asked.

James' smile took a hike. He surveyed the futon. A folded blanket and pillow sat at one end.

"You texted me." James turned to face me. "So I came."

"*I* texted *who*?" I stepped closer to James. Why would I text an ADA even if he was Michael's other best friend?

"Is this a joke? You said you'd had a bad day and needed help."

"Uh, that wasn't her." Michael squeezed between James and me. "I used Corrie's cell. But I also said I'd talk to you tomorrow. Did I forget to identify myself? Sorry. It's been a crazy terrible day."

James scowled. "Yeah, well, it sounded serious so I came right away. And I thought she...needed to talk."

My heart beat with the tempo of torrential rain.

James' scowl shot between Michael and me. "What's this about, anyway? You two fighting?" He set the beers down on the coffee table.

"What? No," Michael said. "We don't fight. I mean, we have small squabbles once in a while--"

"Just tell me what you wanted."

"Don't talk to him like that," I said. "He's only trying to—"

"I walked in on my very dead boss," Michael said. "The police might think I killed him, but I didn't."

"You sure she didn't kill him?" James tossed me a look that would melt a glacier.

"No, it was me. I mean, the real killer is on the loose, but they'll think it was me."

"Why would the cops think that? Were you brandishing a serving spoon?" James asked.

"Just because you don't have his sweet cooking skills—" I started.

"You obviously haven't tried my French toast."

"Guys please, we're talking about a murder, remember?" Michael said. "As soon as we figure out where the body—"

"What body?" James asked.

"There's no body," I said. "Couldn't you have just called?"

"Yeah, I could have. I'm outta here." His sneakers forged a path to the door.

"Wait." I don't know why I stopped him. Except we needed a fresh outlook. "Now that you're here, we might as well fill you in."

In two minutes, Michael spilled the events of the day. James listened quietly. Michael punctuated the facts with panic stricken looks and groans.

"This is serious." James glowered at me. "You sure you wiped the place clean after you left? Michael's prints can be explained, but not yours."

"Of course, I'm sure." Why did he care?

"It's bad enough I might have to bail him out, let alone you, too."

"Well, you won't." I might have been grateful for his help, if he wasn't so difficult to get along with.

"I'm leaving. But I want you to think about possibilities," James said to Michael. "There's a solid chance you know the killer."

"I'll make a list of suspects," Michael said. "And keep my knife handy."

James cocked his head in my direction. "Let her do the work. And handle the weapons. Between the two of you, and with a little help from me, we should be able to wrap this up so you're in the clear by tomorrow."

"Can there be a murder charge without a body?" Michael asked.

"Absolutely," James said.

"But only if there's enough circumstantial evidence," I added. No need to worry Michael even more. "And there has to be a significant amount of it for that to happen."

"Without a body, the case is harder to prove," James said.

"And if this is a first time killer, which I happen to think it is if a common carving knife was used," I said, "they're not disposal smart."

"Disposal as in…" Michael started.

"Amateurs tend to make mistakes, as in amateur killers." James shot me a lingering gaze. "And amateur investigators."

I chose to ignore the last comment. I'd show him I had no amateur stripes. At least, I'd do my best to hide them.

"Thanks, bro." Michael gave him a quick embrace. "Thanks for coming."

James patted him on the back and broke away. "Let me think about how to handle this. In the meantime, stay away from the crime scene." James grabbed the beers and exited.

I turned to Michael. The corners of his lips aimed skyward.

"I feel better," he said and turned to me. "I'll be more helpful. I'm going to buckle up and be ready for anything. I'll even bring a crash helmet. Goodnight." He sank onto the futon, dropped on his side, and pulled the blanket over his head. I stared at him a few moments.

"Michael?"

"Uh-huh?"

"Want to talk some more?"

"Hmmm? Now?"

I blew out a huff. "First thing in the morning."

I slinked back into my bedroom and closed the door. I slipped out of my work clothes and rubbed my bare arms to banish the cold. Where was my sweatshirt? The one Michael had loaned me. The one belonging to James. I mentally retraced my steps. Michael gave it to me in the parking lot. I'd worn it when we hit the dirt, and when we snuck into Big Mac's office. But back at the car I'd been shivering.

"Oh no." I'd left it on Big Mac's chair. What a rookie move.

## Chapter 7

### A Covert Operation

It was a simple plan: return to the president's office well before sunrise to retrieve James' sweatshirt. I'd leave a note for Michael with a mild threat of the consequences if he disturbed my slumber. Then I'd slip out my bedroom window and leave Michael thinking I was sleeping in. If I couldn't get inside Big Mac's office, I'd place a call. I still had Ian's business card with his name and cell phone number. I'd tell him the truth: my boyfriend's favorite sweatshirt was left in the president's office. I had to retrieve it, or else. Okay, so it was a half-truth. Maybe even a quarter-truth. But partial-truths are allowed when helping innocent friends, right? Lying can be helpful, if it's for a noble purpose. It would also be helpful if Ian worked on Saturdays and was an early riser. And lived close by, if not on campus. I said a little prayer for myself and for Michael.

My phone alarm woke me a few hours later. Eyes closed, I slipped into black leggings and a hoodie. I opened the door to my bedroom and tiptoed through the darkness. My penlight blazed a path to the futon. I peered down at Michael's back. A shoulder rose up and down; the heavy exhales meant deep slumber. I stood over him until time paused in the hush of the room. If everything went according to plan, I'd be back just as Michael awoke. If I messed up, well, messing up was not an option.

His small, black, rectangular key lay on my kitchen counter. I scooped it up. His car had the parking pass I needed to get into the faculty lot. Parking is always an issue in Los Angeles, even in predawn hours. Plus, taking my car out of the garage would wake him.

I soft-shoed back to my room, jotted down a few words, and taped this note to the outside of my bedroom door:

*Sleeping in. DISTURB AT OWN RISK.*

That would buy me some time. Before Michael would consider waking me, he'd ponder various outcomes of such an action. If he didn't notice his missing car first. I grabbed an oversize handbag, stuffed a few necessities inside, and climbed out my bedroom window.

The sulky morning curled around me, clinging to the darkness. This was the solitary hour before dawn. Friend to sleep, silence, and the sneaky. Cool, misty air swept me down and onto the concrete walkway that ran beside my duplex. I breathed in salt-sprinkled dampness and scurried in a slightly crouched position. Why I crouched, I can't say. It seemed like it lent credibility to a covert escape. Even though I didn't need to be covert. All light sources had been sucked into a low-lying fog hovering just above ground level. A deep blare mimicking the mating call of a lone moose thundered a warning every ten seconds from the Hermosa Pier. There wasn't a foghorn loud enough to wake Michael. I unlocked his car door and slid inside.

My journey took all of thirty-two minutes, thanks to light traffic and my spirited driving. I turned onto Los Angeles Boulevard and spied an entry leading directly to campus. No thought was needed. I kissed the faculty lot goodbye and executed a sharp turn through an open space in a chain-link fence. I motored down a dirt road leading onto an asphalt parking lot. I maneuvered the car between two legs of an H-shaped building, grabbed my handbag, and slipped into the dimness.

My black sneakers plodded through the grass. Unsuspecting koi lurking near the edge of a natural pond splashed their tails, disappearing into the murky water. I avoided well-lit paths to better blend in. If I had black face paint handy, I could really disappear. I was so busy playing like I was invisible I smacked into someone big and bulky.

## CHAPTER 8

## THE INCIDENT AT THE SCHOOL IN THE NIGHTTIME

"It's you," we both said after a small collision that left me rubbing my shoulder.

Ian stared my way, the blast of fresh surprise blotting his face.

"Nice to see you again." I had to conjure up a handy excuse for why I roamed the school grounds this time of morning. Good thing I'd left the black face paint at home. "I'm not used to seeing anyone but campus security on my early morning runs. I'm a student, you know, that's what I do. Run on campus before classes start." Oh-oh. This was Saturday. "And before I do my homework on weekends." A perfectly plausible reason for my overly early return. I waited to see if he could top my explanation.

"No, no, it's my fault. I worked late last night and went home thinking I'd give my car an overdue oil change and call it a day, only to have Squalley call me back to campus. I wasn't expecting that."

"Squalley?"

"Yeah, you know, Pasquale Piccolino, the guy in maintenance. The poor chap that mops the hall floors and fixes broken pipes and leaky faucets. You've probably never even seen his face, have you? He's always looking down." Ian dropped his head and tipped his chin up a moment later. "His tire's flat. I'm going to help him out with a tow."

I considered asking Ian to unlock the president's office door for me, to retrieve the sweatshirt. It would be quicker than attempting a second break-in. "Can you—"

"Can you...?" Ian asked. "Wait. You first. I didn't mean to interrupt."

My little voice told me to walk away. Go home and call the cops. But I had to retrieve the sweatshirt first. "No, you go ahead. Mine's not important."

"I need a favor," Ian said.

"Favor?"

"Just a few."

Was he asking for money? Drugs? Volunteers for a no good, low-down, dirty deed? That would be my best guess. "A few…what?"

"Oh, sorry. It's a bad habit, speaking in phrases instead of full sentences. I do that when I'm nervous. I need a few minutes. Do you have any? On the other side of campus?"

"Why?" Varying scenarios flashed in my mind. All of which involved unwanted physical contact and possible hand-to-hand combat. My fingers crawled under the flap of the purse that hung from my shoulder. My thumb rubbed against the smooth wooden grip of my pistol.

"Well, if you must know, Squalley spent most of the night drinking. He does that when he works ungodly hours. Who doesn't? Ever since Leo was sent over, Big Mac wants the floors cleaned twice daily. Squalley did half yesterday during lunch, and came back later to do the rest. I hurt my back sweeping, so Squalley's helping me out."

That would explain the extraordinary cleanliness of the president's office.

"He'd been working since three in the morning the day before. Big Mac treats Squalley like sh…well, really bad, and this is how Squalley plays it out: a *cerveza* here, another there, and the next thing you know, he's polished off thirteen beers."

"Thirteen?" I loosened the grip on the gun and rested my fingers on the outside of my purse.

"I drove him home and promised I'd come back to get his car. But I need a hand. I'm going to tow it home and fix it later."

Brilliant. I'd help him and he'd owe me a favor.

"My truck's in the faculty lot."

Yet, he was walking in the wrong direction. "Where were you headed?"

"Oh, to convince Bobby to give me a hand without ratting on Squalley. Bobby's security shift is over in a few minutes."

I must have looked puzzled because Ian added, "You know, he's the guy with the limp. I didn't want to ask him, but I had no choice. I'd hoped I'd run into someone I could trust, and there you were."

Yet, he met me less than eight hours ago.

"I know how you feel about Big Mac, that's why I trust you. Bobby's a good guy, but if he reports Squalley, Squalley gets fired for sure. Which would be so unfair." Ian shook his head and latched his gaze onto the pond. "It's Big Mac's fault that Squalley drinks in the first place."

"Let's go."

"Really? That's terrific. But wait." He bit his lower lip.

Now what? I tapped my fingers against my handbag.

"Can you drive a stick shift?"

First of all, why did I need to drive? Second of all, Dad gave me a lesson or two on driving a stick, back in high school. "Sure. Why?"

"You'll need to drive Squalley's car up to my hitch."

"No worries."

"Do you want to ride with me?"

"I'll meet you there."

"Good idea, my truck's no place for a refined young lady. Just follow the main walkway." He pointed to a sidewalk at the edge of the grass. "Through the double arches, toward the library, and make a quick right. Keep going to the end and you'll be in a dirt lot. Mounds of dirt. It's the construction workers' parking area. Squalley's white Honda's in there. See ya." Ian turned and jogged into the final stretch of dark blueness. "Watch out for the drop-off."

"Drop-off?" The campus was flat. Like the world before Columbus. It's not like any cliffs hung around.

My legs sprang to life. It was my turn to hurry. I needed to get back before Michael awoke.

I leapt onto the concrete path, following Ian's directions. A minute later, I spotted the Administration Hall, where the office was housed. I slowed and pondered. I could make a quick right, hop in through Michael's window, pick Mac's lock again, and grab the sweatshirt while Ian was driving to the lot. I slipped into a pair of black gloves and plowed ahead.

I'd barely taken two steps toward the building when I froze. A black iron lamp stood off to one side of the front entry, barely stretching past the first story. To the right of the light, a woman slipped out of a first story window and dropped to the ground.

I ducked behind a pillar. I peeked out between the stucco slats.

Dressed in black from side-pinned beret to sneakers, the woman took off like she was about to cross the finish line in a relay race. Knees high, shoulders back, arms pumping the air, shoes pounding the lawn. A ginger colored ponytail hung behind her. She disappeared into a clump of trees.

I scrambled after her, past the elms perched along the pond. She turned a corner, out of my line of sight. I stopped and listened to flashes of silence between the wail of a siren. No sound of thumping feet. No trace of her. Since the clock was ticking, I returned to the Admin Hall to complete the task that brought me there.

In less than a minute, I'd pulled open one side of her exit window with my fingertips. She'd barely bothered to shut it behind her. I climbed into a compact office, the same size and shape as Michael's, but messier. And smellier. I clapped a hand to my nose. Stale cigarette smoke smothered a slab of air freshener on the sill. I grabbed a couple of paperclips off the floor and dove for the door. It creaked open. I peeked into the hallway. Dimly lit and empty. Just the way I liked it. The whirring of far off machinery crowded out the quiet. I stepped out and glanced back. The wording on the door read:

*Co-Associate Dean*
*Computer Science*
*Alyce Scerbo*

Alyce was the manly blonde I'd seen exiting last night. And Michael's competition, according to him. But she wasn't the one making the getaway just now.

I'd solve that puzzle later. I had work to do.

I mounted the stairs two at a time, sprinted down the hall, and skidded to a stop in front of the president's office. I massaged my forehead. An army of tiny iron soles plodded on the right side of my head. The beginning of a headache. I took a deep breath. Being back in the Admin Hall was so wrong, yet so right at the same time. It was like eating a slice of chocolate cake when I was already full. I didn't need the calories, but the sweetness was irresistible. At least eating cake wouldn't land me in prison. I consoled myself by the fact that I hadn't broken in either time. Michael belonged in the building last night. Maybe we did break into Mac's office. And entry the second time was...well, let's just say I didn't have an invite, but I had no choice. Oh boy. I gritted my teeth and straightened the paperclips.

I'd barely started the jiggle when a high-pitched ping announced the arrival of an elevator car. I leaned back and peered down the corridor. Who comes to the Admin Hall on a Saturday in the wee hours of the morning? Besides me, that is.

I stuck the second clip in and jiggled them both. "Don't look at the elevator. Don't look at the elevator." Last night's refresher course in manipulating locks got me inside at the same time the elevator croaked to a stop. I closed the door, turning the knob to avoid a slam. I entered the dark room and heard a crackle beneath my sneaker. I turned on my penlight. A white envelope rested on the floor, the President's name handwritten across the front. I picked it up. The scent of gardenias invaded my nostrils. Where had I smelled that before? I shoved the letter in my hoodie and quick-stepped toward the desk. A scratching noise stalled my next move.

I spun around. I sucked in a breath and flashed my beam. The doorknob was twitching. In lightening speed, I stood next to the entry, back pressed to the wall, Taser in hand. Possibilities raced through my mind. Was it the killer? Ian? A random student? I waited. And waited.

"What the hell?" I whispered. I could have run two laps around the room while the intruder fumbled with the lock. I couldn't take it anymore. My hand reached out and turned the lock mechanism, Taser raised. The door slowly opened halfway.

With both hands, I shoved the door against the intruder. I plunged forward with the Taser, but I was pushed back. I stumbled onto the floor and rolled away from the attacker. My penlight lit up his penny loafers. I caught a glimpse of a suit and glasses. A faculty member. I jumped to my feet. The beam of his flashlight blinded me.

"I should have known," a familiar voice said. The beam dropped.

My head nearly hit the ceiling. The last person I expected to tangle with tonight was James. "You're tracking me again." My fists rolled into balls. When I was investigating the homicide at Ameripictures' Newport

Beach studio where I worked, he'd slipped a tracking device into my hair clip. The difference was I'd given him permission back then.

"Hardly." He glared down at me.

His effort to blend in the campus scene almost worked, what with the tweed suit, bowtie, and tortoiseshell glasses. But the slight bulge on the left side of his suit jacket wasn't from a stack of student papers. The bulge came from a shoulder holster. He was packing a gun.

"I knew you'd return to the scene of the crime." A smirk landed on his lips. "Criminals do that. So do private investigators."

"Which I'm—"

"Not. I know." He squinted and scoured the room. The scowl never left his face. Nor did it diminish his fine features. "That would make you a criminal."

I squeezed my lips together. I had a lot to say, but not to James. Now or ever. I'd had a crush on him in high school, the kind that sent me primping and preening every ten minutes, but all he did was make fun of my unruly hair and skinny arms. The final straw came at Michael's twenty-first birthday bash when James planted a kiss right where he shouldn't. On my lips. That kiss kicked my crush to the curb. I was not, nor would I ever be, one of his bimbos. I'd kept my distance ever since. With a few exceptions…like right now.

"You're the only person I know who waltzes into a fire instead of trying to extinguish it," he said.

"You got a problem with that?"

"No. I like it."

I meandered around the office and paused in front of the desk, blocking his view to the chair. "Your lock-picking skills are rusty." I edged along the desk, backed into the chair, and grabbed the sweatshirt.

"Why is my sweatshirt draped over that chair?"

I evaded his question with one of my own. "How did you get in the building?"

"Michael told us his window was unlocked. Isn't that how you got in?"

Now I had two questions to dodge. "Of course it is." Not.

James looked like he was about to say something, but instead recalled his scowl.

"Wait," I said, stretching my eardrums. "Do you hear something?"

"Stop it. Just stop it. I'm sick of your distraction tactics."

"You don't hear that?" A low-grade buzz shook the silence, like a small engine running. "Sounds like a motor."

"This whole campus is one big engine noise." He snatched the sweatshirt out of my hands. "Now stay out of my way." In three long strides, he moved toward the desk, squatted, and pulled out a flashlight from the inside pocket of his jacket. He lowered his head to the floor. The slim beam grazed a path beneath the desk legs. A drawer clattered open.

"You told us to stay away from the crime scene, yet here you are," I said.

He ignored me. I shifted my gaze to the windows. The edges of lingering darkness foamed with rose and amethyst. I'd officially run out of time.

"I'll leave this to the only real professional here and get back to Michael."

James scrambled to his feet. "Where are you going?"

"I just told you—"

"Where are you really going?"

"Okay." I pushed out a sigh. "I only came back to get your sweatshirt. Michael loaned it to me and I accidentally left it behind."

James narrowed his eyes.

"Is the truth so hard to believe?" I asked.

"It is when it's coming from you."

So I'd lied to him about the homicide at Ameripictures. The one he'd helped me with. I'd told him I wouldn't investigate it, but I did. What did he expect? My job had been on the line, not to mention a murderer was on the loose. Seemed to be a trend in my life these days.

I turned toward the window. Daylight would be in full bloom soon. "Meet me back at my place. We'll figure out the next step together."

He moved closer and leaned down. I could feel his breath against my forehead. I unglued my feet and retreated. He spoke in a low voice, "Where are you really headed?"

"Look." I pushed back my shoulders. I was nearly a foot shorter, but I felt taller somehow. I had to feel in charge or he'd get the best of me. "If there's something important we missed last night, we need to know. I need a fresh pair of eyes to scowl…scour this room. No killer is that smart or that clean." A lesson learned from trailing Dad on his cases. "They always leave something behind." I neared the door. "Except the body, in this case. And the resignation letter."

"Any ideas?"

"Not yet."

"You're going straight home?" His tone had quieted.

Truthfulness isn't just about what you say, it's about intentions. I intended to tell the truth. If only I could. "Absolutely," I said. My main intention was to free Michael from a crime he had nothing to do with. And to do that, I needed to meet Ian. And see what he was up to. And what he knew. I didn't want James tagging along and questioning my every move. I knew what I was doing. Most of the time.

I sucked in a gulp of air. At that moment, my heart was made of steel, my limbs iron, and my fingers brass. Of course, I didn't tell James any of that. I forged ahead and threw him a backward glance. He watched me, head cocked to one side, chin slightly lowered.

"See you back at the ranch," I said.

I flew down to Michael's office and headed in. I didn't want to chance being seen exiting out the front or from Alyce's window.

Slipping into the creeping dawn, I hurried off. I hopped over a low stone wall and headed for the archway. A solo lamp spattered light over a portion of the lawn.

Minutes later, I stood in a dry, dusty lot, facing a sunrise that barely rustled the shade.

"I gave up on you," Ian said.

"Sorry, I took a wrong turn." The rumble of Ian's engine shooed away the quiet. The back-end of his ancient pickup stood an arm's length away from a compact white Honda.

The passenger side of Ian's pickup opened and a wiry man spilled out, hitting the ground on all fours. He clapped his hands together in an effort to chase the dirt off his palms. He turned his face in my direction and blinked. "Good thing you arrived. I can't drive. It's bad for the head." He pointed to his temple. "Have a terrific day." With that parting sentiment, he unfolded onto his stomach, flat on the ground.

"When you didn't show up, I went and picked up Squalley thinking he could start the car so I could hook it up to my hitch." Ian shook his head and looked at the crumple he called Squalley. "He's no good to me. You, on the other hand, are just what the doctor ordered. Not that I'm a doctor or been around any lately. Unless you mean a PhD. You can overdose on them around here."

"Didn't you say Squalley cleaned Big Mac's floor last night?" I asked. "Do you remember what time?"

"Let me see. I'd cleaned the sinks in the men's lavatory and rinsed out a Scotch glass. Some professors take nips between classes. That's when Squalley got there. I'd say he finished about five. Why?"

"I was curious if anyone happened to go in after we messed with the stuff in the president's closet. I don't want to get busted."

"Squalley went in way before. But he'd never tattle on you." Ian's eyes widened. "You think Big Mac'll figure out we planted the goods in his closet? He'll suspect me for sure. Maybe I'll get kicked out."

"You were there to do your job."

"That's right." He gave himself a body shake. "Shall we?"

"What?"

"Move Squalley's car. The key's in it. Just start the engine and drive it closer to my truck. I'll hitch it on."

I pulled on the tarnished handle. Squalley's car door creaked open and I slipped inside. The driver's seat was stiff with age. It was like sitting on a block of cement. I gripped the steering wheel and turned the key in the ignition. Nothing. I glanced at the clutch on the floor. One foot slammed on the brake, the other pressed the clutch so it hit the worn rubber mat. I turned the key again. This time the engine spat and came to life.

Ian stood by the hitch and motioned me forward with his hands. I focused on the shifter. Only bits and pieces of the white numbers and letters remained on top.

I rolled down the window. "Which way is drive?"

"Up a notch and all the way to the right."

I took my foot off the brake.

"Don't—" He cupped a hand to his mouth.

I placed my foot on the accelerator and shuffled the stick around.

"Accelerate."

The car shot backward. I pressed the brake. There was a clang as the bumper made contact with wood. The rear end slanted downward. I lifted the handbrake and hopped out. I ran to the trunk. Ian was already there.

A wooden fence post was split in two and knocked to the ground. A deep trench dipped into the dirt. "That's the drop-off you told me about," I said.

"No big deal." Ian kneeled next to the fender and ran a calloused palm against the crinkled metal bumper. "I think the smashed part was already there."

"But I—"

"Oh, that's nothing." Squalley stumbled up to us, brown eyes locked onto the bumper. "That's from before. Way before. I back into things all the time." He sank onto his knees.

Even if it had been mangled, I'd made it worse.

"Get in and drive to the hitch, will you?" Ian said to me. He started jogging toward his truck.

"But I—" I started.

"You can do it." Squalley looked at me and lowered his voice. He flicked a thumb toward Ian's back. "Ian's a good guy, you know?" He lay on his side on the dirt, his head resting on his palm, elbow on the ground. "He helps me out all the time."

Which was more than I could say. I could barely help this one time.

In seconds, I'd moved the heap up, inches from Ian's truck. Ian secured it to the hitch. Squalley pulled himself into a sitting position, reached into a pocket, and pulled out a few bills.

"Here." He waved the money toward me. "We put you to a lot of trouble and made you worry about my wrecked car. Take it."

"I can't."

"You have to." Ian came around. "You'll insult him if you don't."

"Better believe it," Squalley said with a Bronx accent that belonged deep inside a New York subway station. "I don't like insults."

"So I damaged, or worsened any damage to your car, and you're paying me? I should be paying you." I reached into my purse.

"Stop. This is our little secret. No one needs to know what we were doing here today. Or they'll make a stink about me parking where I shouldn't be and wrecking the fence. I'm going home now. You go too. Here." Squalley hauled himself onto unsteady feet and shuffled toward me. He stuffed the bills into my palm. Ian took his arm and pulled him toward the pickup.

"A happy ending for everyone." Ian grinned. "Come on, homie, let's get you and your car back before Luigi gets mad." He turned to me. "His parrot's got a terrible temper."

I stood by the trunk and watched the two get into the pickup's cab. I opened my hand. Three crumpled twenties surfaced. Sixty dollars for smashing his fender?

"Wait! I can't…" I waved my arms and hurried toward the cab, but they'd already motored away. I jogged behind them. The white sedan shuddered and hobbled behind the truck. Something was odd about this whole scene. On impulse, I reached into my handbag and opened a zippered pocket. I pulled out a small, black, PVC pouch with a sim card inside. Stronghold magnets stuck to the back of the pouch. My jog turned into a sprint. The tail end of the car grumbled in front of me. My right hand grabbed for the bumper. The Honda slowed over a pothole in the driveway. I turned to soften my impact with the car, bent down, and stuck the GPS tracker to the chassis. The tracker could come in handy.

My gaze fell to the fender, all twisted out of shape, no thanks to me. My attention was diverted by a strange noise. It came from the trunk of Squalley's car. Was that a burp?

## CHAPTER 9

### TRUST ISSUES

I eased Michael's car into the driveway in front of my duplex, stepped outside, and came face-to-face with the morning. Its chill nipped my cheeks and buried its cold hands beneath my clothes. The fog had lifted into light gray clouds. I pictured Michael fast asleep upstairs. Now I could tell him that I went back for the sweatshirt and all was well. No calling cards had been left behind.

Racing up the back stairs, I paused at the door and listened. Not a sound. He was probably sitting quietly, wondering whether he dared to wake me. A preview of my next words rushed through my head.

"Michael, are you okay? I took your ride out for a quick spin back to campus. After I discovered I'd left James' sweatshirt in the president's office."

That wouldn't work. The ending was too much of a shocker. It needed padding. How about "After you fell asleep I realized I'd left James' sweatshirt in Big Mac's office. What? I couldn't believe it either. I took your car back to campus to use the parking pass. Sorry I didn't ask first, but I didn't want to wake you. Mission accomplished, by the way." That was better. But there was still the little problem of the missing resignation letter. And the missing body.

I slipped the key in the knob, turned the handle, and pushed it open. Shutting the door behind me, I tiptoed through the kitchenette to the futon. Michael's blanket sat neatly folded at one end.

"Michael?"

I peered toward the bathroom. Empty. The note I'd scribbled lay taped against the door of my bedroom. I opened it and headed inside.

"Are you...?" No one was there.

I reversed to the front door. The deadbolt was open. I considered the possibilities. My keys were in my handbag, which meant my car sat in the garage. It wasn't like Michael not to leave a note. I checked my smartphone. No missed calls or texts. Wait, his phone was in his car, he'd said. That meant it had been with me. Maybe he woke up, realized his car and phone were missing, and went berserk. His BMW was his Achilles' heel. There was not a ding, scar or blemish anywhere on that vehicle. If his fingers were calloused and his knuckles worn, it was from cleaning his beloved car. I never should have left him alone. He'd come undone.

I sniffed the air. It smelled like pizza. A delicious pizza.

I stood in front of the oven and opened the door. Inside sat a warm asparagus and mushroom dish with herbs and heavenly cheese. I started salivating just thinking about tasting it. Michael knew the way to my heart.

Two quick raps rattled my back door.

"Michael." I yanked the door open. "Oh. It's you." I stepped back into my kitchenette at the same time James plowed forward. His green stare penetrated mine and flew past to the living room area.

"Where's sleeping beauty?"

I swallowed. "I don't know."

James' eyes bounced back to mine. "Where'd he go?"

"He wasn't here when I got back. He couldn't have gone far on foot."

"How do you know he's on foot?"

"I took his car. Mine's parked in the garage."

"It's not too hard to find transportation these days." He pushed past me. Each of his hands gripped a phone.

"What's with the twins?" I asked.

He gave me a half smirk. "You're losing your touch."

What touch was that?

"Your power of deduction used to be keen."

"Really?" I was offended and flattered at the same time. Two phones meant...oh boy. "You found Michael's phone in the president's office."

"In the closet." James crossed his arms and took a step toward me. "So now, not only is his DNA all over the office, which is passable since he worked there, it's in the closet. How's that going to be explained?"

"Oh please. Big Mac hung his coat in the closet daily. He could have asked Michael to fetch it for him."

James took another step toward me. My head tipped upward. I took a deep step back. "If you both missed the phone during your search, what else did you miss?" he asked.

I stifled the yell that nearly escaped out of my mouth. "Isn't there something more important to discuss right now?"

He moved closer, invading my space further, and sniffed. "What's that smell?" He peeked into the kitchenette. "Now we know what he was doing before he took off."

"Guys!" Michael rushed in through the back door, brows raised, eyes round and unblinking. The waves in his dark hair were crisscrossed, aiming in different directions. His cheeks and chin sported a day's worth of stubble. His shirt was rumpled and untucked, his tie askew, and his pants…well, they still looked good on him. "Sorry I didn't leave a note." He turned to me. "I used your laptop to get an Uber and go—"

"Go where?" James shot a hard gaze toward me that slapped me between the eyes. He didn't say a word, yet a whole conversation swirled around us.

"To Mac's place," Michael replied. "I couldn't sleep so I made the spring frittata and went to Mac's after." He took out two plates from a cabinet and sliced the frittata. "He lives in an old, brick house a few miles from campus. He lives…lived, I mean, alone." His voice dropped a notch. "I thought if someone was staying with him, they'd need to know. I rang the doorbell. No one answered."

"Did you try his phone?" I asked.

"Three times." Michael ran a hand through his hair. "I kept thinking maybe I'd made a mistake. That he could still be alive.. When no one answered at Mac's, I went to the faculty lot. His Volvo was still parked in its usual spot." He handed us our plates and walked to the futon. He sat and looked at James. "You'd better eat and leave. I need to call the police. You shouldn't be here when they arrive."

"Wait." I sat next to him and aimed my stare toward James. "You're the criminal law expert, but one thing's for sure, there's no body. They might hold Michael for questioning. He has no alibi. And I'm clearly involved as well. Ian, the janitor, saw both of us in the office."

Michael pushed out a sigh. "It's okay. I'm ready to face the consequences."

"Are you? You've got motive," James told him. "You were demoted and mad as hell. That couldn't have gone unnoticed. And she's got the skills to help you put Mac down, so you'd both be detained. And that's for starters." He was done eating in three bites.

"We'd be at the mercy of law enforcement and unable to investigate." I jumped up. "James, you know we can't—"

"Tell him about this morning," James said.

"What about it?" Michael shot up. "Did you think of something?"

I sat back down and faced Michael. "I took your car because—"

"It's okay. I know," Michael said.

"You do?"

"You're the most thoughtful, caring person," Michael said and took my hand. "You didn't want to wake me because I went off the tracks last night. Thanks for that." His eyes softened from worry to gratitude. "You remembered I didn't leave my cell phone in the car so you went back to campus to find it."

"Well…" I started.

James held up the phone.

Michael dropped my hand. "Thanks, man."

"That's not why I went back," I said. "This morning, early…I took your car to the crime scene. I mean, LA Tech."

Michael shot up. "When did you figure it out?"

"I didn't. But I remembered something else. The sweatshirt you'd loaned me. I'd left it in the president's office. I went back to get it."

"Wow," Michael said. "I'm surprised we didn't sear our initials on Mac's desktop with a branding iron."

"Probably because no branding irons were handy." My joke slipped by unnoticed. I pointed to James. "He went to LA Tech on his own this morning. Good thing. He found your phone in the closet." I tossed a look at James. "There's something else you both need to know." I filled them in on my morning escapade. I stopped before I got to the part where I drove Squalley's car in reverse and hit the fence post.

"I *knew* you wouldn't listen. What is it with you and taking risks?" James said. "Do you ever ask yourself if you could be making matters worse?"

"Risk can't always be avoided." I stepped forward and tipped my head back to look at James. "You know what? Maybe I should have gone straight home. But then I wouldn't have found our first clue."

"What?" Michael's eyes grew round again. "You know where Mac is?"

"I..." Did I?

James' eyes narrowed. "Well?"

"While I was helping Ian and Squalley, things happened. Things that didn't fit."

"Like?" James asked.

"I reversed Squalley's car and hit a fencepost. I meant to go forward, but I hadn't driven a stick in a while and there was this dip. It could have happened to anyone."

"That is so not tr—" Michael said.

"Instead of getting mad, Squalley paid me sixty bucks for helping out. He insisted I take it."

"You crashed his car and he paid you?" Michael cradled his chin.

"Hush money," James said. "For what?"

"For keeping quiet about his car being parked in the lot on campus. And...for the burp."

"Who burped? Squalley?" Michael looked concerned. "I heard he had a drinking problem."

"It wasn't Squalley."

"Who was it?" James wanted to know.

"Someone in the trunk of Squalley's car. That's where the burp came from."

James' gaze smacked into mine. "You're serious? You actually think you heard a burp in the trunk?"

"Are you saying you think Mac was in there?" Michael's eyes were pinned to mine. "That would mean he isn't dead. Do you think it was him?"

"We don't think anything at this point," James said.

"Don't tell me what I don't think." I magnified his scowl.

"You shouldn't think alone. It gets you into trouble."

If I had a volume control for James' voice, this is where I'd mute it.

"It couldn't be Mac, could it? But if it wasn't him, who could it be?" Michael asked.

"It wasn't a who. It was a what," James said. "People stuck in trunks do a lot more than just burp. You said the pick-up truck was old. It could have been funky engine noise."

"You got Squalley's plate number, right?" Michael asked. "James can do a background check."

My cheeks grew hot. I pressed my lips together. I had an uncanny knack for overlooking the obvious. "I'll call Ian and get to the bottom of this." That's all I was saying for now. My reputation was getting sketchier by the second. They didn't need to know about the tracker.

"No." James tried to reel us in. "We should come up with a plan before doing anything. And stay away from the crime scene. Understand? Don't talk to anyone. Not without me."

I launched toward him and stopped, noting a rustle inside the neck of my hoodie. My fingers reached in and pulled out the envelope.

## CHAPTER 10

### UNCERTAINTIES

"What else have you got in there?" James' gaze dipped down the V-neck of my black hoodie. "A slim jim, or an ice pick maybe?"

"Corrie, stealing mail's a federal crime," Michael said. "Looks like we'll both end up in the slammer, after all. And we won't even be together."

"Oh, Michael." That was the sweetest thing he'd ever said to me. "I didn't steal anything." Paperclips didn't count. "This letter didn't go through the postal service. It was lying on the floor of Big Mac's office."

"What does it say?" James asked.

"Who's it from?" Michael squinted at the small white envelope.

"I haven't opened it," I said.

"Give it to me." James' hand shot out. "I'll find out."

Before James could snatch it, I hid the envelope behind my back. "Michael, put on the kettle, please."

"This isn't tea time," James shot back.

"We're going to steam it open, read it, and reclose the envelope. Then we'll put it back. Like it never happened."

"Bad idea," James said. "Steaming will warp the envelope. It'll look like it's been tampered with."

"Good call. I am so done with tampering," Michael said and turned to me. "How are your forgery skills? We can get a new envelope and you can re-address it or maybe type one out—"

"All we have to do is freeze it for a couple of hours and it'll slip open," James said.

"Brilliant." Michael and James bumped fists.

I regarded the envelope. "Except for one small thing." I held the envelope up. "It's not even sealed."

Michael's smile grew wider. "Yes."

"It was meant for you to find." James' scowl was back.

"That's ridiculous," I said. Unless the killer was smart and detail oriented. That would describe any student or faculty member at LA Tech. Not to mention the janitorial staff.

"Someone knew you'd be back," James said. "For something you'd left behind."

I had never met anyone, except my parents, who had a more suspicious mind than I did until James. "The chances of that are slim to non-existent. Who knew we were there?" I counted Ian, Squalley, possibly the security guard, and anyone else keeping tabs on the building. I lifted the envelope flap. I pulled out a typed letter and read it out loud:

*Dear President MacTavish,*

*I came by your office yesterday, but you were not in. I wanted to let you know that it is unacceptable that you terminated co-associate dean Michael Parris.*

"Terminated? I was demoted," Michael said. "That's not the same."

"Michael, do you mind?" I said.

"It was a temporary demotion. I would have straightened him out. If he hadn't gotten himself killed."

I continued:

*I am the president of the student body and currently in charge of circulating a petition for Associate Dean Parris' immediate and full reinstatement. Although he has been here a short time, he is the most accessible, top-level administrator ever. He holds regular student meetings, listens to us, and eats at the same tables we do. Do not take away the first person on the faculty that students find relatable. I will be in your office on Tuesday morning. We will not give up until he is fully reinstated.*

*Sincerely, Loretta Fink, senior undergraduate major, applied and computational mathematics. Future PhD*

Michael wore a small smile. "I've got to thank her."

"You're not supposed to know about this letter, remember?" I looked up at Michael. "I'm going to add her to the suspect list." I stuck the envelope in my pocket.

"You have a suspect list?" James asked.

"Why is she a suspect?" Michael came around to face me.

"She's a complex math major with the capability of committing a complex crime. She's probably ruthless, judgmental, has no practical skills, and refuses to use contractions. She could have planted the letter to throw off the scent." I pointed to James. "Like he said."

"I didn't say all that," James told me.

"Just the type of person that could snap and stab the president. Probably came in last in cheerleader tryouts."

"We don't have cheerleaders at LA Tech," Michael said.

"Who else is on the suspect list?" James asked.

"No one you know," I said.

"Okay, that's it. This is the part where I *leave*," James shouted the last word and shifted toward the front door. "I didn't give up the Saturday morning surf for people who won't accept any help."

"Bro, this was your Malibu weekend, wasn't it?" Michael looked concerned.

"Both of you. She..." He pointed and dropped his hand. "I'm done." He took a few steps and turned to me. "You have twenty-four hours before I call the cops."

The door slammed in his wake.

Michael's down pillow lay at the base of the futon. I kicked it hard and it smacked against the opposite wall, setting tiny white feathers free-falling. "We need a plan to find Mac's body, and the person who burped," I said.

Michael patted his back pocket and turned toward the kitchenette. In two steps he closed in on the Formica counter and pocketed the key to his car. He retraced James' steps to the front door, opened it, and paused in front of the entry. "But first, I need to find James. He took my cell phone with him."

≑≑≑

Thirty minutes later, I'd polished off the rest of the frittata and stepped into the morning chill. I trudged down the stairs to the garage. Water droplets trickled to the ground when I lifted the door. It creaked its way up and banged to a stop. I eased inside.

I pulled out a flashlight and focused the beam on a metal box hidden on a shelf behind my car. The box housed my inheritance: Dad's weapon collection.

I unlocked the lid and eyed my favorite: a six-pointed shuriken, a weapon of distraction, not destruction. I swore off PI work after what happened to Dad, but every murder case needs a hero. Or heroine. That would be me...even if I was light years away from finding the killer.

Back upstairs, I piled the blankets on the floor and reclined onto the tumble. I pulled out a piece of cheesecloth. My fingers made small circles along the blades of the throwing star. Dad and I spent hours flicking our wrists to hit the target. It got so I never missed. I didn't think I'd need this again. Or at least not so soon. After wrapping up the homicide at Ameripictures, the studio security chief had asked for help in finding his long lost father. Before I could say yes...or no, his dad showed up at the studio. He'd read about the homicide on the internet and saw his son's name. They rode off together in the sunset to start a new home security business. And I was done playing PI. Until now.

I tucked the shuriken in my purse and got to my feet. Time to check in with Ian and Squalley. I turned to my phone and accessed the tracker on Squalley's car. I'd heard something in that trunk. But was that something dead or alive or mechanical? And shouldn't it take more than sixty bucks to keep me quiet if it wasn't mechanical? Silence didn't come cheap.

The tracker showed the car stopped in Burbank. I blew out a sigh. I needed to talk to someone about the events of the last twelve hours. Someone reasonable who'd be willing to take a risk or two. Someone with a legal or police background would be ideal. I'd settle for a K-9 unit.

Four hard raps struck against my front door.

"Corrie, you in there? It's me. Open up."

## CHAPTER 11

### GETTING THE JOB DONE

"Gotta use the bathroom something fierce. Can I come in?"

A plus-size female wearing a turquoise velour jogging suit and fruity scented lotion stared back at me. Her skin matched the color of wet sand. Her caramel colored hair was slicked back in a side-swept ponytail. Veera Bankhead hopped from side-to-side.

"Hold on." I closed the door, and lugged the metal box to my room. I shoved it under my bed and returned to the entry. I pulled open the door.

"Thank you." Veera zipped inside. "Ooooh, like the digs. Real nice. Where am I headed?" She pushed past the tumble of blankets. "Found it."

"Why are you...?"

The bathroom and front doors shut at the same time.

Since Veera was my legal assistant at Ameripictures, she knew where I lived. My official title was associate attorney, business affairs, children's movie division. I handled everything my V.P. boss shoved my way. And then some...like investigating a possible homicide that led to the firing of most of the Newport Beach division. Veera and I were hanging by our thumbs, waiting for lay-off notices or the hoped-for move to the main headquarters in Culver City.

"You stopped by to use the bathroom?" I asked when she came out.

"Nice crib. Minimalist but bold. You know what you need? One of those fuzzy rugs." She eyed the war-torn dartboard, my only piece of wall décor. "This is fine art. Sharp and welcoming at the same time."

"*Welcoming?*"

"Yeah. It screams 'come in, sit down, and play a spell'."

"Veera, you're here because...?"

"This is a great place to chill, re-charge and...hang. Maybe?" She strolled to the window and peeked out.

I opened the door. "I'm in the middle of something."

She turned to me. "Like, you're in the middle of doing laundry? Or in the middle of fighting crime?"

"See you on Tuesday." We were at the start of Memorial Day weekend. Which gave me an extra day to relax…and solve a murder.

"Okay, look. I stopped by 'cause I need a favor."

"'Favor'?" My mind raced ahead. Did she need help with a law school exam? She'd started night law school two months ago. Or maybe she had guy issues. I hoped not. I was worthless in that department.

"It's like this…can I spend the night?"

"I'm working on a—"

"A case? Yes!" She unleashed a fist pump. "Tell me what to do, boss. I've got my PI game on. You know I can help. And you know I can be a generous provider of moral support. Everybody needs that."

"Why do you really want to spend the night?"

Her lips turned inward. "My plumbing's all busted. No running water. No toilet flushing. No tooth brushing. I'm not down with that. You know I can't spring for no motel. So I thought of you. We've got that mentor-mentee thing going on that's meaningful. And I'd sure appreciate staying in this real nice beach pad. It's got character."

Was she referring to the metal cabinets in the kitchenette? Or the wood floor that doubled as a termite campground?

"Is that my blanket you're standing on?" Veera asked.

I took a step back.

"Do you have a case? 'Cause I can help if you do. I'm good for bouncing things off of. Unless you got yourself another bouncer." A frown shadowed her smile.

I pictured Michael and James, heads together, rustling up clues. "Not exactly."

"Then I'm your trusty sidekick. How about it?"

"Okay, but the futon's all I've got."

"The futon's all I need." With a running start of two yards, she landed bottom first on the unsuspecting futon. It slumped, one side crashing to the ground. A short peg leg lay on its side against the floor.

"Oops." She slowly rose. We surveyed the sagging, three-legged excuse for a couch.

"Now my place really has character," I said.

"I can fix that. All I need is a hammer and nail. Or a screwdriver. Got superglue?"

"What I've got is a possible homicide."

Veera's smile radiated to all four corners of the room. "Now you're talking."

## CHAPTER 12

## WHO YOU GONNA CALL?

Lack of sleep and a slow moving Veera didn't prevent me from jogging on the woodchip path between Ardmore and Valley. Even with the sun blazing overhead, the pine-scented trail bore the weight of runners, casual walkers, and an assortment of escorted baby strollers and canines. I jogged up a rogue path that cut through a sea of ice plants above the main trail, inspired by rubber soles bent on avoiding hobby joggers.

"Wait up, girl! Oops."

Veera veered off to one side behind me. She ran between the two trails, trampling the ice plants in an effort to dodge the serious runners and keep up with me. She'd let out an "oops" with every blow of her sneaker, as if she shared the silent pain and humiliation of the plants. I slowed at the corner of Pier and Ardmore and waited, jogging in place.

"When you asked me to go for a spin." Veera doubled over panting next to me, resting her hands above her knees. "I expected you meant in your car. I wasn't prepped for no running."

"You're wearing a jogging suit and tennis shoes."

"These are for looks." She straightened and lifted a thin sole. "See? These are fashion finds. Why we have to go for a run, anyway? We're supposed to be crime solving."

"I think best when I'm in motion. And I think I've got a plan."

I'd filled Veera in on Michael's stumbling upon Big Mac's body, and the subsequent disappearance when we returned to campus.

"What kind of plan? Are we gonna take someone down? 'Cause I'm ready for him."

"It's not always a him. Could be a female student with the hots for Michael. But he'd never fall for her. Because he is too much of a gentleman to ever consider dating a student."

"You got it for him bad, C."

"I just want what's best for him." And me.

"So you wouldn't be disappointed if he got himself in a serious relationship?"

"Course not."

"Good to know. 'Cause I heard he's been seeing someone."

"He'd better not be." I felt my cheeks go green.

"I knew it. You're crazy in love with him."

"That's ridiculous." I wasn't in love. Was I? Maybe I just wanted to dip a toe into the romance waters and see if it felt hot.

"I'm just playing with you. But you got to play it cool if you want to make headway."

"We have a case to solve, remember?" Michael needed to know I had a handle on this. And so did I.

"I get that. Priorities. Only, can we eat first? This run has made me hungry."

I could use a snack. "I know just the place."

Twenty minutes later, bellies brimming with Brazilian BBQ, we made our way back to my pad.

"We're going for a drive," I said. My cell phone showed Squalley's car on the move, heading north on the 405.

"Let's take my car so we can burn off some of that tri tip and sausage," Veera said. "That was straight-up meat lust I was accommodating."

I loosened the drawstrings of my sweat pants so I could breathe. I'd had my share as well as that of two sailors lost at sea for days. The frittata was a distant memory. "How do you burn calories while driving?"

"Live and learn, girl."

We made a right on Longfellow and hustled toward my place. Veera strode over to a lime green Volkswagen bug right out of the sixties.

"This here's a super Beetle," she said. "Never let me down once. Well, never let me down twice. Okay, maybe a half dozen times. How about that?"

"I've got a weakness for German automobiles myself." My twelve-year-old BMW sat in the garage. It conked out on me a few times in the five years I'd been driving it, but always rose from the dead. I retired it for a week after I'd received a gift from one of Dad's former clients: a brand new BMW. But I sold the new Beemer to pay off student loans. My old, mostly trustworthy ride was back on the job.

The Beetle's motor gave a little cough, shook, and spit up smoke like a baby volcano attempting its first eruption. The smell of exhaust seeped inside. I held my nose and glanced behind me. A rear window was popped open. I couldn't reach to close it. Veera revved the engine and turned the wheel. We rumbled up the street.

"It stumbles a little before it gets into its stride," she said. "But don't be fooled. This here's a race horse."

More like a neon-shelled tortoise. The little bug chugged up the hill to Coast Highway. It choked a few times like it was going to roll over and die. But once we got past the rise, the VW toned down to ease into the ride.

"Where we going?" she asked.

"I'm tracking a car belonging to the school maintenance guy, Squalley," I said.

"You get a license plate?"

"I've got something better."

Veera shot me a glance. "We going to drive around and hope we bump into them?"

"No." This wasn't my first nearly clueless, stuck in deep mud, crime scene investigation. "I put a tracker on the car."

"Now we're talking." She began humming a jaunty tune.

I smiled and hummed along.

Minutes later, Veera broke our hum-fest with, "What if the professor—"

"You mean, the president."

"—is still alive and walked outta his office by himself? He could have faked his own death."

"Why would he do that?" I asked.

"For a fresh start. Or to escape a nagging wife, gambling debt, or the kind of mundane existence that sends you spinning down back alleys 'cause you ain't got nothing better to do."

"Michael's certain Mac was dead."

There was one small chance, a minute one, that Michael was mistaken. If the lung was punctured by a knife, it could shorten the breath and make it seem like Big Mac wasn't breathing when he was. I remembered a case in law school where that very thing had happened. Maybe even the killer thought Big Mac was dead and took the body to dispose of it.

"You're awfully quiet." Veera's face pinched together. "You going all 'silence is golden' on me? I'm gathering dust over here when I could be put to good use."

"I'm mulling over a possibility. A slim one. It has to do with the body, and the guys we're tailing. Ian pops up in strange places with strange people, like suspect number two, Squalley." I told her about the noise in the trunk.

"They could be our prime suspects."

"We have to catch up to them. And check inside the trunk without getting caught."

## Chapter 13

## The Trunk Show

It was early afternoon when we hit State Route 14 somewhere north of the Angeles National Forest, Southern California's epicenter for body dumping. It made sense to bury Big Mac's body in the forest and leave him at the mercy of the elements. But the tracking device showed the car stopped in a rural town called Littleton. Population 6743.

A large cross-fenced corral occupied my side of the freeway. Yucca trees spiked the mostly barren fields, accented by clumps of chaparral. Skinny horses grazed, lips to the ground. Older ranch-style homes popped up here and there.

"They're near a small town called Littleton," I told Veera. I'd been reading up on the place for the better part of five minutes. "Close enough to commute to L.A., but far enough to have your own ranch, shooting range, and private dump."

"Did you say *dump*? Like for trash or old cars? Or body parts?" Veera slowed the car.

"We've got to look at all angles."

"Maybe Ian's got a cousin Bob with a mechanic shop on the cheap in Littleton. And that's where they're headed."

"All this way to fix a flat? How does the burp fit in?"

A shiver quaked Veera. "I got a cousin who runs a drive-thru funeral home outta Compton. He also sells concert tickets on the sly. But you know what he says about dead bodies? When they're freshly gone, there's excess air and such the body needs to expel, so it might burp or fart or something. That's what you might've heard."

Why didn't I think of that? "I thought of that. If it's Big Mac who burped, we've found the missing body." And I helped them get away. My temperature topped the charts.

"You think it might be a different dead body?"

"Or maybe a live one."

A smile scattered Veera's worry. "That's right. You got cuffs on you? We're gonna need them in case we get to apprehend someone."

Of course I had cuffs. In the bottom drawer of my dresser where I'd left them. I pointed to the exit. "Let's find the car first. There's a chance no one was in the trunk. Get off at El Torino Canyon and make a right." My cell phone strummed a harp. I answered on the first ring. "Michael? You okay?"

"I'm waaaaay past okay. James and I are meeting with Loretta on campus in thirty minutes."

"Who?"

"The student who wrote the letter you found in Mac's office."

"You told her we found it?"

"No. I'd never do that. I sent her an email commending her on being a model student body leader. Then she asked if we could meet."

"Don't you find that suspicious?"

"It's our chance to find out everything she knows. We're going to do some industrial strength grilling, the kind you rock at. When can you get there?"

I wasn't keen on Michael meeting with a student with the hots for him. But I had work to do. "I can't."

Silence then, "Oh, I get it. You're staying under the radar. Sweet. Why, exactly?"

"I'm with Veera. She's having some issues."

Veera threw me a sidelong stare. "Tell him the truth, C."

"You're in good hands with James." I disconnected. "He's better off without me," I told Veera. "I've got nothing at the moment."

"You are way too busy soaking in that self-pity tub of yours. It feels all warm and cozy at first, but the water turns cold real fast."

"Who's soaking? We have a crime to solve, and I've got to follow my lead. Even if it is a burp."

"Crime solving's no substitute for a good man. No matter how thrilling it may seem to take down a killer. Even if it is for the good of society and making the world a safer place for grannies and little children. Okay, I'm with you on that one."

"We're on a fact-finding mission, and I don't want Michael to know. If this is a bust and we don't discover anything, he won't be disappointed. Move it."

Veera pressed the pedal to the metal and the little engine rumbled down rough, cracked asphalt. There were enough potholes to loosen the fillings in my teeth. The car bounced up and down the pockmarked road, and so did our heads, and anything else that protruded or wasn't strongly fastened in place.

"That's what I'm talking about." Veera's voice quivered with the car. "We're going to vibrate away those extra pounds."

"Veeeeera," my voice quivered back. "There's a reason why people don't use shaking cars to lose weight."

"There sure is. 'Cause they don't know about it. It's just plain ignorance."

"No, it's just plain uncomfortable. It's more than uncomfortable. My organs are coming loose."

"That's not organs you're feeling. It's fat."

And this was how the conversation continued for the next few miles. In vibration mode, until we left all semblance of city life behind. Dry brush, tumbleweeds, and forlorn pine trees straddled both sides of the road.

"What is that?" Veera hit the brakes.

A bloody glob stretched across the center divider. The stink of rotting cabbage fought its way into the car. I could practically taste it. "Skunk." I squeezed my nostrils shut.

"That there's a bad omen."

"No, that there's road kill." Vultures circled above us. "Move."

Veera's sneaker landed heavily on the gas and the bug shot off. "There's trouble ahead. I feel it."

"We're semi-professionals. Let's leave feelings out of this."

We'd barely traveled a mile when the tracker indicated we'd caught up to Squalley's car. "Stop. We're here," I said. Even though I wasn't sure where *here* was. We were at the top of a scrawny driveway bordered by tall weeds and scraggly oak trees.

Veera pulled to the shoulder. "Looks like we're on another planet."

I checked my tracker. Squalley's car had travelled down this road. "Move up a little."

Veera motored ahead and stopped next to an open gate. Dirt overpowered most of the asphalt.

I squinted. "What does that sign say? Something paradise."

Planted about twenty feet down the driveway stood a large, rectangular sign in peeling lemon yellow with white lettering. Much of the lettering was missing.

"An arm and dig paradise." Veera's neck stuck forward to get a better look. "Maybe it's a place where they sell shovels to dig your way to paradise."

"Move closer."

"Closer?"

"Put the car in drive."

"Well, here's how I see it. If we go down this road, we could get arrested for trespassing."

"We won't get arrested. That sign's an invitation, letting us know this is a business. And businesses like visitors. We're legitimate visitors. And, we have a perfect excuse in case legit doesn't work. We're looking for a missing person."

"A missing, dead person."

"Will you drive, please? We're also looking for a maintenance guy I owe money to. That's legit."

"If you say so." She shifted and inched forward. "The closer we get, the sketchier this place feels."

Veera shifted again, and we were off, bumping up and down the dirt road until we reached a rusty, chain link gate.

"Now what? You want me to ram through?"

"Hold that thought." I opened the car door and stepped outside. The dry air smelled of hay mingled with dust and animal droppings. I moseyed up to the gate and lifted the latch. I pushed it open, and waved Veera inside. "Park here." I pointed to a space beneath a pepper tree.

She pulled in and turned off the engine. She stepped out. "Where we going?"

"To find signs of life. There's a business here somewhere."

We traveled the rest of the way on foot.

"I see a red roof over there." Veera slowed and pointed to a tiled roof with missing shingles and an overgrowth of dark green moss. The tiles sat atop a single story, dirty white stucco structure with small windows and a wooden door that could use a few coats of paint. "I don't mind red roofs. What I mind is what I hear. Unidentifiable creepy noises."

Machinery whirred nearby. "Engines from nearby ranches. A tractor, maybe."

"The noises I hear aren't human. Or machine."

We heard cries and a high-pitched wail. "Let's check it out."

Minutes later, we stopped before an entry to a dusty lot near the red tiled roof structure. Ian's truck was parked at the far end. Squalley's white Honda was still hitched to the bumper. A big wooden sign read, "Animal Farm and Pig Paradise."

"See?" I said. "It's farm noises we hear."

"Do you think that's 'pig paradise' as in all the bacon you can eat, or 'pig paradise' as in squeally things with snouts and curly tails running all over the place?"

"Probably a petting zoo."

Clucking, moos and baaahs filled the air. The smell of straw, dust, manure, and cowhide grew stronger.

Veera cupped her nose. "I don't like critters with hooves and fly swatting tails. That's not for me. Closest I ever want to get to a farm animal is in the freezer section of my grocery store."

"Here's the plan." I surveyed the parking lot. Another gate led to an open courtyard littered with overgrown hedges. A cracked cement bench and a leaning birdbath sat on the mangy lawn. "Follow me to Ian's truck and watch out for anyone approaching."

"Anyone?"

"Anyone that looks like a big guy with gray hair around here." I gestured around my head to show Ian's designated hair spots. "And a smaller guy that looks like Al Pacino."

I took off with Veera at my heels.

After a few steps, I heard her whisper, "Hold up."

I froze. Veera stopped behind me, eyes aimed toward the stable area. "There he is."

"Who?"

"Al Pacino. Maybe this place is a Mafia safe house," Veera said. "Or a money laundering operation."

I stared over the fence. A man in a gray suit leaned against a stucco wall. He wore a sullen expression and had dark, messy hair. His hands were buried in the front pockets of his trousers. His suit made him stand out like a quarter on a plateful of pennies. "That guy's the young Al Pacino, like from *The Godfather*. Think Pacino as a senior citizen. With a goatee, gray hair, and stand-up eyebrows."

"Stand-up what?"

"Just look for an older Mafia-looking guy, okay?"

I moved toward the pick-up and stopped behind Squalley's Honda. The flat had been fixed, but the dent in the bumper hadn't been touched. So why was the car still hitched to Ian's truck? "Veera, keep a sharp eye out."

"I only do sharp." She scanned the grounds. "You think the body's still in that trunk?"

I pulled out an extra slim screwdriver and paperclip from my purse. "No, but there should be some sign that the body *was* in there." I hoped.

I shoved the ends of the paperclip and screwdriver into the keyhole. After a good amount of twisting and pumping, the trunk clicked and lifted slightly. "Bingo." I peered inside.

"What do you see?" Veera edged toward me. She leaned in to peek in the trunk. "Oh my."

## CHAPTER 14

## HOG WILD

"Lose something, ladies?"

Veera and I spun around from the Honda and locked stares with a big guy and a smaller one, backlit by the sun.

"In my trunk?" Squalley continued. "Because if you did, I gotta ask what you lost." A hand sliced the empty air in front of him. A gold hoop earring glinted in the sunlight.

I sprang to life. "I never imagined you two, of all people, would be so irresponsible. To leave your trunk wide open like this."

"Really? I thought I slammed it after we…" Ian caught himself and stopped.

"This trunk sure is messy. We been trying to figure out if we should close it or hose it down," Veera added.

"Ian, you were the last one here. Did you shut it or not?" Squalley asked him.

While Ian stammered, I plunged a hand in my pocket. My fist closed around the folded envelope holding Loretta's letter. I planted my bottom onto the edge of the open trunk and reached a hand behind me.

"Smells like a beer party in there," I said. I stretched two fingers, out of sight of the two men, and ran them against the trunk's rubber mat. I'd spotted coarse white hairs smattered in liquid when I'd peered inside. Now those hairs stuck along my fingers. I rubbed them on the inside of the envelope, stuffed it back in my pocket and tried to keep a straight face.

"Yeah, but out here…what is that God awful smell?" Veera raised her chin and sniffed the air. "Smells like rotten fruit and old coffee. Of course, it's hard to isolate the exact description with all these foul odors floating around."

"That's good clean compost you smell," Ian said.

"Is there a tire repair shop close by?" I asked.

"I don't think so. I mean we got it fixed close to campus," Ian said, shooting a glance between Veera and me. "But Squalley was upset, so we drove here, to settle him down before we tackle the bumper. He really loves the animals."

"They bring me peace." Squalley held up two fingers in the peace sign. "It's tough doing maintenance at that ritzy college, so when my buddy says to come to this..." He waved his hands around in empty air. "...Mecca for bovines, equines, lambs and little...what are those skippity things called again?"

"Kids," Ian said and turned to me. "He means the baby goats."

"I got a lot of love for those little guys." Squalley tilted his head and clasped gnarly fingers in front of him. "They're like..." He wiggled his fingers. "Little Gene Kellys."

Progress was sorely missing from this conversation. I pivoted around and scrutinized the trunk. A large, wet rubber mat lay spattered with hairs, each about an inch or two in length. Why would Big Mac shed so much hair? Had he just gotten a haircut? "You're here for a picnic?" I turned to face the duo.

"We are? I mean, yes. We are," Ian replied. "Perfect for a picnic. Who are you, by the way?" He focused on Veera.

"I'm—"

"She's a student, too," I said. "You must have seen her around."

"Yeah, I'm hard to miss. What's your favorite animal?" Veera asked him.

"Why do you ask?" Ian stole a glance toward Squalley.

Veera shrugged. "Well, the kind of animal you like says a lot about you. For example, if you liked sharks, I'd think you might have an evil streak."

"We like them all." Squalley tapped Ian's chest with his hand. "Let's vacate. I'm feeling worn."

Ian started to leave, and stopped to ask, "What are you two doing here again?"

"Someone told us about this petting zoo," Veera said.

"Hey." Squalley held up a hand. "This ain't no petting zoo."

"It's a sanctuary," Ian said. "A haven."

"You've got to experience it before you go labeling." Squalley donned a pair of dark shades.

"Did you touch any of these animals while you were here?" Veera asked.

"Well, sure."

"Then how is this not like a petting zoo?"

"You don't even—"

"A crime's been committed, people," I said.

Everyone froze mid-movement, including a couple passing by.

"What are you saying?" Squalley asked.

"It's a crime to stand around chatting when we could be enjoying the beautiful day. Here." I reached into my handbag and pulled out a post-it. I scribbled my name and number and handed it to Ian. "If you ever want to talk animals, feel free to call."

Ian's eyes widened. Squalley took the note. It looked like Ian was about to talk, but he clammed up.

I pulled out the sixty dollars. "Take this, too." I shoved the bills into Ian's shirt pocket and stepped away from the trunk. "I didn't expect any payment for helping. See you on campus." I zipped off, Veera in tow. I spoke out of the side of my mouth, "Let's look around."

"What was all that hair doing in the trunk? You think it belonged to the boss?"

"Big Mac had white hair." I remembered Michael's description. "There's a chance these two dropped off the body, using beer to mask the smell."

"Dead body smells?"

I didn't want to freak Veera. "Or cologne or anything distinctive. It's too soon for other types of odors."

Veera shuddered. "This is giving me the heebie-jeebies."

Her lips pressed together, her smile disappeared. I turned into the farm entrance and paused next to an oak tree. Veera placed her hand on the scarred trunk and took deep breaths. I shot a look over her shoulder. The two men sat in Ian's truck. The engine rumbled. "You okay?" I asked Veera.

"Mind over murder." In ultra slow motion, she circled her arms above her head and brought her palms together. The tips of her index fingers touched and rested below her chin, eyes squeezed shut.

"Tai chi?"

One eye opened. "This is straight-up prayer. I'm praying we find the body and get the hell out of here before there's a cow stampede or the pigs get loose. All this mooing and squealing makes me jittery." She dropped the pose and asked, "Shouldn't we do something? Like call the cops and tie those two guys up 'til they get here? You know they've got rope in those barns."

"We have no proof yet. But I lifted hair samples to have tested."

Ian's truck ambled down the driveway. I headed toward the stables.

"Where would a couple of criminals dump a body?" I asked.

Veera took a few steps and paused. "Maybe they buried it."

"In broad daylight?" I slowed and eyed two ranch hands walking between animal pens. Each held the end of a large metal bin. They stopped near a small herd of sheep. "They'd be seen. Plus, buried bodies might be dug up by animals later."

"Cows and sheep and horses don't dig. Dogs do, but I don't see any."

"Coyotes dig." I scanned the different pens. "Veera, keep those two busy over there." I pointed to the ranch hands. "While I take a closer look."

Veera's smile revived. "I'm on it." She moved on to the workers. The endless clucking of chickens masked the conversation. Veera chatted them up, and they headed toward a small structure.

I fast-walked past the stables toward the pens. Two brown hens squawked and flapped their wings, jutting off to the side. Goats reclined on the dirt in a neighboring pen, oblong shaped eyes watching my every move. Could Big Mac's body have been dragged all this way? I spied a large wheelbarrow next to a horse trough. It had ample room for an ample body. But nothing made much sense when I thought about it. How Ian and Squalley got the body out of the office without getting caught, why they drove way out here, why Michael abandoned me for James when I'm the one with PI experience, or why I downed five pounds of BBQ beef before realizing I was full. A cat with gray stripes threw me a hopeless stare.

I switched direction. A series of grunts and squeals interrupted the brief quiet. I stopped in front of a pipe-fenced corral. A white snout stuck out, covered with short hairs, the roundish tip leathery and pink. Wing-shaped ears flopped above tiny eyes canopied by snowy lashes. The snout puckered and puffed my way, before reversing to join his pals. A group of curly tailed hogs snorted and squealed in the center of the pen. An object lay on the dirt between them. I caught my breath.

## CHAPTER 15

### CLUES A'PLENTY

I reeled, unsure of what to do. Could I waltz right in and remove the evidence without interacting with the hogs?

"You're not supposed to be here." A small woman stood behind me, arms crossed against her chest, dark blonde hair tucked under a floppy hat. "This isn't human visitor day."

"Human?"

"If you've got an animal that needs housing, then you're good."

"Who're you?"

"Zena, volunteer and animal lover. Most of them, anyway." She threw the pigs a killer look.

"You work the pens?"

"And the souvenir shop. Not always on the same day. Who are you?"

"I came with two guys. Friends of mine. They may have left something behind in this pen. I'm here to get it." I didn't want to say more or panic could ensue.

"Was it food?" She craned her neck and examined the area. "'Cause they're like piranhas when there's food around." She lowered her voice and spoke through closed lips. "Don't tell anyone I said that." She clasped a hand to her mouth and pointed toward the pen. "What's that?"

"A pair of dentures. Can you retrieve them for me so I can return them to my friends?"

"No way. No freaking way. I don't go in there. Uh-uh." She took small steps backwards.

"I thought you worked the pens."

"Pens you write with, okay? Not the ones with pigs in them." She crossed her arms again. "I love animals. But these guys are...boisterous. I've seen them. When there's food, get out of the way." She lowered her voice. "I'll get Freddy." She turned and ran off.

I forced my eyes away from the dentures and examined the pig floor. It was dirt, thinly scattered hay piles, and vegetable cast-offs. No trace of human remains. Was it possible that if they were starving enough, they'd eat a body so quickly? What happened to the bones? And the clothes?

"We're not open to the public today," a male voice said.

Zena had returned with the younger version of Al Pacino. His once shiny black shoes were matted with dust and dirt and possibly more. Veera showed up behind him.

"I'm not here for the farm tour. I came to retrieve my friend's dentures," I said. "They're in this pen."

"Retrieve what?" Veera was all eyes.

"Who's your friend?" the man asked.

"Ian. He was here with Squalley."

The guy smiled. "Good fellas. I'm Freddy, the manager. I'm Squalley's nephew. I'll get the teeth." He unlatched the gate and strolled in. A huge white pig ran full speed toward him. Freddy opened up his arms.

"Oh, mother of…" Veera muttered.

Zena squirmed.

The pig flopped on its side in front of Freddy, who bent down, patted the hog's side, gave it a belly rub and grabbed the dentures. Zena wrinkled her nose. After another hefty dose of belly rubbing, Freddy rose and exited. The pig stumbled to its hooves, shook itself off, and trotted off to a corner.

"Would you look at that?" Veera said. "They're like dogs."

"But a lot smarter." Freddy whipped out a plastic bag and dropped the dentures in. He handed the bag to Zena. "Rinse these and bring them back to…" Zena sprinted away and Freddy turned to me. "What's your name?"

"Uh, Sue. That's what I'm called. That's my name. I work at the school with Ian and Squalley. That was nice of you to let them visit when the farm isn't open to the public."

"Besides being family, they're VIPS. Volunteers in Pig Section. They have permission to be in here. So who did you say those teeth belong to?"

"The guest they brought with them."

"What guest?" Freddy asked. "I didn't see anyone."

He spoke a little too quickly.

"Maybe I imagined it," I said.

"You saying you got an imaginary friend? Hey, who am I to judge?" Freddy grinned and turned to Veera. "Looking forward to adding you as staff. You got a true love for animals. We need more of your kind of love around here."

"That's me, alright. Can't pry me away from them hogs and pigs. I look forward to milking the cows and sheep and anything else that needs milking. Milk does a body good."

Zena returned with the denture bag and handed them to me.

"Thanks. I won't take up any more of your time," I said.

Veera and I hustled down the driveway to the car. We sat inside, and she cranked the engine.

"That was more than I bargained for," Veera said.

"What do you know about Freddy?"

"He owns this place. He inherited it from his gran two years ago and stops by most weekends. And when he's not here, he runs the family cement company." Veera turned to me. "You thinking what I'm thinking?"

"Yeah, that up close he looks more like Chachi on *Happy Days* than Al Pacino."

"*Happy* what?"

"Never mind. What were you thinking?"

"That Big Mac was brought here for a fitting. A shoe fitting. If you know what I'm talking about. The kind of shoes you only wear once."

"Like tuxedo shoes?"

"Like cement boots. It's no coincidence Freddy's family owns a cement company."

I stopped listening to Veera and thought about the pigs. Zena called them piranhas. They seemed tame when Freddy entered the pen. Yet there were documented cases where all that was left of a pig farmer were his teeth and shreds of clothing. It was my turn to shudder. "Let's find out who burped in the trunk."

## CHAPTER 16

### ANIMAL WEARY

There were times my father and I picked up clues the crime scene investigation unit missed. Clues Dad utilized to crack his clients' cases. Clues that needed expert handling. Dad couldn't just parade into the coroner's office or LAPD forensics lab to get evidence analyzed. He turned to PETS.

"No, thank you. I'm all animal-ed out today," Veera said after I told her where we were going. "No pets, no cute little singing birds chirping in the trees, no butterflies even. Nothing with more than one stomach and two legs."

"PETS is an acronym. Physical Evidence Tech Services. We're going to a forensics expert analyst. It's a private lab."

"For real?" Her eyes grew round. "That's exciting." Her brows drew together. "I know I'm new at this PI stuff, but do we even know if this president wore fake teeth? Wouldn't it be quicker to have ADA James—"

"Now, what fun would that be?" My first inclination had been to go to James, but I'd nixed that in favor of later than sooner. After I knew if the clues were viable. To avoid more embarrassment. Mine, that is. "Big Mac had fat cheeks. Perfect for wearing dentures. Once we've got something worthwhile, I'll call Michael."

"All right. Where is this place?"

"Take the 101 north to downtown Ventura, to a lab my father used."

"I can hardly believe it. We're crime scene investigators. Just like on TV. You know we got potential. We should open up shop. Not like we're doing anything at the office these days, anyway."

When I'd scored the dream job at Ameripictures, I'd thought I was set. It turned out there were strings attached. Long, strong ones. The studio security chief did his share of arm-twisting to get me to investigate a colleague's suspicious death. The chief knew all about Dad's PI work, and my role in helping find a big clue in a high-profile case. After I'd fingered the killer at the studio, the executives that weren't fired were shipped to the main lot in Culver City. Underlings like me stayed in limbo in Newport. My boss, Marshall Cooperman, promised I'd move to the main lot soon, but I'd stopped holding my breath. I drove to work, took calls, and drafted contracts with talent too small for the executives, expecting the guillotine to fall any moment.

"We'll call it the Number One L.A. Detective Agency. What do you think?"

PI work was like working in a coal mine, complete with collapsing walls, black lung disease, and oxygen deprivation, with nothing more than the light on the helmet to guide the way. "First up, let's convince this lab to help."

Veera cracked her knuckles. "Convincing is my strong suit. I could convince the stripes off a zebra if I wasn't all done with animals. I hope Michael knows how lucky he is to have you on his side. You sure are a big help to him."

Was I helping by running all over the place? "These teeth and stray hairs belong to somebody, right?" I said. "It could be Big Mac." Or they could belong to someone else.

⧪⧪⧪

Over an hour later, we exited the 101 and drove up Telephone Road.

"Turn right on Market Street. Look for 4123," I told Veera, giving her VW another tour of duty.

"You know someone there who'll take care of us?"

"I will soon." I regarded my smart phone. The PETS website listed its employees by rank. The top dogs were the lab president, manager, and the assistant. PETS was open on Saturdays, but only half-staffed. I was willing to bet the main techs rotated weekends, with an assistant perpetually in attendance. The assistant was one Yoko O'Hara, a millennial with a penchant for popcorn balls and party planning, according to her bio. She also bragged a biotechnology certificate and a T-6 finish in the U.S. Pro Miniature Golf Masters.

Minutes later, the street curved into a stream of single story, industrial type structures, all with the same bland exteriors and strips of shrubbery, squared off and running in place.

"This is it." Veera pulled into a parking lot with a sea of empty slots.

The suites facing us sported limo-tinted windows. A royal blue awning hung above every entrance, as if the added precaution would prevent the sun from throwing in an errant ray.

"You got the goods?" Veera asked.

I spied the dentures between my sneakers. The teeth rested at the bottom of the plastic bag, pink gums hosting pearly whites ready to take a bite. I patted the envelope with the hairs in my pocket. "Roger that." Hopefully, we hadn't bitten off more than we could chew.

## CHAPTER 17

## THE LAB NON-RESULTS

I pushed open a door in the wall of glass and stepped into a cramped reception area. A bell jingled our arrival. Oak chairs sat in single file against one side. An oval table squatted in front of the chairs, hosting science magazines. Reception was unmanned.

"Hello?" I called out in my best *I mean business* voice. The lab employees needed to know right off the bat this was serious.

A youngish woman with a badge reading *Yoko* bounded in through the side door. Limp black strands feathered around her pale face, the rest pulled back in a half-bun. She wore a white lab coat with matching pants and sneakers. "You have an appointment?"

I pulled out my wallet and flashed a silver badge taken off a fallen Los Angeles cop by my father. I tried not to use this ploy too often, as it could have consequences. Like prison. "We're here on a sensitive matter."

"From LAPD?" Yoko asked.

"We ask the questions," Veera told her.

"We're forced to cross county lines and bypass our own lab," I said. "That's how delicate this situation is."

"We're talking wonton skin delicate," Veera said.

I flashed her a *cut the chatter* look and inched closer to Yoko. I lowered my voice. "A VIP is involved."

Yoko's dark stare flashed from Veera to me. "This is not a good time. I'm the only people here."

I couldn't have asked for more. "You're the only people we need."

"We'd prefer someone in top level forensics," Veera said.

"But we're in a time crunch. The accused may go on the lam once he discovers we have these." I held up the dentures in one hand and the envelope with the hairs in the other.

Yoko's fingers slapped her lips when she saw the teeth. "They are evidence?"

"In what could be a serious crime."

"Come with me," she said.

Veera whispered, "Now we're getting somewhere."

We followed Yoko through a door marked *Preparation Laboratory* and into a white-walled, brightly lit space, so compact that two people would rub shoulders passing from end to end. Both sides housed shelves overflowing with boxes, empty glass jars, and tools varying from syringes to tweezers. Below the shelves sat vertical rows of drawers. Small machinery monopolized the counter space. The place reeked of pungent disinfectants.

Yoko's hands snapped into blue plastic gloves. A mask covered the lower half of her face.

"Shouldn't we be wearing one of those?" Veera asked. "This place looks like a germ factory."

"You don't touch anything, you get no germs."

"I got to breathe," Veera said. "And I don't want to be breathin' in bacteria or toxic waste floaters."

"You'll be fine," Yoko said. "I'm fine, and I hardly ever wear a mask."

We took a hard look at Yoko. A butter-colored lump occupied a spot above a sparse brow.

"You've got some funky growth right there." Veera pointed. "I'd better not get one of those."

Yoko patted her forehead with a glove. She rubbed at the lump with her index finger. "That's a piece of ramen noodle from lunch."

"Take a look at these and see if you can determine who they belong to." I handed her the denture bag. "Or anything that makes them unique."

Yoko took the bag in her fingertips, turned, and dropped it on a counter. She unsealed the top, grabbed some prongs and extracted the teeth. She laid them on a Petri dish and prodded the gums with a metal stick.

"She doesn't know what the heck she's doing," Veera spoke out the side of her mouth. "This is a time waster."

"I know who these belong to," Yoko said.

"No foolin'?"

"Why you doubt me?" Yoko asked her.

"How did you get the answer so fast?" Veera wanted to know. "That's just not possible."

"Yes, it is." She turned to me. "You got four hundred dollars?"

"You'll need to send the department an invoice," I told her.

"Cut the department crap. I know who you are. You used to come here with your pop. I have a good memory. He's that famous private eye."

"Investigator is the proper term. I'm with the department now. How come I never saw you before?"

"Because I worked the back office. I was promoted. I have more responsibility now. Which means…" Yoko turned, picked up the teeth with her gloved fingers, and dropped them into a drawer. Then she removed a key from her coat and locked it. "…no money, no teeth."

"Why you scheming—" Veera started.

I held Veera back with my arm. "Four hundred is too much and you know it."

"How do we even know you got an authentic ID on the dentures?" Veera asked. "You could be lying."

"No, she's the liar." Yoko pointed to me. "And maybe you, too."

The phone in my pocket vibrated. I pulled it out. Michael had sent a text:

*Loretta says she saw Mac on campus this morning. Is it possible he's alive?*

My gut told me Loretta was the biggest liar of all. I turned to Yoko.

"We don't need you anymore. Come on, Veera. Let's get out of here."

We headed toward the door.

"No, you wait." Yoko took little steps toward us. "My time is valuable."

"Okay, I got this." Veera jammed a hand into her pocket and yanked out a small pink wallet. She pulled out two bills. She held them between her fingers. "That ought to cover the time you spent taking the teeth out of that baggie."

"Two dollars? Why you so mean to me?"

"Keep the teeth." I walked out the doorway.

"Wait." Yoko gained on us. "I have a positive ID on the dentures."

I turned toward her. "And?"

"I want something in return. Not money. A favor."

What was with favor fever? Everyone from Veera to people I'd just met were asking for favors.

"I've had enough of this gold digger," Veera said.

"We help your pop a lot," Yoko said. "For no money."

"Who's 'we'?" I asked.

"My father is the head scientist. I help him help your pop. Now it's my turn. I scratch my back, you scratch yours."

"That's…" Veera held up her hand. "Never mind."

Veera and I turned our backs to Yoko. We made it down the hallway when we heard,

"When your pop comes in next week, I'll tell him how you acted."

My legs froze. I took a step back and turned to face Yoko. "He won't be coming in."

"He said—"

"He won't be."

"But last week he needed—"

"What?"

"WHAT?" Veera stood close behind me.

## CHAPTER 18

### THE IMPOSSIBLE DAD

"Back up," I said. "So someone who looks like my father—"

"Not looks like," Yoko said.

"Came in last week…" I continued.

"Early Sunday…" Yoko said.

"And asked you to analyze what exactly?" I asked.

"Fingernails. Clippings he'd found on the floor of a men's toilet."

"You're talking about Montague Locke, right?" Veera asked. "The private investigator?"

"Yes."

"He died a year ago," I said. "He was poisoned."

"Pants on fire," Veera said to Yoko.

"I'm telling the truth. He came here," Yoko said. "I asked my pop and he says 'no questions,' so I stay quiet."

"Is it a coincidence you're telling me this when you need a favor?" I asked.

"When am I supposed to tell you?"

Veera grabbed my elbow and pulled me away. "Don't get sucked into her alternate reality. Look at her. That girl's crazy."

Our eyes rolled back to Yoko. One gloved finger fidgeted in her mouth, between her two front teeth. She blinked rapidly and sucked on her finger. I couldn't argue with Veera, but still, crazy people knew things.

I walked back to Yoko. "When is my dad coming in next?"

Yoko slid to a drawer, opened it, and removed a clipboard. She studied it. "He's not on the schedule." She raised her pointy chin. "Sometimes he drops in. Like you did. I'll call you when he's here."

"Not so fast." Veera pushed past me. "You need to give us something more about those teeth."

"I won't. Until she…" Yoko tossed her index finger my way. "Agrees to my favor. It's an even exchange."

"What favor?" I asked. First Mac was spotted and now my father. How could that be? Part of me wanted to set up camp in front of the building to see if the impossible could be possible. The other part wanted to run off to Alaska, and keep running until my feet grew numb.

Yoko backed up to the counter and unlocked the drawer that housed the dentures. She reached a hand behind her, dropped the teeth in the Petri dish, and slid it atop the counter. "The favor is for me. I'm the one who told you about your detective dad."

"That's private investigator. Detectives work for the police." Why did no one get that?

"You'd better watch your language." Veera moved in behind me and flanked Yoko's opposite side.

"What's the favor?" I wanted to know.

Yoko's head flipped between us. "I need another job. I know what job I want. I'll get it if you write a letter," she told me. "My pop doesn't want me here anymore. He's mad."

"Mad, as in mad as hell?" Veera stepped out in front of Yoko. "Or mad as in he's got cotton balls for brains?"

During Veera's babbling, I leaned all the way against the counter and peered into the Petri dish. The set of teeth rested on its haunches, gums parted. I scrutinized the smooth finish, the small hills in each pearly white. Then I saw it.

"Mad angry," Yoko was saying. "He says I can't work for him anymore. Because I used *Wikipedia* to get information—"

"Let's go, Veera." I grabbed the dentures and shot out the door. I didn't stop until I reached the exit. I tossed a look over my shoulder at Yoko and pulled out my business card. "We can talk favors after you get me proof about my dad." I dropped the card on the magazine table and hit the pavement. I leaned my head toward Veera. "I know who the dentures belong to."

"The president?"

"Initials are carved on the gums, behind the last two molars. DVF."

Veera's dark eyes reached for the sky and fell back to me. "Diane von Fürstenberg? She could wear dentures. She's got perfect teeth."

"I doubt she was in the pigpen."

"True. She does have a fashion empire to run. What's the president's name again?"

"Something MacTavish." I blew out a sigh. "Veera, the teeth belong to someone else. And it's possible Michael was mistaken about Mac. Michael texted me that Big Mac was spotted on campus this morning."

"For real? Well, that's good news 'cause it lets Michael off the hook. But you don't seem too happy."

"It doesn't add up."

"You mean like one and one equals seven?"

Yoko ran over to us, clutching a manila envelope. "It's in here. A sample letter. For my favor. Just copy and send it in. Easy-peasy."

"Girl, you got nerve," Veera told her.

"I'm not taking that," I said.

Yoko folded her arms across her chest. "You take it if you want to know about your pop."

"Guess what?" I folded my arms across my chest. "I don't. You didn't see him." I turned to Veera. "Let's go." I landed in the passenger side and shut the door.

Veera took her place behind the wheel and turned on the ignition. She slipped the VW into reverse. "What's that crazy woman doing now?"

Yoko pushed the envelope through the slat in the rear window and took off toward the lab. I turned in time to see her shut the door behind her.

"What the hell?" I stretched an arm and grabbed the envelope.

"That girl is bonkers," Veera said. "Don't go believin' anything she says."

"I'll be back." I stepped out into the brisk evening, ran to the door, and shoved the envelope through a mail slot.

I returned to my seat. "Let's get out of here."

Veera pulled out. I glanced around the building. No security guard. No video cams. But plenty of questions. From me. I'd never seen Dad's body. No way to know if Yoko told the truth. Except one.

## CHAPTER 19

## THE ONE WOMAN SHOW

"What happened here?" I'd barely crossed the threshold when I noticed a rift in the landscape. My living room floor was swept clean, emptied of blankets and sheets. Fluffed pillows posed at each end of my futon. Even the short chrome legs sparkled. A brown wicker basket hosting a pink orchid posed on the kitchenette counter. The air was moist with household cleaning fumes.

"Looks like Martha Stewart broke in," Veera said.

I marched over to the chairs by the back door. I lifted one slightly and rubbed a finger around the square heel. Rubber pads were glued to each foot. "Mother."

"Your mom did this? That was so nice." She lifted her nose. "Is that pot roast?"

I raced into my bedroom and looked under the bed. My weapon box was missing. "Mom!"

Veera raced in. "There's a roast cooking in the oven. Is she here?"

"She's like a human hurricane. She blows in, sweeps the floor, makes dinner, conducts a search and seizure, and blows out, in under two hours."

"Your mom's in the business too?"

"What business?"

"You know, crime fighting."

"She's in fashion. She's great at accentuating the shoulders to make the waist and hips look smaller, but not so great at keeping out of my business. Too bad."

"If someone tidied my place and made me dinner while I was out, it would be too good, not too bad."

"Too bad she's not still here." I spied a note taped to my bathroom door:

*I'll be back at six to take the roast out, sweetie. If you get in first, let me know. You're welcome. Love, Mom*

I grabbed a sweater and headed for the door. "Mind staying here and keeping an eye on the roast?"

"I'll make sure it continues to smell delicious." Veera was about to bounce onto the futon and stopped herself. She gingerly planted her bottom on the seat. "See you soon."

Twenty minutes later, I pulled into Mom's driveway. She still lived in the same home she'd bought with Dad during a lull in the Southern California real estate market. He'd gifted it to her after the divorce.

I pulled out my key and unlocked the front door. A latched gold chain halted forward movement. I put my mouth to the narrow opening. "Mom? I found a speck of dust on my kitchen counter."

A slice of Mom's face appeared. She unlatched the chain and opened the door. "Sweetie! If you're here, who's watching the roast?" She gave me a peck on the cheek, and I bolted inside. "You're wearing sweats? That would mean—"

"That's right. I was exercising."

"You only wear sweats when you're doing what you shouldn't be. How many times..." She stopped and peered closer. She wrinkled her nose. "Oh, honey, why aren't you wearing any makeup?"

"Mother."

Mom was no minimalist when it came to makeup and fashion. Her casual house-wear consisted of a red turtleneck, a black and white checkered pencil skirt, and sling-back sandals. Her lipstick matched her top. Mascara plumped her lashes. She pushed back a stray lock from my face. "I can hardly see you through that jungle." Her heels cut a path to the kitchen. "I'm not saying you have to do anything fancy, but I'd probably have a grandchild by now if you wore lipstick. How about I make us a smoothie?"

"Is Dad dead?" I followed her to the kitchen.

"*What?*" She tripped to a halt. Her hand shot to her chest. "Why would you ask such a thing? Oh my God. Is this because I took your weapons away?"

I spilled the day's pertinent contents and observed her for any shift in expression. My mom was an exceptional liar. She'd honed her skills all those years keeping Dad's private investigation life a secret. Everyone thought he was an academic at UCLA, which he was. Professor of Motion

Picture History. But he led a double life, from which I was excluded...until after the divorce. That's when we hung out on weekends. I never questioned his indoor shooting range or collection of illegal weapons. I thought all fathers practiced target shooting with their kids on Sundays.

"Yoko is obviously insane," Mom was saying. "Did you happen to see glass pipes or magic mushrooms lying around? Was her lipstick on crooked? That's always a sign."

"Mom."

"Nutmeg's a gateway drug, you know. It's a hallucinogenic in large quantities. Did you see any?"

She turned to walk away and my fingers locked around her wrist. Her pulse raced faster than a thoroughbred running the Kentucky Derby.

"Now stop that," she said and twisted her wrist free. "The roast—"

"Okay. These topics are off limits: the roast, thank you very much, my sweats, makeup, wild hair, and things that turn your brain to slush."

"You're really restricting the conversation." Her eyes cut to the pantry.

"I never saw Dad's body," I said. "Did you?"

"You're going to insist we talk about it?" She sank onto the couch and crushed a pillow against her chest. I perched on the edge of the coffee table.

"Your father died and that's all there is to it. There's nothing more to say. It's too painful." She jumped up. "I've got just the thing to pick us up." She strolled over to the hall closet and pulled out her handbag.

"He was your ex. Why can't you talk about him?"

"Just because he chose living dangerously over living with us didn't mean I stopped loving him. Or that he stopped loving us." Mom played with her smartphone.

"Why would Yoko make that up? That's a pretty tall tale for a favor."

"How tall was her favor?"

"I didn't give her a chance to say. Something about writing a letter."

"I can see it now. You do the favor, she strings you along like a harp. Pretending your father was coming in when he wasn't. Then she'd ask another favor. And another. Smart move, not playing into her weaselly hands." Mom walked over to the TV and turned it on.

"Oh no," I said.

"There's nothing that a good tune won't cure."

"Anything but Karaoke."

"We don't even need a mic," she said. "I've got this new app..."

"No."

"One round of 'I've Got You Babe' and you'll feel like a new person."

"Where are my weapons?" I asked. "You had no right to take them."

"Yes, I did, sweetie. I found them when I was dusting under your bed. You should know better. You're a lawyer. A representative of the law. An upholder of the Constitution."

"Which provides the right to bear arms."

"Not the kind that'll land you in jail. If you're caught with those..." Her eyes shifted to the pantry door again and back to me. "Bye-bye, legal career. Hello, Sing Sing."

"What's with the pantry?"

"What?"

"You keep looking at it."

"Of course I do. I'm deciding which blender to use to make that smoothie after our songfest." She played with the TV remote. Lyrics appeared on the screen. "Come on. You'll feel better."

"No, I won't."

Mom sang along with the song on the television.

Were my earplugs still up in my old bedroom?

She sang louder.

"Mother." Her voice grew louder at the chorus.

"Did you see Dad's body?" I shouted over her crooning.

She muted the TV. "Didn't I answer that question already?"

No change in expression. No fidgeting. I turned toward the door. "Thanks, Mom."

"For what?"

"Dinner, cleaning my place, and telling me the truth." I opened the front door.

"Corrie, wait." She hightailed after me.
"Yes?" I turned toward her.
"There's something you need to know."

# CHAPTER 20

## IN DEEPER

"Say what?" Veera's fork hovered over a plate heaping with pot roast slices and mashed potatoes, which she'd whipped up during my absence.

"Mom never saw Dad's body." A large knot twisted around in my stomach, not leaving much room for food. "She ID'd a mole on his palm." Dad had a small brown mole below his left ring finger. That was all Mom saw of his post mortem body. "She said that was all she needed to see."

"She's right about that," Veera said. "No two palms are alike. Did she freak when you asked about him?"

"I guess. But she's not really that type. Except when I borrow her clothes. Besides, she was preoccupied with the roast and the pantry."

"The pantry? You mean like, cleaning it? I have an auntie who cleans her pantry when she's feeling anxious. And when she's watching *Dancing with the Stars.*" Veera took a second helping. "Two things we know for sure. Yoko is crazy. And this roast is good. Did you talk to Michael?"

"What for?" I knew perfectly well what for. I wanted to tell him about Yoko and Dad, how he was missing a good roast, and that Loretta needed to be thoroughly interrogated about her Mac sighting.

"To catch up and get the details. We got no hard evidence."

I grabbed my cell phone and called his number. He answered on the first ring.

"I'm so glad you called." He yelled over thumping music and crowd chatter. "I'm here with a bunch of LA Tech students. Everyone's nice and jazzed and everything, but something's off, Corrie. I'm not just talking about the fake tan thing they've got going...these students don't see much daylight. I'm talking about the Mac sighting—"

"Where are you?"

"At this cool bar in downtown L.A."

"You don't think Loretta saw the president?"

"I'm not sure." His voice had quieted. "How do we find out?"

"Did Loretta speak to him?" I needed something to make the sighting real and not a fabrication.

"No." He lowered his voice. "She saw him from a distance and from behind. I've got a ton more questions to ask her when you get here. You're so much better at interrogation than I am. No one can pull off a headlock like you can. See you soon, okay?"

"Where are—"

Michael disconnected.

"How do you like that?" I said. How was I supposed to get there when I didn't know where to go?

"What did he say?" Veera asked.

"Something about going to a bar and asking questions." I lowered my hand to the table.

"I've been thinking. Somebody's hair was in that trunk. Don't you want to know whose?" Veera had stopped eating. "'Course I don't blame you for feeling frustrated. Getting pig slop on your shoes, pocketing creepy teeth that look like they're about to bite off your fingertips. And ending up with a crazy woman who sees ghosts. What could be worse?"

My phone vibrated in my hand. The number was unfamiliar. I debated answering, but curiosity got the best of me. "This is Corrie."

"Squalley and I've been talking, and we know you know what we did."

My eyes darted to Veera's. I lowered the phone and whispered, "It's Ian. I think he's going to confess about the pigs eating someone."

"Mother of…" Veera stood and pushed back her plate.

I placed the call on speaker. "When did you figure it out?"

"After we drove away from the sanctuary," Ian said. "It was the only reason we could come up with for your being there. Did you see us load him in the trunk?"

Veera's jaw dropped.

"I heard him in the trunk when I helped you hitch up Squalley's car," I said.

"I knew it."

There was quiet, then a mumbling, and phone static.

"Squalley wants to talk to you," Ian said.

"Should I call the police?" Veera asked me.

"No," Ian said. "Please."

"I wasn't talking to you," Veera glowered at the phone. "Criminals. Gangsters."

"Wait 'til you hear us out."

"Why should we, fool?"

I put out my palm and waved my fingers toward Veera. I pointed to her smartphone. She handed it over. I pressed record. "I'm listening."

"It's me, Squalley. How you doing?"

"We just finished this fabulous pot roast," Veera said. "So we're doing good. What about you?"

"Well, nobody makes cannoli like I do. *Delizioso.* But here's the thing, Ian couldn't eat any. Not one bite. And that's not like him. He says you know what we did."

"True story," I said.

"He's worried you'll go to the cops. I want to explain why that's not a good idea."

"Why should we listen?" I asked.

"Because after we explain, you won't want to report us."

Veera's brows dipped. "You askin' us to break the law? 'Cause we don't do that."

"I'm asking you to understand. We witnessed the torture," Squalley said in his gruff voice. "There were blisters and open wounds. The infliction of such pain...well, the only choice was to pass out. We couldn't let that go on."

"Torture? Was there a lot of that?" Veera asked.

"Why didn't you report this?" I asked. How could Mac possibly get away with torturing students?

"We didn't know who we could trust. It was all hush, hush. It's easy to look the other way when your job's on the line."

I couldn't believe my ears. The scene played out in my mind: Ian and Squalley couldn't take it anymore. They stabbed Big Mac, propped him up between them, and dragged his sensible shoes across campus to Squalley's car. Maybe that's what Loretta saw. A dead or nearly dead president being transported. "So you stuffed him in your trunk?"

"He had plenty of beer to knock him out," Squalley said.

"Yeah, we didn't want him to get scared in there," Ian added.

"We freed him from his pain," Squalley said.

Freedom took on a whole new meaning. "He was alive when you put him inside?"

"We weren't going to let him die on campus," Squalley said.

"So you took him to the pigpen?"

"What better place?" Squalley asked. "The sanctuary's full of pigs."

Did they dump Big Mac in the pen? Lack of sleep dimmed my brain cells. I wasn't sure of anything anymore. My mind raced through recent crime files and stopped on a case in Italy where a mobster fed his rival to hungry hogs. "I know what pigs can do to a person. In Italy—"

"Hey, stop. Stop it, right now," Squalley said. "Pigs are not bad. People are. And this does not involve the Mob, understand? This involves two simple, hardworking people bringing about justice the only way they know how. And..."The pause was not only pregnant, it gave birth and watched twins grow up to be teens, that's how long it took him to continue. "If you rat on us, we'll tell the cops you helped slip him into the trunk."

Veera blew out a chuff, like a bull in a ring ready to charge. "Now you listen—"

"She was there," Squalley said. "She had knowledge and didn't stop us."

I placed my hand on Veera's arm. "That's an empty threat." Thorny, but empty. "I'll think this through."

"You're not going to say anything, are you?" Ian was on the line again.

"Give us a few days." I disconnected and turned to Veera. "That'll keep them from doing anything drastic, for now."

"Unless they think we're going to report them. Those two are trouble. We got to hide out or hunt them down. Let's hunt them down and get us some signed confessions." Veera's face took on a fierce glow. "That'll clear us of any involvement."

First Michael had a murder charge hanging over him. Now me. "Let's not overcomplicate things."

"We can't leave them runnin' loose, thinking they're doing good by offing bad people. Can we?"

When Veera put it that way, it sounded like killing Big Mac wasn't such a bad idea. "Let's focus on what we know. Ian and Squalley stuck the knife in the president's back, and got rid of the body by feeding him to hungry hogs. We need to find evidence to tie it to those two. And leave us out of it."

"We've got a confession." Veera held up her phone. "Uh, oh. Guess my phone didn't have enough juice."

I slapped my hand on the table.

"I know it, I messed up. But we're witnesses, aren't we? We heard it firsthand."

"We need better proof than that," I said.

"I just thought of something," Veera said. "If they think we'll talk, they might come and try to feed us to the hogs. There's a possibility we could both fit in that car trunk."

"The trunk is for people they regard as evil. When was the last time you tortured anyone?"

"What do you mean by torture?"

"I've got an idea." I usually fly under the wire, and only under the wire. But I had a sudden hankering to be an upstanding citizen. I'd never tested that route. I used my smartphone to call an LAPD hotline. "I'm calling the cops. Anonymously."

Veera pushed her chair back. "You sure about that?"

"Sergeant Hatfield," a voice answered.

"I want to report a homicide." My upright citizenship was on fire. "Name?"

"Isn't this an anonymous tip line?"

"Of the victim."

"Oh. MacTavish."

"That's it?"

"Yes."

"Where did you find the body?"

"I didn't see it, but I—"

"What makes you think there is one?" His question came out as part of a yawn.

"I heard it," I spoke louder.

"You heard a dead body?" He snorted.

"Aren't post mortem sounds emitted?"

"I'll let you have that one. Why didn't you see the body? Are you blind?"

I fought the urge to answer back. Upstanding citizen all the way. "No, sir. It was in the trunk of a car."

"Whose car?"

"Someone named Squalley."

"License plate?"

This was becoming increasingly humiliating. The facts seemed so clear before I'd placed the call. "Is that necessary?" My father would have been at Squalley's door by now.

"Look, we don't have the resources to investigate each call. Only the viable ones. You know what 'viable' means?"

"I have an address."

"We're not going anywhere. No body, no critical facts, no eyewitness to anything unlawful."

"I've got powerful circumstantial evidence linking the defendant to the homicide."

"Now we're getting somewhere," Veera said.

"Isn't it true," I continued to make my case, "that circumstantial evidence is more likely to be encountered at a crime scene than direct evidence?"

"Well, I'm not at liberty—"

"Motive. That's what this suspect has. Plenty of it. His viable reason for killing the victim."

"And what might that be?"

"The dead guy tortured students," I said. "At LA Tech."

"Hold on."

The line went silent. I was placed on hold.

"Aren't you worried Squalley will try to pull us down with them?" Veera asked. "He said he's gonna say we were in cahoots."

I pushed my shoulders back. "He and Ian have motive. We don't."

"But your boyfriend was fired by the dead guy, and you might have been mad enough to do something illegal to help him out. Isn't that motive? And I'm the loyal sidekick who does as she's told. So I've got me some motive too."

She made a good point. My shoulders dropped. "He's not my boyfriend."

"Miss," the officer came back on the line. "No police reports were filed by students claiming torture on that campus. But we're willing to check it out. Where was the last place you saw this car? We need details."

"Uh...I'll find out and call you back." I disconnected. This was stickier than I thought. I didn't want to be the fly on the sticky paper. I stood, clasped my hands behind my back, and walked to the front door. The only weapons I had left were my shuriken, a knife posing as a comb, and the pistol, which was perfectly legal. It's the shuriken that could be problematic. "We have to take action."

"I'm not going back to that farm," Veera said. "I might end up in someone's pot belly."

I unclasped my hands and paced back to her. "We can do this. We'll bring Ian and Squalley to justice ourselves." My two minutes as upright citizen were officially terminated.

Veera jumped up, face alight, hands balled into fists. "Does that mean we can skip the farm? Now we're talking. We'll break those two in half like a rickety wishbone. What's our first move?"

I needed to pay Yoko another visit. There were still hair samples to analyze. "If we can match the hairs from Squalley's trunk to those on Big Mac's head, that's evidence right there."

Veera slammed her palms against the kitchenette counter. "That lab must have an emergency dial-in, like doctors do. We'll call and get Yoko in there."

"She could refuse to cooperate."

"Let's hold her hostage 'til she does her civic duty."

My eyes shot to Veera's. "I like that."

"Nothing makes someone feel more important than doing what they should be doing anyway."

"I don't know what I'd do without you, Veera. There is one more, small thing. About the farm—"

"I won't do it."

## CHAPTER 21

## THE RIDE-ALONG


I picked up my phone. "All you have to do is call your friend at the sanctuary."

"Al Pacino is not my friend," Veera said. "Least not this version of him."

"We need to find out whose initials were carved on the dentures. For all we know, they belong to a witness."

"Or to another dinner entree." Veera shuddered.

"Just call and say we tried to find the rightful owner."

"The rightful, possibly dead owner."

"Freddy will talk to you," I said. "He seemed genuinely moved by your love for animals."

"I do like animals. Cats and cute little puppies. Not critters with horns and beards."

Before either of us could call, my cell phone vibrated. It was my boss. At Ameripictures. I answered and mouthed to Veera, "Marshall."

"Don't talk to him," she said. "That man never has anything good to say."

"This is Corrie," I said.

"Corrie," a thin voice said. "Go to the Newport office and clean out your desk. Collect your personal items, files you're working on, and anything else you need. Tell Veera to do the same. Do it now."

My heart sank again. I was about to lose my steady paycheck, my excuse for borrowing Mom's clothes, and bragging rights to working for a movie studio. Marshall Cooperman, vice president, business affairs of Ameripictures, was housed safely in the main studio in Culver City, while we outcasts in Newport navigated without a steering wheel. My days of dodging the lay-off notice were over.

"Is this official?" I asked.

"What is that supposed to mean?"

"Shouldn't I receive something in writing?" As head lawyer, he knew that better than I did. There was probably a letter pinned to my office door already.

"Listen," he said. "These have been unsettling times."

I'll say. "I need to—"

"You and Veera need to bring everything when you report to the Culver City lot."

My heart rocketed upward and slammed against the top of my skull, sending me reeling. I'd been waiting, hoping. My throat squeezed shut. I couldn't even down a mint if I tried. "What?"

"Take care of it tonight." Marshall paused. I could hear radio stations changing in the background. Static, tune, talk, static, violins, talk, and finally a baseball game. "Bring everything to The Lot on Tuesday."

"Where's—"

He disconnected.

"My new office?" I lowered the phone on the table.

"New office?" Veera asked. "Are we moving?"

"He…" My voice squeaked and I cleared my throat. "He wants us to go to Newport tonight and pack up our stuff."

Veera pushed her chair back with her legs and stood tall. "We're fired? 'Cause I'm down with that. I'm ready to pull off this PI business. I'm even willing to hang out at that zoo."

"Farm."

"If I have to."

"We're not fired. Starting next week, we'll be working on The Lot."

"Whoa, whoa, whoa." Veera's mouth fell open. "The place with famous movie stars walking around all casual? And that excellent cafeteria?"

"Commissary."

"I hear they got movie premieres where they roll out the red carpet. I've never walked a red carpet before. I hear they even got their own yellow brick road. Whoa ho!"

"There could be a lockdown tomorrow in Newport." That was my best guess. A lockdown not by law enforcement, but by the mothership. The top guns at the main studio wanted to cut remaining cords with what remained of the Newport division. Somehow Marshall had salvaged our jobs. "They'll probably close down the Orange County office."

"That's bona fide. This calls for a celebration."

"What about Yoko? And Ian and Squalley?" I asked.

"They're not going anywhere, are they?"

I pictured Ian and Squalley in Ian's old truck, crossing the Mexican border by night, settling in a shanty town, meeting an old prospector who convinces them there's gold to be panned. No, wait, that was Humphrey Bogart in *The Treasure of the Sierra Madre*. "Okay. We'll tackle them in the morning. I pictured Michael in the L.A. bar. "I should see Michael." I massaged the back of my neck and texted him. In less than a minute I had an address. "We'll go to Newport first."

Veera clicked her tongue. "No, *I'll* go to Newport and pack up our stuff. You meet with your boy and question that student who saw the president. Sounds like she's our witness." Veera was a one-woman fireworks display. "I'm gonna be a while. I got a truckload of stuff to pack."

"It won't take long to pack our files."

"Who's talking files? I'll get them too. But I'm talking supplies that need my personal attention. I got make-up, undies, and my fold-up black blazer in those desk drawers. I don't want anyone else touching my belongings."

"You have all that in your drawers?"

"How do you think I fielded all those everyday catastrophes?"

Of which we had many. "Thanks, Veera."

I left her with a spare key to my place, changed into a black chiffon dress and sandals, and took off to find Michael.

Nearly an hour later, I parked near Pershing Square, and high heeled it over to One Eyed Sal's, downtown L.A.'s signature dive bar on Hill Street, the only joint with a door shaped like a keyhole. Footsore and lay-off free, I arrived and bypassed the cover charge, thanks to fast-talking the big guy standing guard. I exchanged a dollop of legal advice for free entry. How to expunge a criminal record in three easy steps. He was happy and my wallet wasn't any lighter. Sometimes favors are good. Not counting favors for the insane.

I stepped through the entry and waded through a blur of faces searching for Michael. All I got was ear shattering noise, mirrors, and dark corners. I pushed my way past a red-lit bar lined with red pleather seats. Behind the bar, glass shelves housed an array of liquor bottles in all their spirited glory.

I was about to text Michael when my phone chimed. I'd gotten a text from James:

*Walk down the length of the bar to the patio entrance.*

A dozen more steps and I'd entered a tunnel-like hallway with a wooden handrail stuck to one side. The same red lighting that tinted the bar glowed in the hall, bordello style. Three dim chandeliers hung in a row from the ceiling. The end of the hallway gave way to a large patio with an open roof that framed high-rises standing by like starships.

I scanned the patio. Quirky hats, sunburnt faces, and students in t-shirts galore. At the far end, a tall guy leaned a shoulder against a post. He wore a white hoodie, jeans, and a stare aimed my way. A female cuddled against each of his arms. I couldn't see his face clearly, but I knew it was James. No sign of Michael.

I elbowed my way over and stopped inches away from him, my head tilted back. With one quick shake of his arms, the females scattered.

"Hi," James said.

Warm, beer-scented breath swept my nostrils. I pointed my mouth toward his ear. "Can Loretta be trusted?"

I pulled back. A laser beam of warmth shot between our pupils.

"No."

High-pitched chatter encircled us.

"She may be a mathematical genius." James shot a glance over my head. "But she's an unreliable witness."

"Go on."

"She's got a crush on Mikey and would tell him she saw Godzilla roaming the campus if that's what he wanted to hear." James bent his face closer to mine. "Michael's good at tolerating liars."

I had no intention of taking that personally. "My lies are truths thoughtfully reconstructed for a noble cause."

"Since when?"

"Since the current circumstances dictate I play private investigator."

His rugged features softened and the hint of a primitive grunt melted in his throat. "You wear honesty well."

"Corrie? You made it."

James and I spread apart. Michael stood next to me, a happy smile stitched to his mouth.

"Ah, come on, give me some sugar." His arms wrapped around in a tight squeeze, sparking a warm glow in my chest.

"Michael, I…" A mind-numbing perfume burned through my next words.

"Hey." The word spread out in two syllables and sprang from the mouth of a female with squinty blue eyes and a plank-like body that could have served as a diving board over a gym pool. A choppy curtain of ginger colored hair swung around her pale face. "I was told your dad was someone I never heard of," she said to me.

I recognized the over-the-top scent of gardenias. Loretta was the student I smelled when Michael and I hid in the shrubbery. She was also the woman I spotted running from the Admin Hall after she'd planted the letter.

"You wouldn't, in your circles."

"What does that mean?"

"Loretta saw Mac on campus early this morning," Michael said.

"Who was he with?" I asked her.

Loretta's squint bounced off me and ricocheted back to Michael. Clint Eastwood never squinted so well. "Nobody. Who would want to accompany that troll?" She turned to me. "That was a rhetorical question, by the way."

"He was alone?" How was that possible? "Where was he headed?"

"What is with the questions? Oh, I know." Loretta did an eye roll. "Girl detectives are so bland and predictable."

"I'll try to be more entertaining," I said.

"As if you could," Loretta said.

"I'll show you—"

"What a sense of humor you've got, Loretta." Michael's voice pitched on the high side. "It's so unique." He added a chuckle. Then another. "Mac was probably wearing his usual batwing bowtie, wasn't he?" Michael took over the questioning.

"Yes. With his rumpled blue suit." Loretta's pursed lips slid to one side. "And that loathsome beard without a moustache."

"Who does that?" Michael said.

"Amish farmers do," I said.

"And he was wearing those hideous brown saddle shoes," Loretta added.

"There aren't very many guys who can pull those shoes off," Michael said and turned to me. "Doesn't Loretta have an incredible eye for detail? Must be the mathematician in her."

"The devil isn't always in the details," I said. "He could be hiding in the person doling them out."

Loretta shrank back into a shadow.

"Michael," I said. "It's possible Loretta didn't see what she thought she saw."

"I do not make mistakes." Loretta re-emerged, squintier than before. "He was headed for the faculty parking lot. It was him. His hair was uncombed, messier than ever."

"You sure it wasn't Einstein you saw on campus?" I asked.

"I know who it was. President MacTavish's hair sticks up like boar bristles," Loretta added.

Now she had my attention. "Kind of coarse. Like a fishing line?"

"I do not fish," Loretta said and slid to Michael, placing a pasty hand on his arm. "This has been the best night ever."

"Really?" Michael said, wearing a pint-size grin.

"Let's get a drink." James gave my shoulder a tap with the back of his hand.

"I'm busy," I replied.

"I'm thirsty. Thought you might want a little something, too." James tipped his head toward the end of the room and strolled away.

Meanwhile, Michael giggled, head-to-head with Loretta. I distrusted her more than any felon I'd ever encountered with Dad. There was something so conniving about her.

"You coming?" James shouted from across the room.

I dragged my heels over. James pushed open a door, camouflaged to disappear into the wall. We stepped outside into a car-crammed parking lot rimmed by a wrought iron fence with spiked tops. Slender palms stood tall at the borders, brown fronds begging for a trim.

James stopped by a cement partition that separated the lot from the mini skyscraper next door. He unzipped his sweatshirt and slipped it off to reveal a white t-shirt that molded around his statuesque physique. A group of women paused, gazes kneading James from head-to-toe. I couldn't blame them. There weren't too many males around with stampede-inducing good looks.

"I'm listening," I said.

"About the president," James said.

"It wasn't him. Big Mac is dead."

James did a deep scan of my face. It was his personal version of a lie detector test. No twitch, uneven breath, or failure to blink at appropriate intervals would go unnoticed. "Tell me what you know."

"Remember the burp I heard coming from Squalley's trunk?"

James exhaled. "How could I forget?"

He was not going to yank my chain tonight. "The school janitor and the maintenance man killed Big Mac and stashed the body in the trunk. That's why I heard the post-mortem or maybe even near-mortem belch. Afterward, they transported him to a pig farm where he was devoured by hungry hogs."

James allowed his lips to part. He chuckled. And laughed. A full blown, high-pitched laugh that clashed with his manly exterior.

"I couldn't make this stuff up," I said. "They confessed."

"You're serious?" James sputtered.

"I've got proof."

James toned his laughter down. "Like what? Did you witness the pigs feasting?"

"I took hair samples from the trunk," I said. "And dentures from another hapless victim. I'm sure it's Big Mac's hair."

"How sure?"

I was beginning to feel like the village idiot.

"What was their motive?" James wanted to know.

"Big Mac physically harmed some students, maybe to the point of torture, and those two tried to stop him. They probably went too far and had to dispose of the body. The hogs were a convenient means of doing so."

"Don't you hear how outrageous you sound?" James asked.

"It's possible." It seemed so plausible at the farm.

"It's also possible I'll be a stowaway on the next space shuttle, but I'm not counting on it."

"Are you saying you believe Loretta over me?" I asked.

"It's your theory I've got trouble with."

"Theory? That's low, James." He and I were worlds apart, as usual.

James put up a hand. "She could have seen someone posing as him."

Maybe we walked the same street. "Let's say she did. That would mean someone killed him, but wants everyone to think he's alive. Why?"

"To buy time until the corpse can be disposed of."

"Okay. We agree there's a better than average chance Loretta didn't see him. Which still means Big Mac was the victim of foul play. Which also means we just differ over the handling of the body."

"Maybe the body's still on campus," James said.

"We'll need to do another in-depth search."

"Let's do it," James said.

"Where'd you two go?" Michael appeared behind us.

"I was just saying I'm beat. I'm going to call it a night." There was a kernel of truth to my statement, even if it was a stunted kernel. I was calling it a night here, anyway.

"You're looking pretty energetic from where I'm standing." Michael crossed his arms over his chest. "You're not really leaving. Are you?"

Maybe he had his own lie detector test. "Michael," I said. "This is your chance to get to know the students. And to find out everything Loretta knows about her Mac sighting. I was thinking…you should ask her about the missing dog."

"Leo? You think Mac and Leo's disappearance are linked?"

"You'll need to find out. Ask her about Ian and Squalley too."

"She's right. We need to collect evidence about everyone that could have played a part," James added and threw a look my way.

Michael snapped his fingers. "I've got a better idea. Loretta just moved this little shindig to her place. You guys come along and we'll ask together. It shouldn't take long."

"She'll clam up if we all grill her," I said.

"You don't think she saw Mac, do you?" he asked me.

Loretta took that moment to resurface. "Why is everyone out here when the party is in there?" She pointed a thumb back.

Michael's gaze fixed on me. "Corrie's talking about leaving."

"That works," Loretta said. "Because it will be just us LA Techies. And him." She threw her squint toward James. "My apartment is nice. You'll like it. It has a real wood-burning fireplace."

Michael turned to James. "You're up for hanging with me and the LA Tech homies, right?"

"I'm gonna chill the rest of the night. It's been a long day." He stretched out his arms and turned to me. "You can walk me to my car."

"You don't need—" I started.

"I'll feel safer that way," James said.

"Well, okay. I'll stay with the students and talk about…school. Thanks, you guys," Michael said, his eyes locked on mine. "I'll stop by first thing." He squeezed my arm and headed toward the pub.

Loretta lingered by my shoulder. "I may not be as pretty as you or as street smart, but I am much more clever." She swung her hair and marched after Michael, chin up.

"Let's get going." James turned toward the exit.

I took a last look at the bar. Michael let Loretta through and lingered inside the doorway. He tossed a worried look over his shoulder before he disappeared into the tavern. A look that meant only one thing. He didn't believe Loretta, either.

## Chapter 22

## The Unexpected

I followed James out the door and into the street. A cool breeze slapped my cheeks. Horns honked and jets roared overhead, or maybe the roar came from me. I was ready to crack this case wide open. Or at least find a clue leading me to the killer. Leading us, I meant. I gave James a sidelong glance. He headed across the street to the Pershing Square parking structure. I hurried alongside him.

"Let's take your car to campus," he said. "You can drop me off here after."

"No." I needed to show him who was boss. "Let's take yours. I'll drive."

I expected him to argue. Instead, he handed me the keys.

Minutes later, I climbed aboard his SUV. James was already settled in the passenger seat, slumped down low, seatbelt intact, eyes straight ahead. I was surprised he wasn't holding a glass of wine, he seemed that relaxed. Something was up.

"Get real, James."

"This is as real as I get." His head turned my way.

"If we didn't have business tonight, I wouldn't be here."

"I respect that."

I was beginning to sweat in all my sensitive areas. "You're the last person I want to be with right now."

"That's what makes you so endearing."

What was the matter with him? A mellow James was not what I expected.

I reversed out of the spot in one quick move and motored out of the lot. I jetted toward the 110 freeway.

"We've never gotten along for more than ten minutes at a time. This could be a record," I said. "I expect us to argue any moment now."

James sat up straight, head nearly touching the ceiling. "Ever notice that some things sound so much better when they're left unsaid?"

"Some things need to be said."

"Some things need to be done."

In three seconds, he'd grabbed the steering wheel, and the SUV sat in a red zone on Fifth Street, parking brake at forty-five degrees. His lips were on mine. If I wasn't overcome by the shock of his light speed moves, I might have fought him off. But honestly, I was too impressed to bother. I knew he had sweet driving skills, but not while someone else was behind the wheel. I lifted my fist and aimed for the top of his arm. My fist flew and slowed to a stop right before making contact. In fact, it opened. My hand ran along his arm and curled around his neck. I'd discovered a scrap of moonlight that peeked between the clouds. Moonlight tasted fine.

A siren howled by, followed by the whiz of passing traffic. Time probably flew, too. I was too busy appreciating the flame that lit my lips. That is, until James' misty window vibrated with a hard rap. I pulled back so quickly the back of my head knocked against the window.

"Ouch." My hand flew to my smarting skull.

A wide beam brightened the SUV's cab. James continued to face me, heavy lidded, close-lipped smile flanked by deep dimples. The rapping continued. An internal alarm jolted me upright. Not because of the officer that stood a few feet away, but because I'd responded favorably to Michael's other best friend. A man I'd been at comfortable odds with since our last kiss eight years ago.

James rolled down his window. "This is what happens when I let her drive," he told the cop. "She can't keep her hands off me."

"That's bull-crap." My temperature soared.

"IDs for you both," the officer said, peering past James to scrutinize me.

"I'll tell you what really happened." I reached in the backseat for my purse. "I wasn't feeling well. And he…" I aimed a finger at James, "…didn't help matters."

"Mouth-to-mouth works if you're having trouble breathing. Looks like he did a good job reviving you." The cop shone the light on James. He drew his head closer. "ADA Zachary?"

"That's right." James met his gaze.

"Can't keep the women away, huh?" He flashed a lop-sided smirk.

James grinned. "Have we met?"

I leaned across James to pass my driver's license and jabbed my elbow into his rib cage. He grunted. I would have done a whole lot more damage if the law weren't present.

"At the courthouse. Where you two headed?" The officer shone his light on my license.

"LA Tech," James said.

The cop nodded. "Used to work that area."

"Wyatt, right? Officer Wyatt."

The lower portion of his face broke into a smile. "Good recall."

What was James up to?

"Can you get me a read on police activity on and around the campus in the past forty-eight hours?" James asked him.

"Sure. I got pals who work the area. Why?" He passed my ID back to me.

"We're driving out there to interview a witness to criminal activity."

"You're taking your date to an interrogation?"

"I'm not his date," I said.

"She's an attorney and the daughter of a PI you may have heard of. Montague Locke."

"You don't say? I worked with her dad on the Ty Calvin investigation."

This was the part where I felt like an inanimate object.

"I remember now," Officer Wyatt continued. "She's the gal that uncovered evidence leading to Ty's innocence. Good thing because basketball wouldn't be the same without Ty. Her dad was a good guy."

James handed the officer his business card. "I'd appreciate a call if any crimes were reported around the campus, besides small time thefts. Not interested in lifting of tech equipment, keys, or petty stuff. I'm interested in the unusual."

"Will do."

The officer backed away. I swung into traffic.

"Tonight is our lucky night." James slumped down again, an ankle resting on his opposite knee.

"I'll say it's…not." If I were a solitary piece of coal in a bag filled with identical coals, I'd be the one to self-light and burn the whole shebang down, as well as any nearby combustibles, that's how furious I was. Since when did I become so passive?

"If there's something on the police radar, we'll know about it."

"That was uncalled for," I told him.

"I didn't ask him to pull us over."

"He didn't pull...you know what I mean," I said. "You're infuriating."

His body leaned back against the window, head cocked in my direction. "Truth is, you like my company, you like the unexpected, the dangerous, the electrical. I'm just playing to my audience."

"That work in court for you?" I asked. "'Cause it's not happening here."

"We need to loosen up to work together efficiently." He straightened up a notch. "Do you ever relax?"

"Not with you." I barreled onto the freeway onramp. "If you hadn't taken me by surprise and if I wasn't so damn exhausted—"

"Can we move on?" James shifted to face forward. "Maybe..." He ran his hands through his hair. "A different tactic was in order."

"*Maybe?*"

"Have you ever wondered why there's no man in your life? Your boyfriends last about three hours before they're kicked to the curb. You're a tough cookie, but you're a wimp when it comes to Michael."

"You're talking bull-crap again."

"When are you going to pull your head out of the sand? Or are you expecting me to do it for you?"

"I don't expect anything from you."

"Look, I thought a little action might push you in the right direction."

"I'm not a billiard ball. Stick to the bimbo plays you're used to." I motored across to the fast lane. "When was the last time you had a long-term relationship?"

He removed a coin from a pants pocket and flipped it. "Depends on what you call long-term."

"I rest my case. What are you waiting for?"

"Not what." He flipped the coin and caught it on the back of his hand, clapping his palm over it. "Who."

I gave him a sidelong stare and gulped. Not many people affected me like this man did. In fact, no one else did. James continued playing solo coin toss. "I never understood your friendship with Michael," I said. "You're polar opposites."

"Michael is the only inherently good person I know." He stopped tossing and leaned forward. He fidgeted with the A/C knob and leaned back into his seat. "He's honest, loyal, and dependable. He maintains his integrity no matter the situation. He's been like that from the start. In fourth grade..." He stared down at his hands. "When I lost my father, Mikey stuck with me. We didn't talk, but we shared a pizza and played Super Mario all night. He's more than just a best friend."

I loosened my grip on the steering wheel. My foot lightened up on the accelerator.

"You two have more in common than you think," James added.

I lie, I cheat, I'd steal if I needed to. I break in and risk jail-time on the regular. I was one degree away from being a felon. Michael couldn't break the law if he tried...unless he was with me. Then all bets were off.

"You're not always on the up and up," James continued. "But when you stoop to law-breaking, it serves a higher purpose. Usually."

"To Michael, I'm a friend with a skill set he lacks," I said. "I offer a change of pace."

"You're both idiots. Why don't you tell him how you feel? What are you afraid of?"

Ruining a beautiful friendship, for starters. "You don't know how I feel."

"Not only do you lie to everyone, you lie to yourself too."

"So that kiss was an experiment?" I asked. "To help me get in touch with my inner feelings? Get a life, James."

"I didn't do it for you."

Talk about mixed messages. A beehive popped up between my ears. My mind was that noisy.

"What is it you're not telling me?" he asked.

My head flipped toward him.

"Eyes on the road."

I faced forward. "I could ask you the same question."

James squeezed his lips together. I'd been bluffing, but now I knew I was on track.

"Like I said to Officer Wyatt, I have a meeting on campus. Tonight," he said. "You can come."

"Because of my sweet investigation skills?"

"Because two heads are better than one. Even if one of them is a hothead."

"How'd you get—?"

"I've a friend in the district attorney's office who called in a favor. I'm meeting LA Tech security to get my hands on a video showing main entry activity for the past forty-eight hours."

I was impressed enough to toss him a compliment, if I'd a mind to, which I didn't.

"Your turn. What are you holding back?" he asked.

If the pig-eating-human theory hadn't devalued by credibility, my confession would. He'd think I was ludicrous. Yet I needed to tell someone, besides Mom and Veera. "My dad might still be alive."

"I know."

# CHAPTER 23

## BLOOD WORK

"You what?" I sat up straight, braced myself with my left foot, and slammed on the brake with my right...in the fast lane. Fortunately, we'd only been traveling twenty-five miles per hour, thanks to L.A. freeway congestion. Drivers around me landed on their horns.

"Move it," James said.

My right foot rediscovered the accelerator, and we caught up to the car in front. "Have you seen my father?"

James blew out air between clenched teeth. "A few months ago, in the Newport Beach police station, you saw him. Not me."

It was true. Sort of. I'd thought I'd spotted Dad walking the station's hallway. I'd followed, but couldn't find any trace of him. No one in the station admitted seeing him. It was my imagination working overtime when I needed help on the homicide. Kind of like now. My body molded to the seat. I pushed back deeper, increasing the distance between the steering wheel and my chest. I cut off the car to my right and a horn blasted.

"Stay with the program," James said. "Don't snap now."

I edged my way to the slow lane. Time to wind down before I got into trouble. Michael would have been stuck to the ceiling on all fours with my current driving antics. James was mostly chill.

"It wasn't my imagination this time. It was someone else's." I spilled the beans about Yoko.

James maintained a monastic silence until I'd finished.

"No security cameras are aimed at the entry to the lab," I said. "I checked. I need to verify that it wasn't him."

"Sounds like a clear case of manipulation. Forget it."

"*Forget it*? How is that possible? I don't know why I bothered telling you."

"Are you asking me to help?"

I stole a glance at him. His head leaned against the headrest. "Are you on medication?"

"It won't hurt to plant a camera aiming at the door of the lab, to watch who comes and goes. I'll take care of it."

A flash of surprise pulsed through me. Who was this man? Was it possible the real James had been switched with a kinder model? The gung-ho handsomeness was still there, but the usual impatience and irritability were MIA. "You don't have to do that."

"It's what friends do."

I tightened my lips together to prevent word spillage. I didn't want to ruin the peaceful moment.

"Friendship is like a sponge," James said. "You soak it all up, good and bad. And in the end, what have you got?"

"A sponge that needs a lot of wringing out before it can be used again."

A grin lapped around his lips. "Point being, you've still got the sponge."

"Not all sponges are created equal." That was the best I could do, come-back wise, but even I wasn't sure what I meant.

Twenty-five minutes later, we walked the LA Tech campus, headed for the Admin Hall. It was just past midnight. Quiet intercepted the usual campus buzz except for the occasional rumble of a passing car and a random yell into the night.

James stopped when the Admin Hall came into view. "Give me a minute." He scanned the front of the building.

"Note to self," I said. "Four-inch heels weren't made for trekking the distance from the parking lot to campus."

"A note to self means no one else should hear you."

I removed my sandals. "See anything yet?"

"Can't you stay quiet for even one minute?"

"Actually no, I can't."

James stepped forward onto the grass. "Video cam up a tree at three o'clock."

My head spun around.

"On your right." He nodded toward a eucalyptus to one side of the Hall. "I'll be getting a copy showing activity from that angle in about thirty minutes."

"That could unveil a suspect," I said. "Unless, of course, the suspect climbed out a window on the side of the building, like we did. Got tapes for that?"

"You know what we have to do?"

"Sure. Get eight hours of z's, change this get-up, and look more closely at what it is exactly pigs consider food…"

James opened his mouth.

"But first…" I turned my focus to a backpacked student ambling along the lit path. "I'm going to need to break us into the president's office."

His gaze dropped to my bare legs and feet. "About time you made yourself useful."

I linked my fingers together and gazed skyward. "Ah, the thrill of feeling needed." I skipped across the damp grass toward the Admin Hall, sandals swinging in my hand, the ground soft beneath my wet, liberated feet.

Within minutes, we'd climbed through the official entry point: Michael's unlocked window. We took the stairs to the president's office. If James wasn't physically present behind me, I would have thought I was alone. He was that quiet, like an Indian scout creeping through enemy territory. We stopped by Big Mac's door. I'd snapped up two large paperclips from Michael's desk and was playing the insertion game. James rested his back against the wall, eyes on the corridor. I couldn't complain about having him as a teammate. He knew his stuff, had plenty of nerve, and was fearless.

"Ever wonder what life would be like with—"

"Out crime scene investigations?" I jiggled the paperclip in the lock. "All the time."

"I was going to say, without the lawyer job," James said. "You thrive when crime cracking. And you look sexy breaking and entering."

"Dammit." I'd nearly had the lock picked, until that last comment. Now I had to start over. He wore that devastating smile again. I averted my eyes and focused on the doorknob. "Chasing bad guys blurs the line between right and wrong. Every time I do something that could have consequences, I wonder what the heck I'm doing."

"You're helping someone you care about. Nothing wrong with that."

The knob turned, and I pushed the door open.

The room was dark. James pulled out his penlight. I extracted a mini flashlight from my handbag and dropped my sandals on a small rug near the door. Our bright, narrow streams crisscrossed the office.

"We've combed the area around the desk already. And I examined the space near the window," I said. "So we can skip that, too."

"I love the smell of confidence in the dead of night."

"Let's split the room in half, starting with the perimeter. We'll work our way to the center." I regarded James. In a few strides, he was at the opposite end, on his knees. Always a man of action. "Sometimes you remind me of my father."

He sat back on his haunches. "Is that good or bad?"

"Could be night blindness. I'll reevaluate again in the harsh daylight." The part about his being a man of action was good as far as my father was concerned. But Dad was not so good in his child-rearing choices. I couldn't recall a single hug or normal father-daughter time with him. The time for hugs and run-of-the-mill bonding were long over.

James' narrow beam flashed around the closet where Michael and I had hidden. I faced the massive bookcase. Wider than it was tall, four connected cases spanned floor to ceiling. The bottom shelves sheltered newspapers and folders. Books populated the rest of the shelves. I judged the books by their covers and concluded Big Mac was a reader of all things boring. The history of buckets, wagon train journeys, and byzantine artwork. Nothing to indicate he was the sadist Squalley painted him to be. The bookcase was no place for clues. I pivoted a little too quickly and lost my footing. I groped a shelf and dropped my light. The thud brought James out of the closet.

"What are you doing?"

"Thought I'd take a moment to practice a pirouette," I said.

James blew out a huff and moved to a wing back chair.

I kneeled to recover the light and rubbed my throbbing leg. The tip of the beam ended on a dark stain where the floor and the bookcase met, highlighting small, dark spots. I peered closer. Five pinhead size circles, a few larger rounds, and goldfish shaped splattering surrounded the spots. I examined the blobs closer. They smelled of rusted metal. I straightened, eyes and beam climbing the shelves. I paused over level three. Another smattering of the same brownish color with the odd shapes.

"What is it?" James breathed over my shoulder.

I lit up the floor by my feet. "Blood."

James rested a knee on the hardwood floor and scrutinized the stains. "Could be coffee stains."

"The president was murdered a few feet away. The odds play in favor of blood. Besides, I know the smell of dried blood."

"Let's say you're right. That would mean the body was propped against the bookshelf."

"Maybe a chair was used to prop the other side. While the killer cleaned up."

James rose to his feet and took a few steps backward. He ran the light up and down the bookcase.

"There's no blood anywhere else in here," I said.

"Could be this area was missed. The stains landed too close to the wall."

I knelt again, next to the spots. The thinness meant the body hadn't rested there long. "It was done quickly. We know the point of origin. That chair." I pitched my chin toward the desk.

James strolled over to the chair and bent over it. "Which way was it facing?"

"Not sure. All Michael saw was the knife in the back."

"Okay, if the body was dragged here," James said. "That's about five feet from the chair."

"Let's take a step back. What do we know so far?"

"Dead guy in chair. Gone missing. And blood spots."

"A runaway murder. With a killer on the loose." I rose to my bare feet. "I think I should be given credit for not bringing up the pig-eating-body theory again."

"Duly noted."

"What does 'duly' even mean?" I missed the added height of my heels. I felt small in the spacious office. "It's a word no one would miss if it disappeared." Kind of like Big Mac. My heart swelled. I felt sorry for a man I'd never met.

James backed to the center of the room. The narrow beam ran across the bookcase and stopped. "Did you look for clues outside the building? Beneath the windows?"

"There'd be witnesses."

"Not if it was dark and he was lowered in a body bag."

"From what Michael says, the body wouldn't fit. Day or night."

His beam landed on the dog dishes. "How does the pooch fit in?"

"He went missing the day before Big Mac disappeared."

The door swung open and the light turned on. A man entered the room. "Hands up in the air."

## CHAPTER 24

### ENERGY DROP

"Take it easy." James' hands stretched forward, palms facing out. "I'm here to meet with security."

A thin-lipped, muscular fellow faced us, baton raised in one hand. His dark blond hair was slicked back, his eyes beady. He edged forward with a one-foot shuffle. This was the guy who'd made Michael and me duck behind the shrubs my first night out. His baby blues flew between us. "I need to see ID."

Not again. "So do we," I said. "Who are you and what are you doing here?"

"You first."

"ADA Zachary." James reached into his jacket and pulled out his badge.

He lowered the baton and opened one side of his jacket. "Bobby Shemway." He flashed a large ID card along with a can of pepper spray and a high beam flashlight. "Thought we were supposed to meet in the archway." Bobby raised a wrist and checked an oversize watch. "In ten minutes." He put his baton away.

"I got side-tracked," James replied. "We saw someone break into this building and followed him in here."

Bobby shuffled around the room and looked under a chair. "I didn't see anyone. Where'd he go?"

"That's what we want to know." My arms crossed my chest. I puffed myself out and pushed back my shoulders. I was two inches taller than Bobby in my bare feet, and I wanted him to know it.

"Who's she?" he asked.

"My investigator."

"She doesn't look like an investigator."

His eyes swept my legs and torso. It was all I could do to keep from snarling.

"That's the best kind." James shot him a grin. "She looks like a student, so she blends in."

"She doesn't look like a student either. She looks—"

"Oh no." I shook my head and slid close enough to breathe on his sweaty face. "Watch your language when you're talking about me. Especially when I'm standing right in front of you. Because I will make you—"

"She looks like she'd be just as home at a shopping mall as she'd be painting the ceiling red with my blood," Bobby said. "Any reason I shouldn't turn my back on her?"

"I'll give you ten." I closed both of my fists and was about to smack him beneath the chin when James came between us.

"Don't make her angry," James said. "It won't be pretty."

"I can see why you use her. She's hot, but deadly."

"You know." I moved in closer. Bobby held his ground. "I like that. Plus, you sound sincere. Do you have the tape?"

He reached inside his jacket and retrieved a small tape. His hand shot past me. He handed it to James.

I poked my index finger into Bobby's chest. "Why would you do that? Do you not see me standing here? Where were you the night of the murder?"

"What murder?"

Oops. I was getting ahead of myself. My surge of adrenalin had no effect on the sharpness of my brain. I was edging toward burnout. "I was gauging your ability to handle an unpredictable situation. You handled it well, Scotty."

"It's Bobby."

I slid over to James who stood by the door. I grabbed my sandals and slipped them on.

"Wait," Bobby stepped toward us. "What about the guy you followed in here?"

"Probably left the same way he got in," I said. "You need better security."

James shoved the tape inside his jacket and pulled open the door. He looked over his shoulder at Bobby and grinned. "Don't worry, we won't tell anyone." He raced out, with me on his heels.

Not another word was said until we sat inside the SUV.

"What do you think he'll do?" I asked.

"He'll check the doors and find no breach, which means we were lying."

"You were lying."

James shot me a glare that nearly gave me sunstroke.

My head tipped back against the headrest. I didn't even try to get behind the wheel this time. "So, where to view the tape?"

"In the morning—"

"This is the morning." My voice was a little louder than planned. It was nearly two.

"We'll go to my place and watch it."

His place? I thought we were going to the police station or a video lab or anywhere else. I wasn't ready for his place. I'd already gotten as personal as I wanted to get with James. But if I backed out, he'd think I was scared. Which I wasn't. Just uncomfortable.

"On second thought..." I stretched my arms and yawned. "...I'd better get some sleep. I'm done for now." I edged out of my heels, scooped them up, and dropped them on the floor behind James. His jacket stretched out on the seat above my shoes. I pushed back into my cushion and turned my head to one side. I closed my eyes and slowed my breathing. Minutes later, I blew the air out my mouth with every breath.

I kept it up until the SUV pulled to a stop. James cut the engine. I opened one eye. He'd parked inside the Pershing Square lot. I didn't budge.

He shook my shoulder. "Wake up. We're here."

A gentleman would have opened the door and helped me out, not shoved me awake. I turned toward him, blinking. "Huh?" I moved onto my side, put my hands together and under my head, and shut my eyes.

"What floor are you parked on?"

"Three," I mumbled.

The SUV jerked forward and sped around the corners. It screeched to a stop in a parking spot on the third floor.

He heaved out a sigh and opened his door. The moment he stepped into the night, my hand shot out and grabbed the tape from inside his jacket. I shoved it into my purse and resumed my deep sleep position.

My door opened.  Cold air whipped around my legs. "Get your shoes."

I wanted to bolt outside and dive into my car, but I didn't dare. I blinked his way. I even threw in a yawn. He threw back a stony gaze. I grabbed my heels and purse, tumbled out, and landed on the rough asphalt. The surface brazed my soles. The cold grabbed my feet and held tight. I slipped into my sandals and hobbled to my car. A moment later, I'd slipped a key into the lock and sank into the driver's seat.

"Get out. I'm driving you home." James stood by my open door.

I sat up straight. Did he suspect anything? "No, you don't need to do that. I'm wide awake."

He bent over and peered into my eyes. I stared back unblinking. A group of laughing people stumbled along behind us. James pulled away and waited until they moved past.

"Can you give me one reason why I should trust you?" he asked.

I opened my mouth and shut it. I opened it again and said, "No."

His lips might have turned slightly upward, I wasn't sure. He backed off and hurried to his SUV.

He tailed me out of the structure and onto the freeway. And onto Coast Highway. I made a quick right down Longfellow and parked in my driveway. I waited five minutes. No trace of James.

I tiptoed to the street. No sign of him. I took a deep breath and headed back into my car, and onto the road. I had a job to finish. I didn't have a videotape player, but I knew someone who did.

## Chapter 25

## Up and Over

My mother still wrote letters by hand, watched *I Love Lucy* reruns, and had a collection of videotapes from the Eighties, which she played on her VCR, also from the Eighties. She watched everything from workout videos to classic Hollywood films. The VCR was what I was interested in at the moment.

For the second time in two days, I headed to Palos Verdes, to Mom's house. I cut the headlights and turned into her street. I slipped into sneakers and planned my entry. The house key was not an option. On the small chance I woke her, there would be questions. Not to mention a lecture on any number of things from the necessity of getting eight hours of sleep to the hazards of bug bites, which I had on my legs from my barefoot romp across campus. Plus, I looked forward to the buzz I'd get from breaking in through the sliding glass door that didn't latch quite right. As soon as I figured out how.

I made it all the way to the trash area when I heard a car motor. I froze, ears perked. The engine shut off, the headlights dimmed, and a door closed. I soft-shoed along the edge toward the front of the house. An exterior light from across the street backlit the silhouette of a tall, lean man. He sprinted across the driveway in my direction and stopped just before plunging into me.

"We've got to stop meeting at my mom's house, Michael," I whispered. "How did you know I'd be here?"

"Didn't you see me following you?"

I was getting sloppier by the minute.

"I drove down your street in the nick of time to see you turn the corner," Michael continued. "After you made the right on PV Drive, I had a pretty good idea of where you were headed. And here I am."

"What happened at Loretta's place?"

"I cleared out as soon as I got what we needed. *We* being you and I, and Sweet Baby James. Don't tell him I call him that."

"I'm glad you're here, Michael."

"Gee whiz, Corrie—"

"I could use your help."

"Oh. Well, sure, glad to give it even though I don't know what it is yet—"

"Why were you coming to see me?"

Michael took a step closer. "Because." His whisper was softer. "You were right. Loretta lied. She didn't see Mac." His shoulders drooped. "The poor guy was dead when I found him. Just like I knew he was. The killer's still at large."

"How did you get her to talk?"

"I told her it wasn't likely she saw him. That I'd been trying to reach him myself."

"Bet that didn't go over well."

"She liked it even less when I asked her for details about her sighting. She stumbled over her answers. Which meant—"

"She made it up as she went along."

"The real clincher? I asked her to tell it to me backwards. Should've been a piece of cake with her eye for detail, right? She refused and took off. It's not like I asked her to recite Tolstoy backwards."

"That's brilliant, Michael. The backwards part."

"It's a trick I learned from watching James during trial. Are you here to borrow clothes again?"

"We went to LA Tech tonight."

Michael moved closer. "*We?*"

"James and me."

"Now would be a good time to weigh in on why neither one of you could tell me that's where you were headed."

"We didn't want to disappoint you if we came up empty-handed."

"Well, stop trying not to disappoint me. Did you come up empty?"

"Not sure yet."

"So what are we doing here?" Michael asked. "And why do you need my help?"

I told him about Bobby and the tape.

"You took the tape from James? That's not good. That's bad. Look, I know you two don't always get along...I mean, hardly *ever* get along, but he stepped right up to help when asked. He can be the most incredibly kind person if you give him a chance."

I couldn't argue with him. James had done more than his fair share...maybe more than the fair share of a tribe of Maasai warriors...and he'd helped me in the past. It was just...I'd nursed a grudge against him for so long, I wasn't even sure why anymore. Or how to stop.

"Corrie?"

Did I want to stand still or forge ahead? I gritted my teeth. "I'll try to be nicer. Follow me."

I used the usual means to climb onto the balcony, Michael close behind. I jiggled the slider door, but it wouldn't give. I closed my eyes and pictured my high school self on the balcony opening the door. I flicked open my eyes and studied the handle. I grabbed hold, lifted it up and down, and pulled. Nothing.

"Let's use the front door," Michael said. "We'll be quiet."

"Hold up." I lifted the handle again. Up and toward me and down again in a half circle and...it slid open.

"Awesome," Michael whispered.

In five minutes, we were in the family room watching soundless, hazy black and white images. We sat cross-legged, a few feet away from the TV. The screen illuminated the room. Good thing Mom was a sound sleeper.

"This tape runs from six p.m. to six a.m., Friday night to Saturday morning. When was the last time you saw Big Mac alive?" I asked.

Michael linked his fingers together and rested his stubbly chin on them. "Let's see. I stormed off to my office. I sat steaming and finished a bag of chips. I went for a walk, came back and steamed some more. And wrote the resignation letter. That would put me at about six and some change. I was in his office around seven, seven-thirty, and found him—"

"Look for people leaving the building. See if you recognize anyone."

I forwarded the tape and stopped when a man appeared.

Michael pointed. "That's the maintenance guy."

We watched Squalley open the entry to the Admin Hall, exit the building, and scramble down the short staircase. He stopped at the bottom and brushed off his jumpsuit with his hands.

I leaned in closer. "What's he doing?"

Squalley shot off to the right, away from the lens.

I replayed the scene a few times. Both of our necks craned closer.

"He's a maintenance man doing maintenance," Michael said.

"Wait. He could be wiping Big Mac hairs off his clothes." I remembered the hairs scattered in Squalley's trunk. I spilled the details for Michael.

"You think they took Mac to a pig farm and he was eaten?" Michael said.

"It's just a theory, but it's all I've got right now."

"That's horrible. I don't care how awful Mac was. I can't even begin to...wouldn't there be bones or something left?"

"We have another eleven hours to watch before we jump to conclusions."

"Okay. No jumping. I need a drink. An energy drink"

"In there," I tossed my chin toward the pantry. "Please bring me one, too." I needed a whole lot more than one energy drink.

Michael headed for the pantry, opened the door, and disappeared inside.

The tape continued to run with me fast-forwarding every few seconds. Bobby, the security guy, paced across the front walkway with his lopsided gait, shining his flashlight along the perimeter of the building. Students cut across the lawn. A tabby cat strolled past, tail bristled. A woman burst out of the front entry.

"Michael?" I whispered.

He returned holding two cans. "That is the best pantry ever. Stocked with food, drinks, and seven different types of sweeteners. Love the chalkboard."

I hit reverse. "Isn't that your co-dean? The one we spotted leaving the Admin Hall."

Michael took a few steps closer to the screen. I replayed the woman bursting out again. Blonde hair, a black dress and ballet flats.

"That's her. Alyce. *Former* co-associate dean, now sole associate dean, thanks to my demotion." His lips curled downward.

"We saw her just before we climbed in your window."

"You think she went back to clean up the crime scene? She could have stashed the cleaning supplies in her office. That gives us three suspects. Ian, Squalley and Alyce."

"Let's keep watching."

Bobby circled around the building again. "What chalkboard?" I asked.

"Huh?"

"You said something about a chalkboard. In Mom's pantry."

Michael handed me a can and took a sip of his drink. "On the back wall."

I handed Michael the remote and tiptoed to the pantry. It smelled of fresh paint and something else. Something familiar. I looked around. The top half of the back wall hosted a chalkboard with a narrow ledge that sat empty. A cabinet, painted white like the walls, monopolized the bottom portion. There could only be one reason why Mom cut a cabinet into the wall in her already oversize, walk-in pantry.

I popped my head out. "Michael?"

He paused the VCR and strolled in. "Isn't it great?"

"Do you smell something in here? Besides fresh paint?"

He lifted his chin and sniffed. "Ah, yes. The intoxicating scent of a new car. Rich Corinthian leather." He inhaled deeply.

What was a leather smell doing in a pantry? I bent over to open the cabinet. I pulled on the knob. It was a fake. It was not like my practical mother to insert a faux cabinet. If she'd wanted a chalkboard, she could have hung one on the wall.

"Find out where I can get that smell," Michael said and stepped out.

"Oh, I will," I said.

I rejoined him. We continued forwarding the tape and ended up recognizing five people leaving the Admin Hall: Ian, Squalley, Bobby, Alyce, and Loretta.

"Do you recall seeing any of them inside the building that night?" I asked.

"Are you kidding? I was so beside myself, a rhinoceros could have charged in and I wouldn't have noticed."

I ejected the tape. "Let's go. There's nothing more here."

"But we need a plan."

"I'll have one in the morning."

Minutes later, Michael and I parted ways. I motored home with the windows rolled down. A breeze whipped my hair into a frenzy, driving away thoughts of sleep. I turned into my street and slowly drove up the hill, canvassing the parked cars. No sign of the SUV. If James was lying in wait, I needed to know.

I unlocked the front door and slipped inside. The light from the street lamp leaked in between the slats of my blinds, a thin mist coated the window. Veera's back faced me on the futon. In deep slumber, her breath would have registered as a hurricane in the land of Lilliput.

I dragged myself into my room and shut the door. I dropped my purse on the floor and slipped out of my dress. I headed straight to bed, eyes half-shut, and bumped into something hard.

## CHAPTER 26

## OUT OF BOUNDS

James' hand caught my wrist in a vise. "We were getting along so nicely."

"I think we set some kind of record," I said. A thread of light seeped through my blinds, giving James' face an eerie glow.

"You have something for me?"

"You know I do." I tossed my head toward my purse. "It's in there."

James let go and pushed past me. He grabbed my purse, turned it upside down and snatched the tape out of the spillage. He spoke in a low voice. "Why?"

I had a million answers for him, but none that I could say out loud. He wasn't a team player. I didn't like the games he played. He had a bad attitude. He kissed me when he shouldn't have. Even worse, he stood between Michael and me in a way I couldn't articulate.

*Couldn't he say those things about you as well?* said the little voice in my head.

"That's not true."

"What's not?" James asked.

He was close enough for me to see a vein in his neck rise like a snake pulsing through. He lowered his face and turned on the glare. Sweat coated my body.

"I was talking to myself," I said.

He stormed to my window, raised it with one hand, lowered his head, and climbed out into the darkness. I listened to his shoes padding on the pavement until the sound faded.

I sank on my bed and slammed a fist down. He'd let me off easy. It was his fault for being so hard to get along with. Why was he so mean? And why was Veera such a heavy sleeper? I held my head in my hands. James was too hard muscled to serve as my punching bag. I hurt myself every time. I wanted to hate him, I really did. He was the only thing that stood between Michael and me. I knew then that my schoolgirl crush hadn't evaporated. It had changed into something more.

I lay down and closed my eyes. I emptied my body of all air and waited for sleep. And waited. James floated through my head. Tall, handsome, athletic, intelligent James. The guy who always got the girl. He could be abrasive and callous…and a loyal and infinitely exciting friend. I shook my head and pushed him out of my mind. Michael was the man for me. Kind, sincere, and trusting, he needed me to protect and watch over him. And I needed him to bring out the best in me. He thought I was his safety net, but it was the other way around.

I turned on my side and took another deep breath. I thought of Mom's pantry and shot up. There was only one reason she'd install a fake cabinet.

## CHAPTER 27

## A NEW LEAF

"What's that smell?"

Veera was finally awake. I'd been clanging pots and rearranging cutlery for nearly half an hour while she was in hibernation.

She was up and sniffing the air like a bloodhound, nose pointed up. "Is that burnt rubber?"

"That's fresh coffee." At least I thought it was. I lacked a coffee maker, but Michael had left me a can of ground something that looked like coffee. He'd used a pot. I hadn't watched him, but it was like making tea, right?

"It is? That burning odor must be coming from outside. All our stuff from the Newport office is packed and in my car." Veera stood beside me. "Ready for the move to our new office. Wait. Is that oatmeal in the skillet? I didn't know you could cook. I'm proud of you, C. What's that green stuff?"

"Spinach. I'm making us a wholesome breakfast."

She rubbed her hands together. "I'm starving."

Fifteen minutes later, we were seated around my dinette. Veera took a sip of coffee. Her mouth twisted. Gurgling sounds came from inside her throat. She croaked, "Went down the wrong pipe."

"It's that bad?" I asked.

"You know," she sounded raspy. "Tastes like the coffee Gran used to make. Strong." She pounded her chest with a fist and gave a cough.

"I don't drink coffee." I used to. Until Dad's last cup was laced with poison. "Even when I did, I never made it myself. Michael was better at it.

"I need to cut back anyhow. Let me try some of that healthy food." Veera turned to the oats and downed a spoonful. She covered her mouth during her second coughing fit.

I took a taste and spit it out. This stuff would grow hair on an eel. I dropped my spoon in the dish. "Let's find something to eat that won't send us to the emergency room."

I called Mom and asked if we could stop by. As expected, breakfast was ready when we arrived twenty minutes later.

"Gosh dang," was all Veera could say. "Heaven on a plate."

The pancakes were topped with strawberries and served with crispy bacon. Mom helicoptered around, filling our glasses with orange juice.

"The juice tasted like a glass of sunshine." Veera wore her biggest smile. "I'll help clear the table."

"Oh no, I've got this." I jumped up. "Mom, can you please give Veera some pointers on how to dress? We've got to make a memorable first impression. We'll be on The Lot this week and from now on."

"At Ameripictures?" Mom held up two hands for two high fives. Veera and I obliged. "That's wonderful news, sweetie. Come on, Veera, I'll find you some show-stopping pieces."

I followed them a few steps to make sure they were all the way up before I raced back to the kitchen. I slipped in the pantry. Nothing like a few hours of sleep to jump-start the brain. I patted my hands along the chalkboard. I thumped my fist against it. My fingers traced the tray. I twisted the knob to the fake cabinet. I tried pushing the board. I pushed harder. No give.

I filed out of the pantry and cleaned the dishes. I flipped a U-ey and headed back in. I squatted and peered beneath the chalk tray. "Aha." Hinges with springs. My fingers gripped the tray. It didn't budge when I lifted it. My fist gently hit against it, and the tray flipped downward. A click sounded, and one side of the back wall separated, floor to ceiling, displaying a sliver of light. I gave the wall a push, and stepped inside.

I'd found a piece of Shangri-la. Headquarters for Mom's finest wardrobe pieces. Shelves and rods featured a Paris runway collection of sweaters and coats, including a zip front, laser cut, cherry-colored leather jacket that accounted for the new car smell. An array of black pants hung from one section. Dresses from casual to evening took up another whole side. Below the shoe shelves rested a large metal box. The one housing Dad's weapons. My weapons.

I backed out and, with my fingers, brought the hidden door as near to being closed as possible. I straightened the chalk tray. There was a whoosh of air and the wall clicked shut.

I'd barely cleaned the counter when Mom and Veera reappeared.

"I'm going to feel like a genuine VIP tomorrow." Veera carried a Saks garment bag over her arm. "We're going to kill 'em, Corrie." Veera cut a glance toward Mom. "Figuratively speaking."

"Your style says who you are without your saying a word. Or killing anyone," Mom said.

"We gotta go," I said. "Veera and I have another stop to make."

"Where?" my mother and Veera asked simultaneously.

"Mom, do you have any extra food?"

"Is this for Michael? I could make more pancakes."

"No, I need…" To make it up to James. I didn't have a peace pipe handy. "…something irresistible. To weaken a person's resolve." And scrub away his anger.

Mom snapped her fingers. "Pie does the trick. A lemon meringue can make anyone weak in the knees."

I appreciated that she asked no questions. It was enough for her to know it was for someone important to me.

"Who's it for?" Mom asked. "Your boss? Michael? A new man in your life?"

I took back my last thought. "I need to make amends to someone."

Veera's eyes narrowed.

Mom shook her head. "When will you learn to reel in your temper? Patience, grasshopper. Patience is the cure for everything. Except head lice."

"Not pie?"

"Pie and patience." She marched to the kitchen. "Give me an hour."

Veera leaned in and whispered, "This isn't for Marshall, is it? 'Cause that man don't deserve a bread crumb let alone a whole pie. I don't care if he is our boss."

"For James."

"For that sweet piece of man candy? What'd you do?"

I pressed my lips together.

"Get it out, girl. Maybe it wasn't as bad as you think."

"I was mean."

"He's got to be used to that by now."

"This time was different. I felt bad about it." And maybe a little more.

"You are growing up right in front of my eyes, C."

My smart phone vibrated. I answered the call. "Corrie Locke."

"It's a deal. I'll do what you say. But I need my favor done soon." Yoko spilled out her words hard and fast.

"Wrong number," I said.

"No. It's you. Your father—"

"I don't have time for this, Yoko."

"I won't charge you for extra work, if you don't charge me."

Mom was poised to turn on the electric mixer, but her eyes and ears were fixed on me.

"When my pop comes in tomorrow, I'll ask him about your dad."

"Call me later." I disconnected.

"Isn't Yoko that—" Mom stopped and wiped her hands on a towel.

"Thanks, Mother."

"Veera, why don't you help me with the pie?" Mom asked. "My daughter doesn't like to follow directions or answer questions."

Translation: I'll squeeze it out of Veera.

"Veera and I have to go," I said. "But I'll be back in a few hours to pick up the pie."

Translation: I won't let you give Veera the third degree.

"When? I'm going to a fundraiser at four," Mom said.

Translation: Come when I'm home.

"I'll be here way before then," I said. "See you."

Translation: I'll be back after four.

"Wait," Mom said and disappeared upstairs. She returned in a minute with a dress slung over her arm. She held it out to me. "Knock 'em dead, sweetie. But not literally."

The dress was the bomb: a teal lace sheath. Perfect for the first day at the new office. I stared at my mother, all smiles and make-up perfection. I was buttered up, sloshing around in a vat of guilt, on the verge of confessing everything. "It's beautiful." I gave her a quick hug. "Thanks for everything, Mom."

"Oh, honey. That's what Moms do," she said.

"I'll never eat a breakfast that delicious again," Veera added.

"Why, thank you, Veera." Mom wrung her hands and followed us to the door. "Corrie ate breakfasts like this from birth."

"Be hard to chew without a full set of teeth, Mom," I reminded her.

"I made her baby food from scratch. Sweet potato was her favorite. I'd mash and mash, by hand, mind you."

"What was wrong with the blender?" I asked.

"Sometimes," Mom continued, ignoring me, "I arrived late for work and got written-up by my superiors 'cause I was so busy mashing."

"Oh please," I said.

"Now I try to keep her freezer stocked with homemade dinners when I can. It's not easy. After working all day, on my feet, in four-inch heels. Those tile floors are a backbreaker—"

"Mother." I was caught in Mom's steel jaw guilt trap with no hacksaw in sight. "Yoko works in the private forensics lab in Ventura. I'm trying to get her to check on DNA evidence I collected to help Michael. She's the one who wanted a favor."

"The girl who said she saw your father?" Mom asked.

I nodded. I was done lying…for today.

"That's a bunch of—"

"She says he came in last week," I told her.

"Was he dressed in his dark gray suit? Because that's the suit I gave the mortician."

"What if he faked his death for a good reason?"

"There's no reason good enough to cause your loved ones that kind of pain."

"I'll be outside. Thanks again." Veera tiptoed out of the house.

"Unless their safety was at stake," I said.

"Don't you think faking your death is a little extreme? He could have moved to Venezuela. Who'd look for him there?"

"His killer was never caught."

"You think that doesn't keep me up at night?"

I blew out a sigh. "Thanks for making the pie."

"Corrie." Mom followed me to the door and lowered her voice. "Want me to take care of Yoko?"

"What do you mean?"

"Just thinking outside the box, sweetie."

There was a side to my mother I never understood. She could be thoughtful and generous, even understanding of my yen for her high-end wardrobe. But once in a while, the Attila the Hun side emerged. "It's under control. See you later."

Veera stood next to my car. "Got a little…hot in there."

"That wasn't the first time she's squeezed a confession out of me."

I turned on the engine and checked my rear view mirror.

"Hi, guys."

Our heads nearly hit the ceiling.

"Thanks for letting me tag along," Michael said.

"Michael!"

Veera held a hand to her chest. "I nearly jumped out of my underpants. You know how hard that would be for me to do?"

"Hiding in the backseat does not equal inviting you to tag along," I told him.

"I wasn't hiding. You left the car unlocked. I was waiting."

"How do you do that?" I asked. "Know when I'm here, I mean."

"I spent the night at Mom and Dad's." He turned to Veera. "They live half a mile away. Up that hill." He pointed. "I crashed there after we finished the tape last night."

"What tape?" Veera asked.

"Just a little something James got his hands on," I replied.

"And Corrie borrowed without asking," Michael told Veera.

"Ah, I get it now," Veera said.

He turned back to me. "I walked down after I saw your car parked here. I didn't want to interrupt you, so I thought I'd wait. It was warm and, well, I fell asleep."

"I'm a light sleeper myself," Veera said.

"I was up most of last night," Michael said. "I kept thinking, I've got to let the police know. The longer I wait, the colder the leads become. I'll just tell them what happened, and if they think I was involved, so be it."

"Can you even turn yourself in when there's no body?" Veera asked. "'Cause you know they're going to ask what you did with him."

"I didn't do it so how could I know? I'll tell the truth," Michael said. "That I discovered the body, and now it's gone."

"What if they ask why you didn't immediately report it?"

"That I freaked out," Michael said. "Who wouldn't?"

"Then they'll ask who you told, which is Corrie. She's the one who told me. And there's James. They'll wanna know why none of us reported it."

"Easy," I said, turning on to Palos Verdes Drive West. "We didn't believe him."

"Didn't believe that he off-ed the president?" Veera pulled out a notepad and started jotting something down. "Or didn't believe Big Mac was dead?"

"There's something that's been eating away at me," I said. That was poor word choice. I glanced at Veera. "The hungry hog theory. We've got to put it to rest."

"Wait, I've been thinking about that, too," Michael said. "With all due respect, Corrie, it's a little far-out. There's no possible way they could drag Mac's body across LA Tech to the parking lot without being spotted. By campus security, for starters."

"But we did find hair. I need to know whose it is." I handed Veera my smartphone. "Text Yoko and tell her to meet us at the lab in one hour. To get the hair sample analyzed."

"What about the pie?" Veera asked.

"What pie?" Michael wanted to know.

"It's for James," I told him. "To make up for my borrowing the tape."

"That would work on me, not James."

"What softens him up?" Veera asked him.

"She knows. But she doesn't like it."

"Does this involve a hand-dipped, chocolate banana milkshake after a deep tissue massage?" Veera asked.

Both Michael and I threw her questioning looks.

"Just saying."

"Corrie." Michael's head poked in between us again. "You're going to have to—"

"Forget it."

"Why is it so hard—"

"I said no."

"What?" Veera's gaze shot between us. "I can't see anything being hard on you, C. You got what it takes to do anything."

"Tell Yoko if she's not there when we arrive, all deals are off," I said.

"Done." Veera sent the text and looked between Michael and me. "What can she not do?"

I clamped my mouth shut.

"Sorry," Michael said.

"For what?" Veera craned her neck toward Michael.

"She has trouble saying the word 'sorry,' when it comes to James."

Veera nodded slowly. "That is wrong."

"Must be why it feels so right." I picked up speed and got on the freeway.

James had ignored me during most of high school while I'd nursed my crush on him from afar, daring to hope one day he'd realize I wasn't like the usual pack of females that fawned over him. Things changed after the kiss at Michael's birthday party. I'd resented that he'd expected me to swoon at his feet in exchange for a speck of attention. I'd excelled in ignoring him after that, and pushed away his efforts to diffuse my anger. To his credit, he'd even tried to apologize to me, but I wouldn't let him. Years passed and we barely saw each other. And when we did, I made sure he knew he was just another pretty face in my book. Until he stepped in to help with the homicide at the studio. And now, here he was helping again. I needed to make amends.

Nearly an hour later, we pulled into the parking lot of the lab. Only one other space was taken.

"That better be Yoko's car," Veera said.

Michael squeezed out of the backseat. "Can I see the hair sample?"

I pulled out the envelope and lifted the top. Michael examined the contents.

"I'd recognize those thick white strands anywhere."

Veera and I peered in the envelope.

"He must have had some head of hair," Veera said.

"Over here." We heard a shout behind us.

Yoko peeped out the open doorway. She backed into the office. We hustled inside, single file.

"Before we go on," I said, "what exactly is your favor?"

"Who's he?" She pointed to Michael.

"On a need to know basis. Talk."

"You have to write a letter," Yoko said. "To send to the Stalwart Club in downtown L.A."

"I know where it is," I said. "It's a men's only club that's been there for three hundred years."

"Since 1878," Yoko said.

"Math is not her strong suit," Michael told Yoko. "I heard there's a ten year waiting list for membership. Even men can't get in easily."

"You stay out of this," Yoko said.

"Are you saying that because I'm a man?"

"You're acting exactly the way those men's club members act," Veera told Yoko. "You gotta be the open mind you want to see."

Yoko turned to me. "You want to know about your pop or not?"

"What about him?" Michael asked.

I hadn't bothered to tell him since chances of it being true were slim to non-existent. "She claims she saw Dad last week."

"Like in a dream?"

"No." Yoko inched toward Michael, tilting her head back. "Like in here. In this room, mister. Where you're standing. He's a big man. Hard to miss. Even for a short little, pigeon-toed girl like me."

Our eyes shot down to her white tennis shoes.

"Take it easy." Michael put up his hands. "If I had a club, I'd gladly let in women. Most of them, anyway. If they had a good attitude."

"And brought something worthwhile to the table," I said. Truth was, if she hadn't dangled the bit about Dad, I would never have come back. But that was wearing thin. The more I thought about it, the more likely she was using me. "Are you trying to get a woman into the Stalwart?" I asked.

"They have a job opening for assistant manager of event planning," Yoko said. "That's me. Women can work there, even if they can't be members."

"An event planner needs good organizational skills, a flair for décor, and most importantly, she has to be personable," Veera said. "You got that last part?"

"I'm nice. Very nice. You saw how I tolerated her." Yoko pointed to me. "Even though I knew she was lying." She turned back to me. "I need a reference letter from you."

"Why me?"

"Your pop had clients who are members of the Stalwart. Your name on the letter will get me in. You can mention him."

"Why don't you ask my father to write the letter?" Now I had her.

"You expect me to ask a client a favor? My pop would get mad."

"You expect me to believe that?" I asked.

"You believe what you want."

"Wait a minute," Veera said. She pointed to me. "She's a client. You can't ask her, either."

"She didn't pay. Your two dollars doesn't count." She turned to me. "If I can ask your pop without mine knowing, I will."

"You just don't get it, do you?" My blood was simmering. "My dad didn't come in last week."

Yoko held out an open appointment book. "I saw him. And he's coming in next week. It says so in Pop's book."

I peered at the page. Next to Monday morning, someone had scribbled Dad's name.

"She will not write a letter for you and neither will this…father figure you've conjured up." Michael stood between Yoko and me. "You don't know Corrie, but if you did, you'd know that she's a woman of steel. Nothing fazes her, except the people she loves. You took one of those people and are using him as a tool to get your way. Well, it's not happening, missy."

"Got that right." Veera towered over Yoko, but Yoko didn't back off.

"Why you keep doubting me?" She scoured our faces and stopped at mine. "To prove I'm what I think I am, I'll take care of your business. No charge. You're going to end up doing me my favor."

I didn't hesitate. I'd deal with the living dead later. "We need this hair sample analyzed." I held out the envelope.

Yoko snatched it from me and peered inside. "Is this for drug testing?"

"We need to know who the hair belongs to."

"I'm not a magic man." Yoko cut her stare to Michael. "Or woman. I need actual hair from the suspect to make a match."

"Drat." How could I have forgotten such a simple thing?

"You don't have any?" Yoko asked. "Sheesh."

"Does that mean…do we need…?" Michael's forehead crinkled.

I grabbed his arm. "We'll be back." We headed out the door.

"I've never been to a crime scene before," Veera said after I'd parked the car in the faculty lot.

"It's disturbing in a nightmarish, wake-me-when-it's-over kind of way," Michael said. The car vibrated to the tune of his bouncing knee. "But I'm up for it."

"I'll be in and out in a flash," I told him. "You wait here."

"But where will you find Mac's hair?" Michael said. "The office was scrubbed clean."

"I won't be back 'til I find some." Veera's foot was out the door.

"You're not coming, either," I said to her.

"How come? I'm good at keeping watch. And cracking ribs if I need to."

"You keep him company. And no rib cracking." I opened the car door and looked back at Michael. "I'm going straight for the closet. Big Mac's coat is bound to have stray hairs around the collar."

"Okay, but if you don't return in fifteen minutes," he said, "we're coming in."

Veera rubbed her hands together. "That's right."

"You won't have to." I hurried away and didn't stop until I reached the pond. I paused beneath an olive tree. I took a few sidesteps and peeked around the trunk for a straight view of the Admin Hall. A man shuffled along the side, dragging a rubber sole near the shrubbery lining the building. It was Bobby again, jabbing the bushes with a black walking staff, like the kind used for hiking. If that wasn't suspicious, the fact that he stopped beneath the president's window and gazed up certainly was.

A minute later, I stood behind him. "Nice day, isn't it?"

He spun around, resting the tip of the staff on the grass. "Got my tape?"

"The ADA has it. Why are you poking around?"

He turned back to look at the bushes. "A lab animal escaped. I'm search and rescue."

"What kind of animal?"

"That's confidential," Bobby said.

"How am I going to help you find it if I don't know what it is?"

"Good play, but it's not gonna work."

"Wasn't your shift over hours ago?" I asked.

He moved closer and tilted his chin back, squinting down the rising sun. "What are you, the overtime police? I know why you're really here. You were sent by MacTavish to chronicle breaches, so's the school can get a new security team, right before we get our annual raises."

"We're investigating an accusation made by a faculty member. That's all I can say."

"This has nothing to do with security?"

"Not today." I turned, knowing I'd better get cracking. "Tomorrow could be a different story."

"Don't forget who got you that tape."

"You're in our good graces, Bobby. For now. I'll keep an eye out for the monkey."

"Not a monkey, it's a…oh, you're sly, aren't you? You'll know it when you see it."

He shuffled away from the building. I returned to the path, shooting glances behind me until Bobby escaped my line of vision. Before I reached Michael's window, a tallish woman in a white linen dress appeared, taking the steps to the front door of the Admin Hall. It was

Michael's co-dean, Alyce. She pulled a card from her handbag and swiped it over the security entry-box.

I climbed up the steps to the building and clamped a hand on the door before she could shut it. "Thanks."

"Who are you?" Her voice was deep, her words curled out like steam. A strand of silky, blonde hair fell over one eye. "It's Sunday."

As if I didn't know. "I've got a letter to slip under the president's door." I lifted the envelope with the hairs out of my purse. "A protest to the demotion of the dean."

"That's co-associate dean." One side of her lip turned up, frosty blue gaze took a lap over me. "Come on in."

I followed her through the dark tiled entry and up the stairs. "Where are we going?"

"I'm escorting you to MacTavish's office," she replied.

"Good. You know him well?"

"Well enough."

I followed the back of her black ballet flats up the dark brown, carpeted stairs. "Why did he demote Mi...Mr. Parris? It was so unfair."

"I can't say. But it wasn't because of me. Michael and I are congenial, except when we're with Mac. He enjoys pitting us against each other. Must get a jolt out of making us bicker."

"He likes to be jolted?"

"A lot. But mostly he likes to do the jolting."

"You hate him, don't you?"

"Mac or Michael?"

"You tell me."

She stopped and swiveled my way. "MacTavish is like a father to me."

"I find that hard to believe. Unless you like bossy, bloodless, cold hearted dads. You're the first person who's said anything remotely nice about him."

"All I want is to be the whoppingest best dean I can be."

"Co-associate dean."

"And Mac understands that."

"What about Michael?"

"Oh, he's sweet, isn't he? But if you know him like I do, you'd realize he's not cut out to be a top dog."

My hands balled. "You know him well?"

"Well enough." She continued down the hall. "What's your major?"

"Math." I was cooked if she asked any math questions beyond elementary multiplication. I went to law school for a reason.

We stopped in front of Big Mac's office.

She opened her oversized handbag and took out a cigarette. "I would have pegged you for a liberal arts major." She tossed her head toward the door. "Show yourself out." She headed down the corridor. I watched her until she hopped down the back staircase.

"Here I go again." Before I could set a speed record for breaking and entering, my cell phone vibrated. "I'm on a time crunch, Yoko."

"I don't need the hair sample."

"What?"

"What you gave me is not human," she said.

"It's from an alien?" She wasn't just crazy. She was raving mad.

"Are you insane? It's from an animal."

## CHAPTER 28

## A HAIRY SITUATION

"It was a perfectly logical mistake," Michael said after I told him about Yoko's call and the white hair. "Pigs and humans have a lot in common. Just read *Animal Farm* and you'll see."

"So the pig burped?" Veera asked. "What kind of a person keeps a pig in the trunk?"

"The kind that rescues it from a school lab to secretly transport it to an animal sanctuary." I'd put a few pieces together. I tried calling Ian for confirmation, but he wasn't picking up. That must have been what Bobby was searching for. The missing lab pig. What a fool I'd been.

"I'm...I'm...going to take a nap." Michael reclined in the backseat. "A Rumpelstiltskin nap. Wake me in a hundred years."

Veera's hand slapped her knee. "Wait a minute. Does that mean those two are innocent? They still could be killers. Those dentures didn't belong to any pig."

"Calling the farm." I picked up my phone. "To verify the pig was donated and to find the owner of the dentures."

"Don't forget the body," Michael mumbled from behind.

"We'll find that, too."

"We can't give out donor information." Zena had picked up the phone. "But Archie arrived yesterday."

"Can you describe him?"

"He's young, a hundred pounds of pure fat, and has big floppy ears all pink on the inside and hairy white on the outside like the rest of him. He's a little cut up, but we expect him to be fully healed. They're surface wounds. He hasn't stopped eating since he got here. The glutton."

"White hair?" I glanced at Veera. "Did he seem abused to you?"

"Not really," Zena replied. "Just needed to spend more time outdoors."

"By the way, we were wrong about the owner of the dentures. Do you know who they belong to?"

"One of our volunteers lost them two days ago. She's been sipping her food through a straw ever since. Can't understand a word she says."

"How did she lose the teeth?"

"She took a coffee break in the pigpen, and took them out to hose off. She left them out to dry, and when she came back, they were gone."

"Thanks." I disconnected. I held up the plastic bag with the dentures. "We'll send these back."

"Girl," Veera said. "Our clues just up and disappeared."

"We still have suspects. Good ones," I said. "Now all we have to do is link at least one of them to the missing Big Mac." I tapped my index finger against my forehead. What was the name of the cop that recognized James? "Officer Wyatt."

"Who?" Michael asked.

"Never mind." I called the station and asked for him, hoping he was on duty.

"Ernie Wyatt here."

"This is Corrie Locke. Monty Locke's daughter." I threw a glance in the back seat. Michael had one eye open, fixed on me. I turned and spoke quietly into the phone. "I was with the ADA last night."

"Who?"

"ADA Zachary. You stopped us downtown."

"What?" Michael straightened up. "Why?"

"I stopped a lot of people," Officer Wyatt said.

"We were the ones in the SUV."

"Huh?"

"We were…" I could feel Michael hanging on my next words. Even Veera was leaning in. "Fogged in."

"Oh, the kissing couple." He chuckled.

Oh boy. "I'm supposed to meet the ADA on the LA Tech Campus in a few minutes. He asked me to call to confirm the information you provided." I crossed the fingers of both of my hands. This lie was so far-fetched it belonged in the Milky Way.

"What makes you think I got anything new since the ADA and I chatted an hour ago? No clarification necessary about the ice cream truck report."

My pulse quickened. "I understand, but James wants to know if you verified the story yourself."

"Listen, young lady. This is not the way your father operated. You only had to tell him things once. The truck was stolen in the wee hours, Saturday morning. Probably just a bunch of kids." He disconnected.

Or a bunch of killers.

Michael's head appeared over my shoulder. "Why were you and James pulled over? What fog?"

"That's not important. Here's what we know." I turned to face them. "Someone stole an ice cream truck near campus, early yesterday morning. Why?"

"You wouldn't be asking if it didn't have something to do with the Big Mac attack," Veera said.

"To store the body in," Michael said and shot his head between us.

"Or...this here truck was hijacked to use as a getaway vehicle," Veera said. "No one would chase down an ice cream truck. I know how the criminal mind works. I'm taking a criminal law class right now."

"But that doesn't explain how they snuck him off campus," Michael said. "That's nearly impossible without being seen."

"You're both on the right track," I said. If that track was part of the Siberian Railway. "But I'm thinking, like Michael, it wasn't the truck they wanted. It was what was inside. They either needed to cart ice somewhere or a place to keep something cold...like a body."

"See, that's what I'm talking about," Veera said.

"All we have to do is find the body," I said. "Yet we can't find any trace of it or any witnesses. What does that tell you?"

"It was chopped into itty bitty pieces and taken out in a bunch of suitcases?" Veera said.

"That the body's still on campus. Maybe even in the building," I said.

Michael's eyes grew large and round, mirroring Veera's.

"The basement," Michael said. "Why didn't I think of that earlier? It's the perfect place to store him. Cool and dark. Hardly anyone goes there."

"Is there a basement?" I asked. Basements were scarce in Southern California.

"And a sub-basement. And twisty tunnels running under campus," Michael said. "It's like an open secret everyone knows about, but it's on the down-low. Freshmen consider breaking into the sub-basement a rite of passage."

"Okay. It's midday and the co-dean is going to his office with two students."

"Which students?" Michael wanted to know.

"Fake ones. Veera and me."

"I can do that."

"We're going to explore the underground," I said. "The ideal place to hide a body until it can be safely transported."

"So you think the ice cream truck was used to haul ice in?" Michael asked.

"You're doing damn fine without any evidence," Veera said.

"The less evidence the better for her," Michael said.

"All we've had are false leads," I said. "We need to comb the underground to determine if the body is or was stored there."

"You know, I'm thinking this here president is hiding right under our noses and we've got vision problems." Veera slapped a hand on Michael's shoulder. "Let's go look up close."

Michael led us to an unmarked door near the Admin Hall's back entrance. He tramped down a flight of cement stairs into a small, stuffy room. A panel of lights above the elevator indicated only two floors, B and SB. I turned. Veera remained in the stairwell, fingers propping open the door.

Veera's eyes were glued to the panel. "What kind of floor is this SB?"

Michael pushed the button. "The sub-basement? I've never been. The regular basement is filled with labs used by students and faculty conducting experiments. Big Mac wouldn't be there. He'd be in SB."

"How did you know about this elevator?" I asked him.

"The faculty tour guide brought us here. We took a quick spin, but I remember her saying the sub-basement housed out-of-date items LA Tech couldn't unload. Old telescopes, furniture, files, and books. Science equipment, too. They could be valuable someday. We didn't go all the way down. Wasn't part of the tour."

"That's suspicious right there." Veera backed up, one arm still on the door. "I suggest we spend time questioning our suspects and not go exploring a sub-basement where we might need to wear HAZMAT suits."

"She's right," I said. "You two stay here. I'll take a quick look."

"I've got a better idea." Michael turned to Veera. "You wait here and get help if we don't return in thirty minutes." The elevator door groaned open and Michael stepped inside, one hand slammed against the door's mid section. "Be our lookout." The door pushed hard against his hand and clanked back.

"Shoot," Veera said when I stepped inside. "You don't know what's down there. Maybe that's where they torture the animals. Maybe they're even doing experiments on people."

I slid closer to Michael so my shoulder touched his upper arm. Warmth shot through me. "Or maybe it's just for storage. Only one way to find out."

The door inched shut, the elevator shuddered, and we began our slow descent.

## CHAPTER 29

### TOES TO TOES

The elevator grinded to a halt, crushing the ground beneath our feet. I swallowed hard to push my stomach out of my throat. The door groaned open.

"Now I know what a crash landing feels like." Michael took a giant step out.

I followed him into a tiny foyer. A black sign with gold lettering read, *Sub-basement*. We turned into a long corridor where the air was thick and lifeless. A pump grumbled in the distance. Exposed pipes ran across the ceiling, hissing and sputtering. A round, gaping hole pierced the cement wall on our right, forming the bottom of a steep chute that ended in the sub-basement, perfect for transporting a large box, a chair...or a body.

"That's disturbing," Michael said, staring at the hole. A dark strip stained the center where the bulk of the weight traveled. "We're in the belly of the beast and this is the mouth. Do you think he—?"

"We're here to find out." I stepped closer and stared up the hole into the blackness. I flashed my penlight. No end in sight. The cement floor below looked clean. The odor of chlorine drifted down the hole. I turned and inspected the hallway in front of us. Cardboard boxes, stacked three high and thickly wrapped in cellophane lined the walls. A blue handled broom leaned on the opposing wall.

"Holy crap," Michael said.

I turned. Michael's hand gripped the knob of an old wooden door that he held open.

"It's a graveyard in here."

I hurried over and peered past him into a small, dark room littered with debris.

"Do they not know that there's an afterlife for old computer parts? These could be screened and recycled and put to good use."

I did a mental eye roll and backed away. "What's that smell?"

Michael tilted his chin upward and sniffed. "French fries."

"Want one?" A voice from behind us asked.

We jumped and turned. In one quick movement, my wrist was poised with my shuriken behind my back.

Squalley's hand cradled a red carton, half filled with fries.

"What are you doing?" I asked and slipped my shuriken back into my handbag.

Squalley stuck his neck out, chicken style. "Um, I work here."

"I mean in the sub-basement."

"That's what I mean. I spend half the day down here, moving stuff around."

"You mean taking things upstairs and downstairs?" Michael asked.

"No, I mean moving stuff around. You know, like I put the broom over there in case I need to sweep. I threw some of those old wooden crates in the garbage. I organize. And keep an eye on things."

Michael and I exchanged glances.

"Like what things?" I asked.

"My swing set for one. Speaking symbolically." He carved a path between us and into the closet-like space housing the spare computer parts. He squatted and pushed apart the tangle of metal sitting front and center, and revealed a small refrigerator, the kind found in hotel rooms. He pulled open the door. Cans tumbled out, clanging to the floor. "Want one?" He held out a can.

"That's a lot of beer," Michael said.

"I can neither confirm nor deny your accusation." Squalley shut the door and straightened up. He pushed the computer parts back in place. "I don't know who this stuff belongs to. I only found it here. For all I know it could be yours." He pointed to Michael.

"It's not. I would never—"

"Oh, calm down. What I wanna know is why a dean and a..." He squinted at me. "Who are you again?"

"I'm the girl you paid off to keep quiet about the pig."

"Oh." Squalley straightened. "I thought you'd understand after we told you about the torture."

"I thought you were talking about torture of people, but it was animal lab testing, wasn't it?"

Squalley ambled out of the tiny room and shut the door behind him. "Animals need our protection." He wagged his finger at us. "Did you know a middle-aged pig's got as much smarts as a three-year-old human? Pigs can adapt to complex situations because they have the ability to learn new skills. Most humans can barely adapt to simple changes in situation. Think about that next time you reach for the bacon."

Michael mouthed to me, "I like bacon."

"They can even play video games with joysticks."

"Really?" Michael said, coming around to face Squalley. "That's genius. But if you're talking about animal abuse at LA Tech, you're wrong. I've been looking into that. The only pig on campus was Archie, the mascot in the physics lab. LA Tech doesn't use pigs for experiments." Michael turned to me. "We have a committee dedicated to ensuring animals involved in research receive humane care. They're never hurt or mistreated."

"Yeah, well, that's not what Ian says. Besides, what we did was take Archie out of the way of temptation. He's at a place where no one will ever think of frying his brain in the name of science. He's a free pig. We took...what's it called again?"

"Pre-emptive action?" I asked.

"That's it."

"Squalley, we took the elevator down," I said. "Is that the only way in?"

"There's a stairwell that's kept locked from the outside, in the building across from Admin."

"That's it."

"That's what?" he asked.

I hadn't realized I'd spoken aloud. "The only elevator. I don't like walking up stairs."

"I suggest you take the stairs, and not be so lazy. That elevator doesn't always work." He pointed over his shoulder and shuffled away. "Look for the door marked *Exit,* two hundred yards down that way." He pointed. "There're few twists and turns. It's so people who shouldn't be here can't come back." He turned and aimed his gaze on Michael. "You gonna report me and Ian?"

"Not if you don't report us," Michael said.

"Deal." Squalley disappeared down the corridor.

We spent the next ten minutes poking around. We came up empty handed.

"The only thing that makes sense is that the body was sent down the chute to the sub-basement and stashed here somewhere," I said.

"But it doesn't make sense if the way out is either with an elevator that works or doesn't. Or a door that leads to the wide open," Michael said.

"Unless there's another exit that Squalley didn't tell us about," I said.

"Or doesn't know about."

We returned to the elevator.

"I'm willing to risk the elevator," I said. "You?"

Michael's eyes were locked on the light panel above the door. "That's strange. Did you push the button?"

"Not yet."

"Then why is it coming down?" Michael asked.

"Maybe Veera got tired of waiting."

The elevator rocked to a stop, the door slid open, and Veera spilled out followed by Bobby.

"See," Veera said, joining us. "I told you."

"You again," Bobby said to me and moved closer, dragging his bum foot beside him.

"You know him?" Veera asked.

"He's night security," I said.

"He snuck up behind me without announcing himself," Veera said. "Do you know how wrong that is?"

"I wasn't sneaking," Bobby said.

"Why is it you turn up in all the wrong places?" I asked.

"You're the one that doesn't belong on campus. I work here, remember?"

"Last I checked, we've got a few hours to go until sundown. Yet you're always here."

"I got a right to be," Bobby said. "I'm going to write you up."

"Go ahead." If only I had an emery board. This would be the part where I'd lean against a wall and file my nails to perfection while I spoke.

"I'm sure your higher-ups would be happy to know that you loaned a security tape to an assistant district attorney from a neighboring county."

He raised his chin. "You don't scare me."

"Already did." I waved him aside and stepped into the elevator.

Michael paused a moment before following me. Veera scurried in right behind him.

"Up, please," I said.

Michael pushed the up button and we waited. And waited. The door remained open.

Bobby leaned against the cement wall, hairy forearms crossed against his chest. His thin lips curved upward. "Nowhere to go, little lady?"

I stepped out. "You think I don't know about the other exit?"

His chin tilted upward again and his torso leaned forward. "You were expecting me down here, weren't you? How did you know I was coming?"

What the heck was he talking about? "That's classified."

"You're stalking me."

"In your dreams."

His slicked back hair remained motionless despite a quick head turn toward Veera. She shot him a menacing grimace, fists facing each other, elbows jutted outward. She didn't back down. He turned his beady blues back to me. "She's a plant."

"Why should I tell you anything?" I asked.

"Because," he said, "you need me."

"Ha! Did you not notice?" I eyed his muscular arms and lean body. Despite his diminutive stature, it was possible he had the strength and stamina to drag an over-grown man to the elevator and down to the sub-basement. "I never work with the untrained. Besides, why would I need you?"

He inched closer to me. "To get you stuff."

Michael stepped up. "She doesn't need any 'stuff.' She's got plenty."

"Aren't you the guy MacTavish fired?" Bobby asked him.

"Fired? I was demoted," Michael said. "It's not the same thing."

Bobby chortled out of the side of his mouth. "Demoted? To the sub-basement?"

I shot out an arm to keep Michael from charging forward. "Define *stuff*."

"I got you and…" his gaze shifted to Michael and back to me, "…your other guy the tape. Next time you might want a book, a key, or maybe a map."

Why didn't I think of that? A map was exactly what I needed. "Why would I want any of those things?"

"I'm not the one you should be watching." His eyes darted between us. His torso leaned forward even more. He whispered, "The maintenance guy."

"Squalley or Ian?"

"The Italian. He's been spending a lot of time in the Admin Hall. Makes you wonder."

"Why is that suspicious?" Michael asked.

"Now you see him, then you don't. I watch security tapes at the end of my shifts. One minute Squalley's in the president's office and the next, poof! He's gone."

I shot a glance at Michael.

"Maybe he knows you're watching and he's playin' with you." It was Veera's turn to step forward. "Like you were watching me when I was sitting on the stairs."

"It's not a crime to observe. It's what security guards do."

"Don't talk to me about security guards. I worked top level security for the Chinese Mafia before I took up the study of law."

Veera was partially right. She'd worked as a guard in the parking lot of a warehouse for a company that reproduced antique Ming vases, women's hosiery, and computer parts—a wide array of goods, so naturally she suspected Mafia ties.

Bobby rolled his eyes over Veera and nodded. "That explains your keen sense of hearing."

Veera turned to me. "I clobbered him when he tried to twist my arm behind my back." Her eyes shot back to Bobby. "That was excessive force. Is that what you do to the students? Or just to helpless females?"

"You grabbed my hair and took a swing at me." He smoothed back his hair.

"You shouldn't have snuck up like you did."

"I think you're right, Bobby. We can help each other. Get me a map of the campus," I told him. "We're interested in the big fish, not you. And remember, if your boss is found doing something underhanded, the school will need a competent replacement."

Bobby gave a straight-face nod. "I can be a turncoat. Meet me in twenty minutes by the arches. I'll have a map of the underground." He shuffled down the corridor.

Michael bunched his lips. "This is getting more and more complicated."

"The theory of relativity is complicated," I said. "A Rubik's Cube is complicated and so is color coordinating with leopard prints. This is not." My hand landed on his arm.

"Hang in there, boy," Veera said. "We're gonna get to the bottom of this."

"We sure are." I stepped into the elevator.

"But don't you see, Corrie?" Michael followed close behind. "If I'm silent and his body turns up and my note is found and the fact that I was the last one to see him comes out and that I was furious, I'll be the prime suspect. This is the time to call the police. Maybe they'll cut me some slack for coming forward. I won't tell them about you," he said to me. He turned to Veera. "Or you. Or James or anyone else. It'll be just me and Mac."

"Maybe we'll solve this tonight and you won't have to," Veera said, stepping into the elevator. She pushed the first floor button. "It's possible."

The elevator wouldn't budge.

Michael shook his head. "That's about as possible as my being promoted today."

"Try the elevator again," I said.

Michael pushed the button. The doors shuddered and closed.

"Finally," Veera said.

We stepped out of the elevator and onto the first floor of the Admin Hall.

"Michael?" The woman with the silky blond hair shimmied toward us. Michael's co-associate dean. Her sleek locks made mine look like a marshland plant, the type that provides cover for waterfowl and spawning fish. I didn't need a mirror to know my sweats were baggy, my sweatshirt stained, and my sneakers bulky. I eyed Alyce's perfect, pouty pink smile.

"I was hoping we could speak." Alyce flicked a glance between Veera and me. "Alone."

"Why?" Michael stepped forward. "Because of all the crazy stuff going on? Or because I'm a sparkling conversationalist?"

She slipped in closer to Michael. So did Veera and I.

"Mac has a request of you," she told him.

"What?" Michael's jaw dropped. "Are you kidding me? Haven't I been through enough already? The surprise demotion—"

"He wants you to act as interim dean of the department while he's away."

"What did you say?" I asked her.

"I'm not talking to you," Alyce replied.

"Who are you?" Veera asked her.

Alyce hesitated, and said, "I'm not sure anymore." She smoothed her hair. "I was co-associate dean with Michael." She tossed a vague smile at him and focused on me. "I saw you here before."

"So what?" I said.

"Are you a student?"

"They're with me," Michael said. "So Mac told you to tell me to act as dean? Did he tell you in person?"

"No. His text said he'd be out this week."

"You got a text from him?" I asked.

"This is not your business," Alyce said.

"The reason why we respect LA Tech," I said, "is because of the transparency between faculty and students."

"That's right." Veera nodded.

Alyce lowered her chin and fastened her gaze on Michael. "I got a text, an hour ago. From Mac."

Michael took a moment to chew on a knuckle. Veera's eyes grew to the size of golf balls. And me, well, I kept watch on Alyce, whose head-on stare bounced between us.

"A text?" Michael was on high alert. "From *his* phone?"

She leaned in close to his ear. So did Veera and I.

"He said he wanted to rethink the events of Friday."

I poked my head between her and Michael. "Why wouldn't you be the one to step in during his absence?"

"That's a fair question. More than fair considering Mac made me a junior adviser," Michael said. "But he left out specifics. Who are my advisees? What does a junior adviser even do? Can I wear flip-flops to work?"

I was afraid of this. Michael was having a melt-down.

Alyce tossed her tresses over her shoulders and slipped an arm through Michael's. She led him down the hall. "He feels bad over what happened."

I was on the heels of her ballet flats. "Why didn't Big Mac text Michael himself?"

"Or better yet, why didn't he call if he wanted to smooth things over?" Michael asked.

"Who said anything about smoothing? He's reevaluating." Her blue eyes were skewers on me. "Step away, would you? You're violating my space."

"Answer the question." I stood firm in my sneakers.

She turned her square jaw to Michael. Even in her flats she was nearly as tall as he was. Alyce dove a hand into her oversize handbag and pulled out a cigarette. She tapped it against her pale wrist. "There's only one question that needs to be answered. Will you be acting dean until Mac returns?"

"This makes no sense," Michael said.

"I don't get why Big Mac contacted you," I said to Alyce.

"There's nothing to 'get.'" Alyce clasped the cigarette between her fingers and held my gaze. "Mac encouraged me to persuade Michael to say yes. After what happened, he expected Michael to march off, never to return. Mac's not stupid. He realized his decision was rash." Her eyes flipped back to Michael. "I'm guessing he's offering you the interim spot to soften you up, to encourage you to agree to return to your post." She moved closer to him. "He had a breakdown on Friday and you..." she took Michael's hand, "...bore the brunt of it."

"Did Mac tell you all this in a text?" I asked. She had too much insider information.

"It's what I surmised from the text and the events."

"From what we heard," Veera said, "this president was no shrinking violet. Doesn't sound like him."

Alyce dropped Michael's hand and smiled at Veera. "You don't know him like I do."

"You've been co-dean for a few months. How did you two grow so close?" I asked.

"Haven't you ever met someone you felt you've known your whole life?"

I cut a glance at Michael and a campfire ignited inside, enough to keep a whole Girl Scout troop warm. I turned back to Alyce. "This is a pile of—" I started.

"You heard from him today?" Michael asked.

She smiled a queasy smile. At least it made me feel queasy. "Yes."

"That's not possible," Michael said. "Someone's pulling a fast one and I'm not falling for it."

"Can I see your phone?" I held a hand out to Alyce.

She turned my way. "That would be an invasion of my privacy." She faced Michael again, phony smile plastered in place. "Sleep on it." She whirled away and disappeared through the exit door.

Veera scratched her head. "What just happened?" She turned to me. "I know I been standing here the whole time, yet I can't make sense of it. Could there be any truth to what she said?"

"Not one iota," I said. First Loretta claims to have seen Big Mac, and now Alyce receives a text from him.

"Why would she make up such a huge lie?" Michael asked.

"To cover her butt," I said. She was a lot bigger than Bobby, which meant she could have the strength to drag the body off all by herself. Those toned and hairless arms were tentacles. "She killed him. And now she's toying with us."

"She doesn't know I found Mac with the knife in his back," Michael said. "So she's throwing the scent off her back-stabbing hands by telling me Mac texted when he didn't."

"She refused to show Corrie her phone," Veera said. "That's guilt right there."

"I'll bet she's spreading rumors," I said. "To delay an investigation until the body's moved."

"When I found Mac," Michael said, "It was awful...I blocked it out. But I remember something now. There was blood, a lot of it. On his coat. On the chair, on the floor, everywhere." He turned to me. "But it was clean when we got there. Shouldn't there be drops of blood...something...somewhere, if he was carried away? They couldn't have cleaned everything. That would take a while."

I remembered the bloodstains near the bookcase in the office. "The body doesn't bleed all that long after the heart stops." A visit with a coroner connected to one of Dad's cases taught me that tidbit. I turned to Michael. "Does that chute in the sub-basement reach the second floor of the Admin Hall?"

Michael thought a moment. "No. But there's one on the first floor next to the fire extinguisher. He could have been carted to the elevator, taken to the first floor, and stuffed in the chute."

"Would that work?" Veera asked.

"You two check the hallway outside of the office. Here." I reached into my handbag and pulled out a small flashlight. "Use this." I turned and walked toward the exit. "Look for any signs of blood along the way. Check out corners and hard to clean spots."

"Aren't you coming with us?" Michael asked on my heels. Veera was right behind him.

"I have to meet Bobby and get the map." I stepped outside and made a beeline for the archway. "We'll meet up outside your office once I get it." If there was another way out of Admin, I needed to know.

Moments later, I spotted Bobby at the far end of the arches, lost in the shadows. And he wasn't alone.

## CHAPTER 30

## THE LOST AND FOUND

I moved forward in slow, deep strides down the archway. Bobby spoke to a tall, broad shouldered man wearing a navy baseball cap over wavy brown hair. The rest of him wore jeans and a navy hoodie. James' back faced me. How could someone so drop dead gorgeous end up with the personality of a pincushion? He looked soft and inviting, but grew sharp and prickly with contact. At least he did with me. Bobby was pointing to a map in his hand. My map, I guessed. He handed it to James moments later. My workload just doubled.

I halted a few paces back. James gripped something in his other hand. A manila envelope housing a rectangular bulge.

"The map?" I held a hand out.

"He's got it." Bobby pitched his chin toward James.

James' stare rolled over me and shot back to Bobby. "Thanks." He slipped the envelope inside his hoodie and made off down the archway.

"You are not scoring any points with me," I told Bobby.

I nipped at James' heels. I was close enough to lunge forward, grab him around the waist, and tackle him to the ground. I had a feeling I'd miss on all counts.

"Wait up," I said, hurrying to keep pace.

He hustled across the lawn toward the tree-encircled pond.

"I've got information. I've been to the sub-basement. The body could be there." The whole time I babbled, he didn't slow down. "Michael got a text from Big Mac!"

James halted so quickly, I smacked right into him. His chin dropped to his chest. He turned my way. "Make your words count."

I spoke fast. "The text was from Mac, but didn't go to Michael. It was sent to Alyce, the co-dean. She said Mac's out of commission next week, no surprise there, and she claimed he wants Michael to act as interim dean in his absence. To make up for the demotion."

James picked up speed again. I hurried at his heels.

"I don't believe her either."

He paused beneath the olive trees that framed the entrance to the pond. "Did you see the text?"

"She refused to show it to me."

He held up the hand that grasped the map. "I know about the sub-basement already. Get it? I've got everything I need, so why would I waste time with you?" He resumed his racehorse gait past the pond. Colorful Koi fish splashed tail fins and whipped away. Students snapped to attention when James swept past.

"Wait." I forged ahead. I caught up and jogged backwards in front of him. "I'm sor...I'm so..." I gulped. "I apol..."

He continued without slowing.

I sprinted by his side, trying to mask my panting by talking in spurts. "I'm...truly...I am." Swallowing a bullfrog would have been easier.

"You're what?" He stopped and faced me.

I stood mute before him.

He turned to leave. My fingers latched onto his wrist. He could escape in an instant. I knew it and so did he. But he didn't budge.

"I..." Why was this so difficult? He brought out the worst in me. "I didn't mean to upset you. I shouldn't have taken the tape."

He yanked his hand free and strode off, but his gait slowed. I continued alongside. He shot a glance my way. "We're done."

"We can't be. We have a unified goal. To help our best friend. Plus, you know we couldn't possibly get along if we were civil to each other. Wouldn't it make you suspicious if I started to act nicely all the time?"

His pace tapered to a stroll.

"In fact, my niceties would make you downright uncomfortable."

He turned and stared me down.

"It...it wouldn't be the real me." My neck tilted nearly all the way back. I was highly conscious of my makeup-free face, limp hair, and the mixed scents of sweat and wet lawn. "I do cooperate now and then. I've only really let you down, how many times..."

"I can't count that high."

I stepped right into that one. "I'm sorry." I leveled my chin and massaged the back of my neck. "I really am." I felt like I'd fallen down a hole, but managed to climb out with only a scratch. I should apologize to James more often.

He continued walking at normal speed.

"May I see the map?" I held out my hand. "Please?"

"You should ask about the tape."

"I watched it already."

"You didn't see this one. Bobby handed it to me ten minutes ago."

"You called in another favor?"

"No, it was the same one."

"Must have been a tall favor. What's on it?"

"Wrong question."

"Really? Okay. What's *not* on it?"

"That's better."

At least I was on the right track. "Part of it was erased?"

"It's missing the portion between the time Michael saw the knife in Mac's back to the time you two returned to the office."

"Which tree was this camera on?" I jogged alongside his fast stroll.

"It's interior, covering the back stairwell on the second floor."

"How much is missing?"

"Nearly an hour."

Enough time to hustle up the stairs, into the office, grab the body, and drag it off somewhere close by. And clean up afterward. "What else?"

"Twenty-five minutes between five and six a.m. are missing."

"What can a killer do in twenty-five minutes? Wait, this was after the ice cream truck was stolen?"

"You know about that?" James asked.

Now we were getting somewhere. My investigator sense was on fire. "Squalley said the elevator to the sub-basement doesn't work all the time. Which means they wouldn't chance transport in an elevator on the fritz. It was sent down the chute." I loved it when the pieces fit together. I told James about the chute in the sub-basement.

"What if he got stuck along the way?" James asked.

That was possible. "So the killer or killers came back. Not long enough to remove the body off campus. He's stored in the building, short term. And—"

"School starts Tuesday so the body—"

"Will be moved ASAP before the campus is back in full swing. Great minds think alike." I expected a pat on the back or some acknowledgement of my rationale, but I got nothing.

"Where's Michael?" James asked.

"With Veera. Looking for traces of blood in the hallway outside Big Mac's office." My eyes fell on the folded map clenched in his hand. "What do you say?" I held out my hand. He slapped the map on my palm. I unfolded it and studied the sub-basement. "It's more of a maze than I thought. Chambers, labs, and utility closets galore."

James checked his watch. "It's almost two-thirty. We'll meet at your place at five."

"Why not here?"

"To regroup and divvy out portions of the map to cover more ground." He held out a hand.

"I'll give it back when we meet up later."

James snatched the map out of my hands and walked away.

"Where are you going?" I asked.

"There's something I have to do."

He picked up speed and left my line of vision. The power play was wearing thin. I watched him swagger away. There was something I needed to do as well.

A crime scene was a little like a large amusement park. They both warranted multiple visits to be able to see everything. Clues always popped up in crime scene re-enactments. Which meant I needed to break into Big Mac's office yet again. And visit the sub-basement. Without getting caught. The odds in my favor grew slimmer each time.

I retraced my steps back to the Admin Hall and hid behind a canopy of trees by the pond. Students wearing backpacks weaved their way around. A guy in a dress shirt and slacks stumbled along, nose-to-textbook. They paid little attention to each other, but there were no head-on collisions. I stepped forward and retreated fast. Bobby paced the perimeter of the building once more, eyes on the surrounding shrubs. Was he looking for the kidnapped pig, missing dog, or something else?

I retreated into the clump of trees and fast-walked in the opposite direction. I'd run out of excuses for breaking into the president's office, let alone the Admin Hall. I had no excuses left for being mean to James, for not telling Michael how I felt about him, and for pretending to be a private investigator when I was hanging by the seam of my skirt to the entertainment attorney job.

"Hold it, young lady."

I spun around. Ian stood behind me. His sparse hair was combed, his smile full steam. He wore a black and white gingham shirt with jeans, and held a small, brown paper bag in one hand.

"I know a Koi lover when I see one. Are you here to feed them?" he asked.

"Actually, I…yes. But I forgot my Koi kibble."

He held up his bag. "I got plenty."

I followed him down a narrow, dirt path to the pond's cement rimmed edge. He crouched and motioned me beside him. I obliged.

"I saw Squalley today," I told him.

"Oh, you did?" He shook a few small kernels from the bag into his palm. They looked like dog food.

"What kind of kibble is that?" I asked.

"Wheat germ pellets." He cradled a few in his palm and held one out almost touching the murky water. The kernel disappeared as a foot-long glutton stuck out lips that sucked loudly on Ian's fingers, spitting out bubbles of appreciation. "Here." He dropped a few morsels into my hand.

"Thanks." No way was my skin touching those whiskered lips. "You guys work weekends?"

"I can't speak for Squalley, but I don't. I was in the library, studying. I'm on a break." More Koi splashed near his outstretched hand. "How about you?"

"Me?"

"Are you studying too?" Ian asked.

"Oh, yes. Too confining to study indoors. I was…" I waved my hand. "On a bench. Where are your books, by the way?"

"In my locker. I'll get them later. Go ahead. They're famished."

Round, suction cup mouths scanned the liquid surface. I took a deep breath, closed my eyes, and plunged in a hand. I plunged a little too much and slipped back on my bottom, one sneaker drowning in the pond. "Dammit." I pulled out my dripping shoe, untied it, and slipped off the slimy sneaker. Water spilled out.

"You're an exuberant feeder, aren't you?"

I wiggled my wet toes.

"Can't let you walk around campus with a naked foot." Ian stood. "Be right back." He hiked up the path and out of sight.

I had a feeling he was going to fabricate a shoe out of leaves and mud.

My foot was dry, but my pant leg damp when Ian returned holding a recyclable cloth bag. "I only brought right shoes."

"Right?" I got to my feet.

"For your wet foot. The left one's dry, isn't it?"

I nodded.

"Bare feet used to be popular at LA Tech. Before Big Mac took over," Ian said. "Now students are fined if they go shoeless. Of course, you may only have to pay half the fine..." He reached in his sack and pulled out a large moccasin.

"Too big."

Next came a boat shoe in a faded maroon.

"Too small." I leaned in to eye the inside of the bag.

"What size do you wear?" Ian asked.

"Eight."

Out came a black combat boot. "They're water-proof. Isn't that great?"

It wasn't like I was going near the pond again. Ever.

"I bet they're also flame retardant and cushiony inside. You'll thank me later."

I lifted my bare foot and examined my sole. Dirt specks stuck to the bottom. Not to mention pebbles, a pill bug, and a Koi kibble. I regarded the combat boot. I swiped my sole with my hand, took the boot and yanked it on. It fit comfortably. I laced it up and tried to ignore the shoe clash. "These are so—"

"Dope, right?" Ian nodded and grinned broadly. "You're going to set the campus on fire with your protesty fashion. Geeks love this off-kilter stuff."

I climbed with uneven steps up the short dirt path and into the civilized world. My sneaker was light and foamy. The army boot was clunky, with an inch on the sneaker, platform-wise, which encouraged an up and down gait.

"I don't suppose you have the other boot?" I asked Ian.

He shook his head. "That style came in a onesie."

Passersby slowed, stares glued to my footgear.

"As seen in the fashion section of last month's *Popular Science*," I said.

"Hey, wanna be my study buddy?" Ian's face lit up.

"Sorry, I've got to meet someone," I replied. "Thanks for the boot."

He turned a thumb up. "There's going to be a lot of buzz about that on the internet." Ian trotted back to the pond.

I shook off the stares and lopsided it toward the Admin Hall, concentrating on making my way to the underbelly. I edged along shrubs and dirt lanes, the better to keep an eye on things, periodically pausing to look in disbelief at the combat boot. That, the lack of sleep, and breaking and entering overload threw me off my game.

As I got closer, I spied a familiar figure by the Admin Hall, sitting beneath Big Mac's office window and patting the ground.

# CHAPTER 31

## THE INTERROGATION

I dove behind the nearest hedge and squatted behind it. Loretta stood and toed the dirt beneath the window with black, patent leather pumps. A Burberry trench coat covered her red sheath dress. I stepped out into the open and hobbled fast and unsteady toward her.

She heard my approach five yards out and shot off, away from the building. Normally, I can ramp up my sprint, but the army boot placed me at a disadvantage. Meanwhile, even in heels, the girl ran like a doe fleeing a flaming forest. I managed to yank a green pinecone off a tree, and aimed it at the back of her head. I missed, but the cone popped her one on the rear. She didn't flinch. Worse, she gained ground.

Loretta darted around a corner of a building along Los Angeles Boulevard. Moments later, I turned the same corner. There was no trace of her. I stopped and bent over, hands on thighs, panting. I scanned the surroundings. A student trudged toward me.

"Did you see a girl in a red dress race by?" I asked.

The student nodded. Her gaze dropped to my feet.

"Which way did she go?"

"Dunno. Cool granny boot." The student moved on.

"That's combat boot." Man, was she way off. Like I was right now with Loretta.

A minute later, I stood in Loretta's spot next to the Admin Hall, peering at the series of arcs she'd toed in the dirt. She'd either expected to find something beneath or was experimenting with a new art form. I called James, hoping his brain was in better working order than mine.

"What?" he answered gruffly.

I deserved that.

"Why aren't you in the car, driving back to your place?" he asked. "What's the holdup?"

"How did you...never mind." I fell for his bluff. "I'm waiting for Michael and Veera. Why would Loretta search the ground beneath Big

Mac's window?" My heart skipped a beat. The answer seeped into my head. Would James' reply match mine?

"I know what you're thinking," he said after a beat.

His voice changed to two degrees less harsh. Or maybe a different kind of harsh. Like going from vodka to prune juice.

"You're thinking she killed MacTavish and left evidence under the window," he said. "She's covering her tracks."

"Close." That wasn't even close. "She hired someone to kill him. Maybe Big Mac was squeezed out the window…somehow." Would cutting off an arm or two get him to fit? "And she's making sure the job was done right."

"You're saying she hired—"

"A professional." She lacked the charm to convince someone to do it without a payoff. Her Burberry trench coat indicated she had the bucks.

"If a professional was hired, the body won't be found any time soon. They're paid to see a job done," James said. "I thought you said MacTavish couldn't fit through a window."

"Maybe he was semi-chopped up." My theories sounded better in my head.

"If I had time on my hands like you do, I'd find out who sent the text."

"If there was a text."

"Why fake it?" he asked.

"To throw us off."

"Someone could have sent it to her, knowing she'd go to Michael. Who's your main suspect?"

"Everyone connected to this campus is a suspect, except Michael."

"You're stretching. You know what'll happen if you stretch too far? You'll snap." He disconnected.

I hobbled a few steps and thought of Bobby. He shared Loretta's interest in the building perimeter. Were they both seeking the missing lab pig? Or the dog? Or something else?

My head dropped down. I got on my hands and knees and patted the dirt with my palms. "Ew." I lifted my finger. A small, dark round pellet stuck to my finger. It looked like a cocoa puff. Or maybe animal poop. I shook my hand and stood.

"Why are you in the bushes?"

"I can explain." I straightened and sucked in my breath. "Oh. It's you."

Michael and Veera stood a few feet off. I stepped out of the shrubs and onto the lawn. "Any news?"

"No. And yes," Veera said. "No clues to show he was dragged out into the hallway. Or that he was even killed in his office."

"What happened to you?" Michael asked.

He and Veera eyed the mismatched shoes.

"My foot took a dip in the pond. How'd you know I'd be here?"

"We ran into Ian. He said you were headed this way."

"What did you mean by 'yes'?" I asked Veera. "You find anything?"

"We sure did," Veera said and turned to Michael. "Tell her."

"I thought of something," Michael scooted closer, his voice dropped a notch. "When I came back earlier today, I noticed a big, metal, roll-away dumpster parked near campus by the faculty lot. Nothing strange about that, except I'd remembered seeing cats sitting on the rim, licking their paws—"

"Cats are cleanaholics. They won't even poop if they don't have a proper facility. You don't usually see them hanging around dumpsters," Veera added.

"Alley cats might," I said.

"There are no alleys on campus," Michael said. "I figured there had to be something enticing in that dumpster. To cats, anyway. So I climbed a wall nearby and peeked inside. You wouldn't believe what I saw."

"Dead rats?" I said.

Michael shook his head.

"Ice cream," Veera said. "In every delicious flavor."

A light bulb hovered over my head.

"Sundae cups, crunch bars, popsicles, push-up pops...everything that used to be in the freezer of the stolen ice cream truck," Michael said. "Dumped out to make room for something."

I sucked in a wad of air.

"We need to find the truck," Michael said.

"Wait. We still don't know how that text to Alyce fits in," Veera said. "Why would she lie about it? And if she wasn't lying, who sent it?"

"How are your phone hacking skills?" I turned to Michael.

Michael put a finger to his lips. "Shhh. We don't use that word around here. But I'd bet most of the campus could get into phones. All geeks have sweet hacking skills."

"Sweet enough to pull out texts?" I asked.

Michael nodded. "You want me to confirm Alyce really got a text from Mac."

"Won't that take too long?" Veera asked.

"I'll need a few minutes to download a phone spy app," Michael said. "Enter the activation license, and read the texts."

"It's that simple?" Veera scratched her head. "Seems like something I could do."

"There is one more step."

I was afraid he was going to say that. "The app has to be installed on the target phone."

Veera wiped the smile off her face. "How we gonna do that? Wait." Her smile reappeared. "Maybe I could distract her, while C swipes it. I've got some dance moves that are mesmerizing."

"Why look at the impossible? Or the somewhat difficult?" Michael's face was alight. "I'll send her an email, with a download that contains the spyware."

Veera's nod turned into a headshake. "Isn't that a geeky talent? If she works here, she must be a geek too. She'd know all about hacking."

"Her background's in the arts and marketing. She's co-associate dean responsible for promoting public understanding of science, international education, and research, not tech stuff."

"What do we send that she'll be sure to download?" I asked.

"A picture of a happy Michael, as thanks for the temporary promotion," Veera said.

"She won't open that," Michael said.

"Veera's on the right track," I said. "Send Alyce a letter as an email attachment and ask her to proof it. A letter to Big Mac apologizing for the misunderstanding. Make obvious errors. Ask her to correct the document, and send it back to you for one last look."

"I don't make mistakes like that. She'll be suspicious. Maybe I should casually drop by to talk about working together more in the future. About team spirit." Worry played the starring role on Michael's face. "Except, she's not a team player."

"We don't want her to think you've got trust issues. If she did kill him…"

A familiar cleft fell between Michael's brows. "You think she's the murderer?"

"Let's get that email written. Your mistakes don't have to be major. Just enough to make her revise. Lead the way to your office."

I was on his heels until he got to the Admin Hall entry. "Michael, you got this. I'll continue poking around the building some more with Veera."

"What are you looking for again?" Michael wanted to know.

"Not sure yet. Work on pushing that app through. That could give us what we need. I'll tell you if I discover anything."

Veera and I returned to the side of the building where Loretta did her toe-art. I replayed Loretta's nosing around, and running off once she was spotted.

"We need to shakedown that girl," Veera said. "I am so in the mood for a shakedown."

A student veered off the concrete walkway near the pond. He carried a heavy backpack and walked like a camel, sinking and rising with each footfall. Dark curls, sallow skin, and horn-rimmed glasses confirmed his student status. He wore a green t-shirt and baggy shorts ending below his knees. He sidled up to me.

"That is so tactical." He pointed to the army boot. "Are you collecting empirical data?"

"Aren't we all?"

He snickered and took a few steps backward to better study my choice of footwear.

"You," Veera said to him.

He blinked a few times and refocused on her.

"I got a question." She curled her index finger, signaling the need for him to move closer. "What do they call you around here?"

The guy turned his head to one side and crept forward. "Marty."

"Marty what?"

"Um, why would I tell you that?"

"You like living on the edge? Let me rephrase that. You like living?" I asked.

"Pantz," he said.

"Marty Pants? Really?"

"Is that for real? Or like a code name?" Veera looked at me. "Doesn't sound real to me."

"It's on my birth certificate," he replied. "Only it's Martin. And Pantz with a 'z'…"

"What do you do around here, Marty Pantz?" I asked.

"I'm a second year student. Biomedical engineering."

"Get this, Marty," Veera said. "We're new on campus, and we never met the head guy. But we've been hearing things. Any of them true?"

I had to hand it to her in the vague questioning department.

Marty leaned in and said, "I'm not sure."

"Really? 'Cause I am sure you know something." Veera shot him a glare out of one eye. "Why don't you go ahead and say it?"

"I will for a price."

"Oh no, you won't."

I placed a hand on her shoulder. "Define price."

His bifocals shot downward, and he pointed to my lone combat boot. "That looks like it would fit me. Let's do a trade."

I eyed his flip-flops, and the Wookiee feet planted in them.

"No way."

"I've got to go." Marty turned to leave.

Veera grabbed hold of a strap on his backpack. "You're not going anywhere 'til we say so." Her grip was firm. Her eyes skipped to mine. "Tell him who we are."

"And blow our cover?"

"We don't have to worry about that." She turned the evil eye on him. "Know why?"

Marty tried to wriggle free.

"I won't even have to cut the whole thing out," she said to me.

"You'd have to cut most of it off." I re-focused on his backpack. "Got any washcloths in that knapsack? To mop up the blood."

His struggle continued, but Veera's grip had no give.

"I'll talk." Marty turned to face us. "What was the question again?"

Veera shook her head. "I thought these students were supposed to be smart."

"They're only book-smart. Prove us wrong, kid." Why I threw in "kid" I have no idea. He was only a few years younger than I was, but it made me the authority figure. "What's so special about the area under this window?" I was banking that rumors floated around about a body.

He licked his lips and turned his head away. In two quick moves, three sharp points from my throwing star indented his scrawny neck.

"Is that a real shuriken?" he asked.

"Want to find out?"

He shook his head.

"We're listening."

"I just thought of something." Veera's upper body leaned toward me.

I pulled my torso back, shuriken in place. We whispered while keeping an eye on Marty.

"Is this strong arm tactic going to force him to lie to get us off his back?" Veera asked.

"Good point. He'll have to provide corroboration if he wants to survive this interrogation."

"I got you."

We returned to Marty.

His words spilled out. "There's a coalition against the president. Comprised of faculty and students. It's all anonymous."

"The purpose?" I asked.

"To boot him out. We have documentation of wrongs that prove he's unfit to run this school. But we made no progress. Until…" His Adam's apple bobbed up and down. His eyes darted to one side.

"I'm getting impatient," Veera reminded him.

"About a week ago, when Leopold arrived."

Veera and I swapped glances.

"I hope that's not all you've got," Veera said. "We're going to need some ham 'n cheese in your meatless sandwich before we take a bite."

"Leo's the dog, right?" I asked.

"Yes. A toy poodle. He was sent to the President by a big donor. But Leo had an accident."

"Accident as in he did his doodie on the carpet?" I asked.

"Accident like he fell out that window." One finger pointed toward Big Mac's window.

"Details," I said, my mind a blur. Just when I thought I'd made sense of things.

Veera tightened her grip on his arm. "This better be good."

The Adam's apple bobbed up and down again. "Leo was a gift, from a Japanese donor. MacTavish had to keep Leo because the school's in talks to get a big donation. Leo was trained. Any time he had to pee, he'd ring this little bell to go out. But…"

"Go on," I said. This opened a whole new motive for killing Big Mac.

His eyes shot between us. "He'd send the little guy out in a basket with a rope tied to the handles, and he'd lower it out the window. Leo would do his business, get back in, and be pulled up."

"I didn't see any trace of dog poop beneath the window," I said.

"MacTavish calls the janitor and it's cleaned up pretty quickly."

"Why couldn't Mac or an assistant just take Leo out when he needed to do his doodie?"

He leaned in. "MacTavish's assistants never stay longer than a week. He's had no one for a while." Marty leaned closer. "But word is MacTavish had to take care of Leo himself. That was a condition. The donor didn't want Leo to bond to anyone but the president. So on Thursday night, Leo was lowered and…"

The rest of the story unfolded in my head. The basket broke off and down it went. The little guy fell out and—

Veera clicked her tongue. "Is Leo in doggie heaven?"

"Not exactly. No one knows what happened, but Leo's missing. Maybe he ran away. Or someone took him. MacTavish made a big stink.

The cops were involved. That's who I thought you were, but you're not. You with PETA?"

Veera and I exchanged looks. I loosened my hold on his shirt and put away the throwing star. Veera released his arm.

"Close," I said. "We're with NASCA. National Animal Safety Commission of America." I had a soft spot for acronyms. "To investigate whether the president should be fined. Or jailed."

"Jail would be cool," Marty said.

"We can't seem to locate the culprit. Seen him lately?"

"Not since Friday," he replied. "But…"

"Yes?"

Veera was about to grab his arm, but I motioned her back.

"There's a rumor," Marty said.

"Of course there is." Rumors circled the globe. And once in a while carried a germ of truth.

"Someone saw the president yesterday morning being escorted off campus by guys in shades and suits," he said. "He was forced into a black SUV. Government grade."

"Just like in the movies," Veera said.

"Did he make a scene?" I asked.

Marty shook his head. "Someone said he looked pretty laid back, considering. Maybe he was gagged or drugged."

"Just who is this 'someone'?" I asked.

"I don't know," Marty said. "I heard this third, maybe fourth hand. So you guys didn't arrest him?"

I shook my head.

"Then who took him?"

"That's what we want to know," Veera said.

"I'll put out a campus-wide APB and get back to you," Marty said.

"What does that mean?" I asked.

"I'll text my peeps."

"Is that the best you can do?" Veera wanted to know. "Geez. Here." She handed him a piece of paper with her name and number. "In case you need someone to teach you how to fight or duck."

"Cool," Marty said.

"She means call us when you have useful information." I handed him my card as well. "You understand we need to find MacTavish sooner rather than later."

"Um, no, I don't, because you didn't say exactly what you're going to do to him—"

"You expect us to share top secret information with you?" Veera reared up. "Un-freaking-believable. This here is confidential. Do we need to have another little talk?"

I pulled Marty by the arm and quick-stepped him away from Veera. I pointed him toward the paved path. He stumbled and eyed my combat boot. "Listen to me, kid." It was my turn to rear up. "If, and that's uppercase if, you find some crucial information and that's—"

"I know, uppercase." His torso leaned away from me, as if that minor distance would prevent me from putting him in a headlock should he make a wrong move.

"If you lead us to him…" I lifted my foot. "This boot is yours."

"Is that, like, my reward?"

"Move it."

He shifted down the pavement. I watched him until the trees around the pond swallowed him whole.

"What's going on here?" Michael jogged up to us.

"Did you take care of the delivery?" I asked.

"I did my part," he replied.

"So we're waiting on Alyce's response?"

"Yep. *If* she responds. Did you two find anything?"

I filled him in on Marty.

"Maybe whoever's got Leo has Mac," Michael said.

"Do you think the attack on the president had to do with little Leo?" Veera asked Michael.

"Hard to say," Michael answered. "There's not a person on campus who didn't have a motive for messing with him. Mac, that is."

"Maybe it was a mass conspiracy," Veera said. "Like that group Marty Pantz talked about. They might have gotten together to designate an individual to inflict the death wound. Then they appointed a special committee to dispose of the body. No wonder we can't find him. Since these students are geniuses, they came up with a full-proof plan. And nobody's talking. 'Cause if one talks, they're all accessories to murder."

"Maybe we'll never find him," Michael said. Tiny red jagged lines crowded the whites of his eyes. His lips were dry and cracked.

"There's zero percent chance of that happening." I crossed my fingers behind me.

"I'm so grateful you're here, Corrie. And you, Veera." He took our hands in each of his. "I hope this is over with soon. Maybe we should go eat your mom's pie. We could use a break."

Veera's smile broke loose again. It didn't just reach her eyes; it pushed past the trees, skyrocketed through the ozone layer, and hit the solo cumulus cloud hovering above. "Good idea. We'll eat pie and talk this out, nab a killer or two, and live peaceably ever after. That's a win-win for everybody. See, I told you we're gonna crack this case sooner rather than later."

"Let's get out of here." I took his arm.

Veera took his other arm. "We're gonna knock this outta the park for the win."

I cast a look back at the Admin Hall. I'd be back. Sooner rather than later.

## CHAPTER 32

## THE UNEXPECTED

My mother had taken the liberty of baking two lemon meringue pies. But you'd never know it twenty minutes after our arrival. Not a crumb remained. Michael texted James on the drive over, and he'd joined us in the feasting. Mom was nowhere to be found.

The pie plates were cleaned and dried, courtesy of Michael. And everything put away, courtesy of Veera and James. I was nowhere in either equation. I don't cook, and cleaning was only on a need-to-door-die basis. Instead, I grabbed an energy drink and headed upstairs. If Mom was hiding her prized wardrobe and my illegal weaponry in her secret room behind the pantry, what else was she hiding in the house?

The door to her bedroom closet sat wide open. Suits and blouses hung on either side. Cashmere sweaters and shawls lined the shelves on top. All the good stuff was hidden in the secret room.

"Looking for something?" James leaned his hip against the wall behind me, arms crossed over his chest, biceps bulging from his short-sleeved t-shirt. I bet he could do pull-ups, one handed, without breaking a sweat. In fact, I'd never seen him sweat.

I tore my eyes away and stepped out of the closet. "I'm looking for motive. I think I know who's got a doozy of a motive." I opened the cap of my drink and took a sip. Did I? I took another sip.

"Do you plan on sharing this information any time soon? My foot's falling asleep."

"The texts Alyce received—"

"If she received any." He uncrossed his arms. "She lied because she's the killer."

"I disagree."

"That's what you do best."

My sparring gloves had fallen off when I wasn't looking. And I had no interest in finding them. I took another sip hoping the energy booster would whisk away the fog clogging my brain.

"So who's your culprit?" he asked.

"Ian. He has the strongest motive. He's been trying to get into the school for years. Big Mac was the only thing standing in his way."

"Proof?"

"That first night he said he came in to plant rats in Big Mac's closet. But he'd really wanted to make sure nothing was left behind."

"Why was he carrying around rats?"

I shrugged. "He's an animal activist. Maybe for a proper burial. It's possible Alyce is his cohort."

His eyes shot down to my feet. "Want to talk about that?" His finger pointed to the combat boot. I forgot I was still wearing it.

"I don't do well around bodies of water larger than a fishbowl."

Our gazes caught and held. James knew very well that I had the swimming skills of a pet rock. I took a dip in the Balboa Island Bay a few months ago, thanks to a murder suspect I'd been baiting. James had been there to fish me out. My heartbeat pounded in my ears. I took another sip and turned away.

"The ice cream truck was located." James continued to stare at me. "Parked behind a grocery store, a mile from campus."

"Any sign of a body…or body parts…in the freezer?" I asked.

"The truck was empty, including the freezer. We can rule out the corpsicle theory," James said.

"That is one bad joke." I walked into the hallway. I stopped and pivoted around to face him. "The ice cream was dumped in a garbage container at LA Tech. Michael and Veera spotted the goods this afternoon. The freezer could be Big Mac's transport compartment."

"The getaway car?" The shadow of a grin lapped around his mouth. "My turn to disagree. An ice pack was found on the floor of the truck."

"And that means…?"

"The goods were dumped so the freezer could store ice transported to campus. In large bags or sacks. Or even an ice chest. Who would question that? Which means the body's still there, like I said."

"The body's still where?" Michael stood on the square landing, mid-stairs.

Before I could answer, my phone vibrated. I pulled it out. "It's Marty Pantz," I told them.

"Isn't that the guy—" Michael started.

"That's him," Veera shouted from the foot of the stairs.

"Who?" James asked.

"The student we held hostage," I said.

"Do I want to know why he was a hostage?" James asked.

"Because we know a punk when we see one," Veera said. "And he had information about the president."

In less than thirty seconds, Marty told me a teacher's aide heard a dog bark in the Admin Hall on the first floor.

"She couldn't pinpoint the exact location," he said.

"What else?" I asked.

"Don't forget about the boot."

I disconnected. "A dog was heard in Admin about twenty minutes ago," I said. "First floor."

"Let's go." Michael headed down the stairs.

"Hold up." Veera blocked Michael's path, arms outstretched, one on each banister. "Is that the right move for us?"

"No," I said.

"But," Michael looked at James and me. "Maybe whoever has Leo has Mac. Shouldn't we take a closer look?"

I maneuvered toward Michael. "We won't find anything. The killer's been two steps ahead of us the whole way." An idea was heating up in my head.

Michael looked at me. "I've been trying to reach Alyce. She won't pick up." He looked down. "Maybe you're right. There's nothing more for us to do right now." He turned to James. "Hey, bro, I need a favor."

"I'm already recording the *Doctor Who* marathon for you," James said.

"You are? Thanks, buddy. This is a different favor. You've got that exercise room in your building. And I'm feeling the need to work off excess tension. And the pie."

"Now?" James asked.

"No better time." Michael turned to me. "I need some serious shuteye, which I'll get after exercising. So I can think things through." He straightened up and patted James on the shoulder. "You ready?"

"Hold up." Veera climbed the few remaining stairs. She took turns looking at each of us. "Did I hear right? Are you sayin' we're done for today?"

Michael opened his mouth and shut it again.

"Don't we need to know what's up with the bark and the body?" Veera's gaze made the rounds. "Shouldn't we be doing something? We should at least have a plan."

I ran a finger along the wrought iron banister. It felt cold and hard. Like my life at the moment. "I think it's a good idea to let things lie. We'll pick this up tomorrow."

Veera scratched her chin. "I guess we can wait. And check how things have…percolated."

Michael hustled down the stairs like a man on a mission. He stopped at the bottom and looked up. "Thanks, guys." His gaze latched onto mine. "You've been beyond awesome. I'm stoked we're done running around for now. You know what I always say: walk before you run."

"You've never said that," I said.

"Crawling is good, too. It's time to crawl."

James made his way down the stairs. Veera and I followed.

"I still think—" Veera started.

The door shut before she could finish.

"What's that boy up to?" Veera asked.

"He wants to check out the barking dog, but James will talk him out of going."

"How do you know James'll talk him out of it?"

"All we've hit are wrong turns and dead ends. That bark could be a decoy." Someone was anticipating our moves. I needed a clear head to deal with that someone. "Besides, I've slept maybe four hours the past few nights. I need to hit the sack."

"We could get up early and look around."

I handed her the car key. "I'll get some snacks from the pantry for later. Meet you at the car." I scrambled to the pantry and closed the door. I stood in the dark and blinked a few times. I fumbled with the chalkboard and cocked the panel. I heard a click and the vertical opening appeared. I stepped inside and scanned the room. The only sound came from the whirr of air conditioning through a wall vent.

I faced a hanger featuring stretch leggings with a zipper trim at the ankles, and a fitted jersey tee with long sleeves. Suede boots stood beneath the pairing, all in covert operative black. In one quick turn, I whisked them off the hanger, grabbed the boots, and folded them into a cloth bag hanging on a hook on the wall. Nothing quite says confidence like high fashion, stealth style. I looked at the metal box that held my weapons. I grabbed it and shut off the light switch.

"Corrie, where you at?" Veera had gotten impatient.

I stepped back into the pantry and closed the fake wall. "Be right out." I returned to the family room nearly colliding with Veera.

"Did you get the snacks?"

I stepped back into the pantry. I grabbed two boxes of strawberry pop tarts, a bag of tortilla chips, and a jar of salsa. I stepped back out. "Sure did."

She eyed my bag. "Are those all snacks?"

"I might have borrowed a few other items," I said.

"I didn't hear that. While I was waiting, I placed a call."

"To?"

"Our informant. Got the number off his backpack."

"Marty?"

She nodded. "He's going to take a walk around the Admin Hall and listen for more doggy noise. He's gonna be our eyes and ears. It'll be like we're there, only we're not. I told him to call us if he hears or sees anything."

We stepped outside into the fading afternoon, past the rose trees lining the short path to the driveway. In the center of a square patch of lawn a stout palm waved a tired crown of arching leaves that flapped in the breeze.

"Uh-oh," Veera stopped in her tracks. "I just thought of something. These geeky types are always getting themselves into trouble. What if Marty's arrested and fingers us?"

I shrugged. "He doesn't know our names."

"What if he picks us out of a police line-up?"

I threw the bag in the trunk and swiped a look over Veera. A thin film of sweat coated her forehead.

"We have to be arrested first," I said. "Or brought in as persons of interest before we end up in a line-up."

"But—"

"We haven't broken any laws." At least we'd not been caught breaking any. "There's no evidence to tie us to anything." I would argue that the president's office was unlocked. And that I got lost and accidentally ended up in the sub-basement, owing to my poor sense of direction. "We're good."

"Squalley might—"

"He won't."

"Ian—"

"We're fine." I landed behind the wheel and cracked open the window. The breeze slithered through.

"You got any pizza or mac n' cheese?" Veera plopped down next to me. "I could use some comfort food."

Me, too. The pie was a distant memory. "We'll stop and pick some up on the way."

≢ ≢ ≢

Three hours later, we were fed and watered and dressed for bed. Or Veera was. I waited in my room, outfitted in my new black duds, ear pressed against the door. I turned the knob, opened it, and listened. A one-note techno tune poured out of my refrigerator. Veera's breath slipped out in slow blasts. I tiptoed to the futon and stared at her face. Too soon for rapid eye movements. I debated flicking her cheek with my finger. What if I flicked too hard and woke her? Then I'd have to take her with me. I needed alone time. The slow breaths continued, and I returned to my room.

I gathered my hair up in a high ponytail, grabbed a spare bed sheet, and a few other necessities: a crowbar, a small toolkit, a Taser, and night vision goggles. I stuffed them all into a backpack. Everything a girl could want for a covert operation. I pulled out my shuriken belt, and buckled it in place, slipping my throwing star into the five-pointed buckle. I quickly removed the belt and refastened it so that my shuriken was secured behind me, where it wouldn't be easily spotted. If I did have a run-in tonight, the throwing star would be hidden. I pulled a comb out of the metal box holding the weapons and fastened it to the back of my belt. A comb could come in handy. Especially one with a knife hidden inside. And for the final touch: a pocket pistol tucked snugly inside my boot. I lifted the window above my bed and climbed out. It was back to school night.

## CHAPTER 33

### NIGHT VISION

Mom never approved of Dad's career move. He went from UCLA academic to channeling Sam Spade faster than you can say, "One lump or two?" at high tea. It was hard, if not impossible, for an impressionable teen like myself not to be swept away by his work. Who can resist hunting down bad guys and saving the innocent? Besides Mom, that is. She steered me toward a tamer career where the only weapons were sharp words used to puncture facts…not skin. I caved after watching Dad receding into a shadowy life. Plus, death threats and assassination attempts clashed with my preference for living by the beach, and just plain old living. Yet, my first lawyer job led me right back to PI work. And here I was again, playing PI for my best friend.

I drove fast and nimbly toward LA Tech, with the glimmer of a plan to capture Big Mac's killer. Something right out of *The Thin Man*. It was all I had, but I was going to make it work.

I accelerated onto the freeway and gave my head a fast shake. I lowered the windows and merged into traffic. The cold whipped around my face, sending thoughts of slumber running for cover.

Forty minutes later, I exited the freeway. It was late Sunday evening, which meant parking was plentiful and inhabitants scarce at LA Tech. I pulled into the dirt lot on campus, grabbed my backpack, and padded onto the nearest path. Gravel crunched beneath my boots. A honking horn punctuated the drone of passing cars. I aimed for the usual destination: the Admin Hall.

The few students lurking around barely gave me a glance. I reached the Hall and circled the building in a wide arc, keeping close to the trees. The swaying branches shook twiggy fingers my way. One low hanging bough smacked me on top of the head.

"Ow." I rubbed my crown and returned my attention to the building.

"Yo. What are you doing?"

I spun around. "Don't you ever go home?"

Bobby's large flashlight pointed to my chest. "Answer my question first." His beady blues canvassed my black get-up.

"We need to talk," I said.

"Because I turn you on?" He chuckled and lowered the flashlight.

"Why were you so quick to give information to ADA Zachary?"

"I'm all set to move up the ranks. He's writing me a letter of recommendation."

First Yoko, now Bobby. Apparently, reference letters were all the rage.

"I had trouble figuring how you fit in. Now I know." He shoved the flashlight into the pocket of his cargo pants. "I'm clean, you hear? I got nothing more than a few moving violations. The other charges were dropped."

I loved how a gap of silence encouraged a confession. I also appreciated people who thought I knew things I didn't. "Is that so?"

"Look, MacTavish lied to you. The pig wasn't snatched on my watch, see? And the dog...I don't know nothing about his whereabouts, either."

"What kind of security guard are you?"

"I'm gonna find them. I just need more time."

I shifted my attention to the Admin Hall. External lighting was dim, the second floor offices dark. No sign of life. I turned back to Bobby. "The map," I said.

"What about it?"

"Why don't I have it?"

"Can't you share it with your D.A. boyfriend?"

Instead of lashing back, I studied him for a moment. I thought about the long hours he spent on campus, the bum foot, the ever-present insecurity. He nurtured an overpowering need to prove himself. I leaned in close to him. He smelled like budget cologne and cherry cough drops.

"You're better than this job," I said.

He lifted his chin. "Don't I know it."

"I can help you."

"Yeah? How?"

"There's a meeting tonight. At midnight in the president's office. To get questions answered. Questions that could put you full steam ahead."

"What am I supposed to do?"

Was he involved in the Big Mac affair? He could have helped Ian or Alyce. I locked my eyes on his until he pushed his head back and circled it around his neck. He was more uncomfortable than defensive. But I was off my game tonight, so it was hard to tell. "I need muscle. That's where you fit in."

He raised a brow. "You mean like moving furniture around?"

"I mean like helping to apprehend a fugitive." I pulled out my phone and swiped to my notes page. "I need the cell phone numbers for these people." I showed him the list.

He stared at the phone screen. "Why them?"

"You'll find out."

"No way. You've got a VIP on the list, students, and employees. I don't get involved unless I know. Now."

I shoved my phone in my pocket. "Never mind." I sauntered toward the Admin Hall and stopped below Big Mac's window. My arm reached over my shoulder and into the backpack, and my gaze flew in Bobby's direction. He watched me like a dog on the prowl. I stood in a pool of lamplight and pulled out a pair of night vision goggles. I slipped the headset on. The surroundings took on an otherworldly green glow. The less outside light, the better they worked. I moved toward the back of Admin. A rustling, too unsteady to be wind-driven, broke the quiet. I shoved the goggles in the backpack and headed away from the building, head down, eyes up. The rustle was joined by a shuffling that grew closer.

"I'll do it," Bobby said from behind me. "And I'll get you the map."

I faced him.

A piece of paper lay between his middle and index fingers. He held it up. "Here're the numbers."

I reached to grab it, and he jerked back his arm.

"First, I need something."

I let out a huff. "This is not about your needs. It's about mine." I pushed forward. He stepped back with my every move. "I need a week-long siesta, maybe a whole month. I need a boss that doesn't rankle me every time he opens his cranky lips. And I need you to need nothing from me."

"I just want to borrow something. Geez. The goggles."

My bait had worked. I swallowed my smile. "For what?"

"You want a map of the sub-basement?"

I sure did. And parting with the goggles would suit me fine. It could be symbolic of my breaking free from PI life for keeps. I'd donate the spy gear, one covert item at a time. Did the Salvation Army take this stuff?

"Give me twenty minutes," he said. "But I'll need the night vision thingees so I don't raise suspicion."

"Who would be suspicious?" I stopped in my tracks.

"The only other map of the sub-basement is in my supervisor's office. I can't use any lights. Unless I want to be caught."

"Why would I care if you were busted?"

"You want the map or not?"

I grabbed his wrist and checked his oversize watch. "Twenty minutes, it is." I reached into my backpack and pulled out the goggles. "Depth perception is shoddy with these. Don't mess up."

Bobby grabbed hold and broke out a smile. It was like giving a little leaguer his first baseball mitt. "Cool." He handed me the paper and shuffled away.

I stared at the phone numbers he'd written down for Big Mac and my official suspects: Alyce, Ian, Loretta, Bobby, and Squalley. I pulled out my phone and texted this invite to each of them:

*I know what you did. I won't go to the cops if you come to MacTavish's office tonight, at midnight. The door will be open.*

Curiosity was a powerful magnet. There was a chance Big Mac's captor had his phone, so I texted his cell too. I figured if a suspect had nothing to hide, he or she wouldn't show up. Anyone who played a hand in the killing would either disappear into the night or show up to see how this would play out. I was hoping for the latter occurrence. I texted Marty, too, in case he had any light to shed. I threatened him with action from Veera if he didn't join the party.

I heard a scratchy sound against the paved path. I spun around. A twig tumbled along the cement. Paranoia would not get the best of me. Not tonight.

I slipped into the shadows and watched students amble by. A light wind pushed snippets of conversation in my direction. Night joggers breezed past.

Twenty minutes lumbered by with no sign of Bobby. It was just past ten o'clock. Barely two hours to explore the underground before my meeting.

Another batch of students tripped across the lawn under the lamplight. Shoulders hunched, heads down, one of them chattered about mathematical formulas and other uninteresting blather.

"Excuse me." I shot out and blocked their path.

The talker looked up first. He paused and the others put on their brakes.

"I'm new on campus," I told them.

"You're a student?" The talker blinked beneath wire framed glasses.

"She's no student," another egghead chimed in. "Rhytides."

"What did you call me?" I asked.

"You've got crow's feet, either from advanced age, crying too much, or lack of sleep."

My hands flew to my face. I needed to kill the feet off the crows. "I don't cry."

"How've you been sleeping?"

"I haven't."

"That could explain it," the talker said. "Are you a student?"

"I'm a lawyer. Here on behalf of a client."

The gang moved in, exchanging glances.

"Is the school being sued?" one of them asked.

"Not yet. I need to get down to the…" I leaned in closer and pointed downward. "The tunnels. The sub-basement. How do I do that?" My time at UCLA taught me that students knew everything there was to know about tunnels under campus. Including how to get in and out without being caught.

They pulled back and mumbled.

"Okay, look. I'm investigating a missing persons report. There's reason to believe they are down in the sub-basement. Involved with a secret project. The family is worried about them." Who doesn't love secrets? "I've been in the tunnels under Admin. I want to explore the opposite end."

The students huddled together, nodded, and the talker turned to me. "This way."

They took a hard left across the lawn to the end of campus. Terra Street ran parallel to the last structure. And that's where they stopped. The leader pointed to a dent in the ground. A steep staircase led to a closed door.

"It's locked." His eyes flicked to his comrades and back to me. "But we hear it's easy to open with the right tools."

The others mumbled in agreement. The leader turned to leave and stalled. "One more thing," he said to me. "The elevators are monitored. Don't take them unless you like hanging around security."

So that's how Bobby had discovered us. "Thanks."

I waited until the students were out of sight before reaching into the backpack for the toolkit. I pulled out a screwdriver and penlight, and hustled down the stairs. My hand rested against a wooden door. "Now we're talking." Metal would take extra skills and a pry bar to work it loose. Wood I could handle. I stuck the penlight between my teeth and aimed it at the knob. I jammed the screwdriver between the door and the frame, gave one quick pull and, "Bingo."

I stepped inside, penlight in the lead. The door eased shut behind me. I hurried down a short flight of stairs to another door. I pushed it open and inched into a dark tunnel. Warm air smashed against my face, wrapping dank, steamy tendrils around my neck. An overhead pipe stuck to the low ceiling. Cracked cement walls and floors surrounded me, spotted with hasty artwork, weird symbols, and random scribbles. Discarded wooden crates littered the ground. I took a few steps. Signs warned against going forward: *Alien sub-station: Humans Beware.* Gotta love those nerds.

I plodded ahead down the twisty corridor, scattering nervy rats and brawny cockroaches. A vertical shaft with rusty ladder rungs was cut into a wall, leading up to a dark climb.

I wiped my face on a sleeve. The air grew warmer and thicker. My clothes clung to my skin. I crouched, sucking in threads of air at ground level. That led to a coughing fit. The urge to escape jetted me forward. I pressed on until I reached a fork in the passage. On my left, the rounded archway formed the entry to a craggy, cramped looking corridor. Straight ahead the passage was more civilized, meaning the walls had paint and the floors looked swept. Both were equally dark. Maintenance meant people. I'd have to go the craggy route.

This was the part where I'd pull out the night vision goggles. If I had them. "Damn."

*Spark and motion won't help you out of a jam, sweetheart.*

I couldn't remember if that was something Dad had said or whether I'd heard it in a Bogart film. Either way, I'd uncovered a new problem. The penlight scanned the ceiling and walls. Both tunnels were outfitted with motion sensors about ten paces out.

I lowered the light and studied the ground. I could crawl on my belly, but the backpack would stick up too high and set off the sensor. I slipped out of the shoulder straps, unzipped the center portion, and rummaged around. I'd emptied out half the bag before I pulled out what I needed: the bed sheet.

Sheets were useful, not just for sleeping and protecting furniture when painting walls. They worked as solid ropes when tied together to escape from a second story window. And they helped people impersonate a ghost when needed. Like right now. Sheet in hand, I refilled the backpack and slipped it over my shoulders. I faced the tunnel that jutted off to one side. Twenty paces would take me into more darkness. But it had to be better than where I was.

I pulled out a knife, cut two slits for my eyes, and covered myself, head-to-toe, with the sheet. Caspar had nothing on me. Except that he was naturally cool, if I knew anything about friendly ghosts.

The heat doubled beneath the cloth. I moved forward with slow, measured steps. My heart hammered, my nerves stretched paper-thin. I'd never tried a sheet shield, but Dad had claimed it worked against motion sensors.

I edged forward, movement slow and minimal. I made it halfway without alarms, bells or whistles.

A minute or so later and more than ten paces ahead, I exhaled, removed the sheet, dropped my shoulders, and checked the passage behind me. The worst was over. I faced forward, penlight in hand. No more sensors. Just a glow a few yards ahead, around a bend. The whirr of machinery was louder, but the air had cooled. I inched toward the glow and stopped. The surrounding concrete grew smoother. An upside down crate lay against a wall. On impulse, I removed my backpack, lifted the crate, and dropped the pack on the floor with the crate over it. I didn't need the extra weight. Or anyone getting hold of my supplies.

I closed in on the light, step by step. I stopped. The glow streamed out from an open doorway.

## CHAPTER 34

### ALL TIED UP AND EVERYWHERE TO GO

A smart PI would have gone in, gun in one hand, Taser in the other, cuffs in pocket. Body armor would have been helpful. Clean hair and fresh makeup would have put a spring in my step. But since I wasn't too smart, sleep deprived, and not a PI, all I had to offer was limp hair, fashionable attire, and a dead weight on my neck. The pocket pistol was tucked in my boot. Not quite as handy as I'd like, but at least my belt played host to a knife and a throwing star. My weapon check haunted me from days spent with Dad.

I leaned sideways to peek inside. Light radiated from a small lamp on a wooden desk in a space the size of a dorm room. A laptop sat open on the desk, facing me. The steady tick of a clock on the wall scattered the silence. I ventured inside. A green loveseat rested against one wall. I peered at the laptop. It was a mini Mac, open to the home page. Why wasn't it sleeping? And why was it facing the door?

"Oh no." The answers came too late.

A commotion erupted behind me, but before I could hop to it, a rough, burlap sack was dumped over my head, scratching my nose and cheeks. A thick, wide strap wrapped tightly around my waist, pinning my arms to my sides. Hands shoved me sideways. I stumbled and knocked against the loveseat. My head slammed against a hard cushion. Pain lashed at the side of my skull. I squirmed, pushing out with my arms. My wrists were grasped and twisted behind me. Nylon strips cut into my skin, forcing my hands together. I kicked out and hit air. Another tight strip wrapped around my ankles. My knee rocketed upward, freeing my foot. I kicked straight out again. The heel of my boot thumped into something hard and bony. A knee. I heard a groan and a gush of air.

I yelled and torpedoed forward. My fingers wrestled with the comb stuck to the back of my belt. I pulled off the top half to free a three-inch blade that sliced against the nylon ties. A few slashes and my hands were free. I jabbed the air with my knife.

Rubbery fingers clasped my wrists. My knife hand was wrenched upward, twisted back against my shoulder blades. The comb clunked against the cement floor. I was pushed back onto the sofa.

*The first thing to do in a restraint situation is to be passive. Fake it, sweetheart.* My father's words thundered through my ears.

I went limp, doing a fine impersonation of a wet noodle. I slowed my breath. My attacker was strong, wore gloves, and was not caught off guard by my presence, thanks to the laptop's camera. He or she was at least my height and exhibited some fighting skills. I moaned and unleashed my inner cry-baby. I blabbered and wailed and, in seconds, the grip loosened. My hands were tied again, but in front this time. I heard a quick shuffle, followed by a swish. He was rummaging through a bag. Solid objects knocked together not far from me. I estimated my attacker was a few feet away. I shot up, executed a solid roundhouse kick, and slammed down on the back of an arm.

"Suck an egg, bitch to the tenth power." A low, deep voice grumbled.

Is that how geeks swore? "I know who you are," I said. A sharp jab pierced my upper arm. A needle plunged through my shirt. Coldness washed through me. I kicked my foot up and was shoved back, crashing against the sofa's rock-hard armrest. My ears rang like a chorus of angry crickets. A moan escaped my lips. Moments later, the moan fizzled and the pain slunk away, replaced by a floating sensation, like I'd sopped up a bottle of champagne.

"Are we flying?" Did I say that out loud?

"What's your name?"

The deep voice was familiar. So was the heavy breathing. There was something mechanical about both. Cold and confident, like the voice of a movie villain.

"Diana Prince." My words slurred together in a jumble. "No relation to the pop star, but I like the color purple—"

"What are you doing here?"

"Ha, funny you should ask." Using my elbows, I tried to sit up, but a bad case of giggles grounded me.

"Michael Parris."

Michael's name fell off the wicked tongue in pieces that crashed to the floor. I recognized the mechanical, laboring breath. It was Darth Vader. Did that make me Princess Leia? And if so, could I use the Force?

"How well do you know him?" The villain asked.

Michael strolled into my head wearing a t-shirt, jeans, his black Chuck Taylors and dazzling smile. The only guy who could look hot and nerdy at the same time.

"How well?"

"Let's just say I've seen him in his *Star Wars* boxers. You can relate, can't you?" My answer put me in hysterics. While my body convulsed, my mind began to clear. Who was channeling Vader? Alyce had a manly voice. Bobby hadn't come back. Loretta would try something cheesy like this. Then again, Ian and Squalley snuck all over campus doing who knows what.

The belt around my wrists loosened, the bag yanked off my head. I blinked and struggled to rise.

"Whoa. You're who I thought you are," I said. The fearsome black mask and bulbous eyes belonged to Darth Vader. But the polished finish was scratched and dented. "Man, that must have been some battle." Instead of a cape, a loose dress shirt with long sleeves monopolized the top half. Baggy pants and leather gloves covered the remainder, all in basic black. Vader stood by the desk, brimming with laboring breath and intimidation. The laughter continued to explode in my chest. "You look like a crow whose beak had a run-in with an artillery truck. Ha, ha, ha."

"Who are you?" Vader asked again.

"Cor...Corrie Locke." Was that my real name?

"Why are you on campus?"

"To help my best friend slash future boyfriend because he's good and kind and smart and cleans dishes and dusts my crib without my asking." I inhaled. "He does windows, details my ride, and treats me like I'm the only bar of gold left on earth."

Vader leaned in closer. "Help him with what?"

I clicked my tongue against the roof of my mouth. "Finding Big Mac, silly. He's missing."

"What's your profession?"

"Law and order. Only I'm better at breaking the law than maintaining order. But I've never been caught. That ought to count for something. Do you know how many times I've broken into Big Mac's office? Some might even say I'm a badass private investigator."

"Investigator? Did you find Mac?"

"If I told you, I'd have to paint your tongue with sulfuric acid." Where did I come up with that one? "But no, I didn't." Did I say that out loud? "I'm going to kick out my foot in a minute and throw you off balance. Did you hear that?"

Vader took a step back. "What do you know about Mac?"

"He's...he's...who?" My eyelids grew heavier and heavier; it was hard to keep my chin up.

"MacTavish."

"He's dead." I yawned. "And missing." My head lolled to one side. "Do you know?"

"Know what?"

"Where he is?"

I felt a blow across my cheek, but there was no pain, just heat. Half my face was on fire. I popped back up. "Get the extinguisher."

"Where is he?"

"He's..." I was slipping again. "Isn't that funny? I'm looking for him too." I toppled sideways into darkness.

## CHAPTER 35

### UNDERGROUND MEET-UP

"Come on, come on, wake up already."

I'd finally gotten some decent shuteye and Veera was shaking my shoulders. "Five more minutes," I said.

"In five minutes, you could be dead, honey."

A Bronx growl bounced between my ears. I knew the voice, only I'd forgotten who it belonged to.

"Did Veera let you in?" I mumbled, eyes pinned shut.

"No one let us in. The door was wide open." The voice changed. The pitch was higher, the words quicker.

"Wake up now or face dire consequences." Back to the gravelly voice.

Not as dire as the consequences he'd face as soon as my eyelids cooperated. I turned onto my back, my neck straining against the cement-filled pillow. What happened to my fluffy one? I lifted my left arm and a streak of pain cut to the core. I moaned and heard a click. A powerful light burned through my eyelids. I tried to breathe, but the stink of stale beer and cleaning solution bullied the fresh air into submission.

"Why isn't she up already?" There was that higher voice again. I heard the crinkle of plastic. "I have just the thing."

A moment later, my face was drenched with cold water. With superhuman effort, I shot up and flicked open my eyes. "What do you think you're...?"

Two men stood over me, one with a tanned face, saddled with bags beneath droopy brown eyes. And the other looked like a hairless, overgrown elf hosting a hundred-watt smile. He held an empty water bottle.

"That's better," Ian said.

I closed my eyes and opened them again. They were still there.

What were Ian and Squalley doing here? My gaze darted around the small room. Wherever here was. No windows or ceiling lights. Sparse furnishings. A rough, scratchy green couch with a slab for an armrest was my resting place. I wiped my face on a sleeve and pushed back wet strands of hair. "I'm on campus. In the sub-basement."

They straightened and looked at each other. Ian turned serious. "Tell her."

Squalley put his hands out. "This is where I found you. Look, it's imperative you get up. Now. Or never."

My head ached like a meteorite had nicked it. "What am I doing here?"

Ian took my arm and helped me up. "That's our question."

I began the upward ascent. "How did you find me?"

Squalley pointed a gnarly finger. "I saw the light and came in. You were sleeping. I thought you were fending off an all-nighter, but then I see this guy in a mask behind me. I ask what he's doing, and he shoves me against the wall and runs out. Just like that. I don't take kindly to that sort of behavior, especially seeing that I was courteous and showed due respect by asking nicely. I went after him. But he got away."

"What kind of mask?"

"Huh?"

"You said the guy wore a mask." The fog gave way to clouds and drizzle. I massaged the side of my head with my hand.

"Like the guy with the respiratory issues. From that movie *Star Trek*."

"He means *Star Wars*," Ian inserted.

"Vader's still at large?" I asked.

"Looks that way," Squalley said.

"Let's get you up and walking." Ian helped me to my feet.

I blinked again to lift the remaining fog. "What time is it?" I strolled the room with Ian.

"Nearly eleven," he said.

A dark hallway had led me here. My gaze landed on the desk behind Squalley. A laptop sat closed. I broke away from Ian and wobbled over to the desk. "I have an appointment."

"Gotta keep up the pace," Ian said. "The stuff will wear off quicker."

Squalley took my arm. He wore gray coveralls, and his usual wild swoop of electrified gray hair. It was his turn to squire me around the room.

"What stuff?" I turned to Ian. "How do you know when it'll wear off?"

"You might have guessed that we're not your average maintenance men," Squalley said.

"You're not?"

"Me and Ian, we got talent." His finger pointed to Ian. "He's a mathematical genius." The finger switched direction and pointed to his own chest. "And me, I'm a scientist."

"We've got our share of projects," Ian said. "And some of them might be considered breakthroughs."

"That's right." Squalley picked up the pace. "I've invented a new strain of sodium thiopental. Potassium thiopental. Potassium is better for you than salt. It's not so hard on the kidneys, prevents bloating, doesn't lead to hypertension—"

"Can it cure my raging headache?"

"No, but it only temporarily messes with your brain. You come out of it faster, memory intact. Give yourself ten minutes, and you'll have instant recall. Unlike the sodium version."

"In plain speak, what is potassium theo…?"

"Truth serum," Squalley replied.

"A new, more practical strain," Ian said. "Isn't that nifty?"

We continued our circular stroll. The events of the last hour unspooled in my head. "I was shot with your truth serum?"

"Someone broke into my cabinet," Squalley said. "I keep it locked. Needles and a tube filled with potassium thiopental were missing. I was searching for the thief when I saw the door to this place open."

"Who knew about your discovery?" I asked.

"Just me. And Ian. And MacTavish."

"I came down looking for Squalley and found him in here," Ian said. "With you."

"Did you see the guy in the mask?" I asked Ian.

"I must have just missed him."

"How tall was he?" I asked Squalley.

He put out a hand, above his head, then he lowered it to chin height, and went back and forth. "I'd say about average."

"Any idea who it was?" I asked.

"I got a better question," Squalley said. "Any idea who'd want to dope you up to get you to talk?"

That was a loaded question. Could be anyone from Mom to Homeland Security. "Nope. Why?"

"Someone must figure you know something pretty important to steal my new, improved, patent pending truth serum to squeeze information out of you. Gee, you're lucky. That stuff is lethal in high doses. It coulda killed you."

Which told me two things. I was close to the killer, and I needed to... "Thank you. You saved my life."

"Who, us?" Squalley said. "Nah. I was trying to find my serum."

"And I was looking for him. Finding you was a happy byproduct," Ian said.

"My backpack." I swerved around the room and headed out the door. I tossed the crate aside and rummaged through the backpack. All accounted for, I slipped it over my shoulders.

"I know you and your fellow students love this cloak and dagger stuff, but what were you thinking?" Squalley followed me out the door. "Besides nearly getting killed, you coulda been expelled."

"We students..." My lie fell flat and heavy, like an elephant stepped on my boot. "Truth is, I'm a risk taker and thrill seeker." I could feel most of my toes again.

"Get your thrills elsewhere. There're confidential items down here. You don't want to get mixed up in any of it."

That would explain the motion sensors.

"An education is a valuable commodity," Ian said. "You know I'd trade places with you in a nanosecond. Hey, are you part of that student group looking for Leo?"

"Everything will be explained at the meeting tonight," I said.

"Is the meetin' gonna be an..." Squalley's hands circled each other, "...inquisition?"

I tried to turn my head toward Squalley, but it squatted atop my neck like a bowling ball, heavy and cumbersome. I turned my whole body. "There's a problem Big Mac wants to discuss."

"Count me out. I don't want nothing to do with him," Squalley said.

"Me neither," Ian agreed. "Especially if he's blaming me for something he thinks I did. Which I didn't. Most likely."

"There'll be an announcement you'll want to hear. Trust me." The clouds in my head gave way to blue sky. Squalley wasn't kidding. My brain was up and running again, in full force. "What's the quickest way to the surface?"

Ian walked to the entry. "Hang a right. When you pass the chute, the elevator's on the left. Want me to come with?"

"I'll be okay. Thanks." I stared hard at Ian, aka my prime suspect. At that moment, it was hard to peg him as the killer.

"Be careful, will you?" Ian said.

"I will." I stepped out of the room and hurried down the corridor.

Minutes later, I recognized the stained chute from my first trip to the sub-basement. A shudder ran down my spine. I could almost see Big Mac's body sliding down, fast and heavy, landing with a thud. He had to be down here.

Padded steps echoed behind me. Was Vader tailing me? I pointed my feet toward the elevator, pushed the button, turned, and quietly made a right down the hallway. I pressed my back to the wall and waited. From my vantage point, I'd see anyone entering the area housing the elevator.

The steps grew louder. The back of a man appeared, tall, slim, dark tousled hair, dressed in layers of black.

I pulled the shuriken out from my buckle. I tensed my fingers, pulled back, and... accidentally knocked down a pail behind my boot.

The man dove off to one side. His palms slapped the ground. I raced over, throwing star in hand. He lifted his head and eyed me.

"It's you," we said simultaneously.

## CHAPTER 35

### RENDEZVOUS WITH ONE TOO MANY

"You're the last person I expected to find down-under," I said.

"Is that how you dress when you go stealth?" Michael picked himself off the floor and gave me a slow once over.

Goose bumps ran up my arms. In a good way.

"You look nice," he said.

So did he in jeans and a blue button down beneath a gray hoodie. Was it possible he really was in love with me? Only love could be that blind. "Thank you, Michael."

His hand reached out and touched my cheek lightly. "I am so sorry."

"For what?"

"For what I've put you through. If I'd just called the police, your cheek wouldn't look like you had a massive toothache."

I rubbed my aching arm. "It's not my tooth that hurts."

"Let's get some ice on it while you tell me what happened."

"I don't need ice…"

He led me to the room with the old computer parts. He shoved them aside and opened Squalley's fridge. He took out a beer can and wrapped it with a paper towel.

"Press this to your face." He held it out to me.

"What are you doing down here?" I took it and held the can to my cheek.

"I figured this was my last shot at finding Mac's body. What happened to your cheek?"

The cold burned my skin. "Darth Vader took me by surprise, tied me up, and injected me with truth serum."

"Did you hurt your head too?"

"Someone dressed up as Darth Vader, stole this new improved truth serum Squalley invented and attacked me."

"Are you kidding me? That's it." He pulled out his phone and dialed 9-1-1.

"Wait. Please." I placed my hand on his arm. "Wait one hour. And I promise we'll call the cops."

He placed the phone next to his ear and disconnected a moment later. "All circuits are busy, anyhow. But Corrie, you shouldn't have come back here alone," he said. "You know that, right? You should have brought James or me or Veera with you."

"Where's James?"

"He dropped me off. Said he'd be back soon."

"Did you find anything?" I asked.

"I wish. If I could just find something to hand to the police...I've been like a ball and chain around your ankle this weekend. You and James and Veera have been so incredibly tolerant."

"Oh, Michael." I took his hand and held it. "I don't mind you're being my ball and chain. Not that you are. You're a sound-minded guy who unraveled after a terrible thing happened. I help because I want to, because I care about you. And because—"

The elevator door pinged and opened.

"You did it," Bobby said to me. He shuffled out of the elevator, sandy strands hanging on either side of his face, night vision goggles in one hand, baton in the other. "I should never have trusted you."

"Put that thing away before you hurt yourself," I said.

"What happened to your face?" Bobby peered closely at me.

"As if you don't know," I said. "Show me your knee."

"You first." He put away the baton.

"Uh, why do you need to see the knee?" Michael asked me. Then he turned to Bobby. "And what did she do?"

"She sent me to the security office, then bashed me in the head when I got what she needed."

"That makes zero sense," I said.

"What was he—" Michael started.

"I needed a map of the sub-basement," I told Michael. "I asked Bobby to get one for me. As much as it would have given me pleasure, I didn't bash him."

Michael pointed to the headset. "Don't you have goggles just like those?"

"I let him borrow them."

"I got the map, then got slammed in the noggin." Bobby's chin dropped to his chest, the back of his skull pointed toward me. "I saw stars, like in a constellation. Because of you."

"You okay? You should see a doctor," Michael told him. "I never realized how much violence there is on campus."

Bobby rubbed his head. "There never used to be. Til she showed up." He tossed his chin my way.

Michael bent his knees and stared into Bobby's eyes. "Your pupils look normal. Did you get a look at the attacker?"

"Didn't need to. She hit me from behind."

"Why would I send you to get the map and attack you once you had it?" I touched the back of his skull. My fingers pressed around to find the bump.

"Hey!" Bobby's head shot away. "That hurts."

"How do we know you were even attacked? I didn't feel a bump."

"And you're not gonna, 'cause you're not touching me again," Bobby said.

"Why would I need to steal it if you were going to give it to me anyway?" My suspicions shot off the charts. What was the real reason for his delay? His coveralls were loose. He was probably still wearing his Vader duds. "Open up your zipper."

"What?" Both he and Michael asked at the same time.

"What are you wearing beneath that uniform?" My patience was stretched to the thinness of a French crepe.

"I'm not showing you my privates."

"I second that denial," Michael said to me. "Why would you ask that?"

"This is why." My hand shot out. A moment later he was zipped down to the crotch area. "Aha!"

A hairy chest, six pack abs, and an itsy-bitsy, teeny-weeny man bikini were all I took in. I slowly moved the zipper upward. He snapped my hand away and took over the job. "This is sexual harassment. I'm gonna report you."

"Whoa, whoa, whoa. You've got to excuse her, Bobby," Michael said. "She hasn't slept in days, and her reflexes are shot."

"You're not getting away with this." Bobby told me and puffed out his chest. "I feel so violated."

"You need to take it down a notch or two," I said. "I was caught off guard by a guy dressed up as Darth Vader. How do I know it wasn't you? Show me your knee."

"Haven't you seen enough?"

"I kicked my attacker in the knee. Show me."

"You're not seeing any more skin," Bobby said.

"How did you know I'd be down here?" I asked and massaged the side of my aching head.

"You think this was the first place I looked? I searched all over. Then I saw this guy." He nodded toward Michael. "On the cam, taking the elevator where he shouldn't be going. Figured you were together."

"You're lying," I told Bobby. "Where's the map?"

"Right here." He tapped his pants pocket. "On my phone. I took a picture before you stole it." Bobby reached inside and dug deeper. "It's here. Dang it. My phone's missing."

"I've been straight with you," I said. "This is how you reciprocate?"

"You're as straight as a snake about to strike."

"You are so wrong." A snake can strike from any posture. And so could I. In one quick move, I had him in a headlock. It felt so right, so empowering, that I barely heard Michael's words.

"You're choking him, Corrie."

Bobby spit out gargling sounds.

I slackened my hold. "Talk before I flex my muscles again."

"I took a photo of the master plan of the Admin Hall and the tunnels beneath."

I let him go. "Can you recreate it?"

He massaged his neck. "You're stronger than you look." He shook his head. "I didn't look at it too close. I was a mugging victim, remember?"

"Yet another crime's been committed under your watch. You're going to be blamed for being clueless. How does that make you feel?" I knew exactly what he should be feeling.

"Look, what's this all about?" Bobby asked.

"Murder," I said. "But the body's gone missing."

Bobby arched a brow. I didn't need X-ray vision to know he pictured himself finding the body and being declared a hero. "A student was killed?"

Michael and I swapped glances.

"Not a student," I said. "First, how can someone leave Admin without being seen?"

"Now I know why the map is so important." Bobby backed up. "It's so's you can sneak around without being caught. Who'd you kill?"

"Do you want this to get ugly? Let's find out what your level of pain tolerance is."

"Wait." Michael held up a hand and turned to Bobby. "We can't share details right now, but starting tomorrow, law enforcement will be all over this campus if we don't make some headway tonight. Would you rather get questioned by the police? I think it'll be a whole lot easier talking to us."

Bobby regarded me through half-closed lids.

"That's it." I lunged forward, but Michael came between us.

"I can't hold her back much longer," Michael said.

We heard a chime and the elevator door slid shut. All of our eyes turned toward the panel above the doors. The elevator stopped a few moments. And started again.

"Somebody's comin' down." Bobby's eyes punched up to mine. "What do we do?"

Before I could open my mouth to reply, the door slid open.

## CHAPTER 37

## LIGHTS, CAMERA, ACTION!

The elevator door barely slid open when we heard a small pop. The room turned pitch. Someone yelled. Scrambling feet drummed the cement floor. I fumbled in my pocket for the penlight.

"You're not going anywhere," I heard Michael say.

Heavy breathing fanned the air. I found the penlight and lit the room. Veera was grasping Michael's wrist. A clump of her hair was gathered in his fist.

"What are you doing here?" I asked her.

She dropped his wrist. "Sorry," she told Michael. "The lights went out and, well, I ran for my life, and there you were."

He released the grip on her locks. "No, I'm sorry. I thought you were...well, I didn't really know who I'd grabbed—"

"I didn't break anything, did I?" Veera asked.

Michael moved his joints. "No, I'm still in working order."

"That's a relief." Veera turned to me. "I was sound asleep until Marty called to say he'd be late to your meeting tonight. So I got to wondering, C.'s having a get together? Why wasn't I invited? Should I bring snacks? So I came here to ask you in person."

"You could have called," I said.

"I tried, but no one answered."

I'd forgotten to un-mute my phone. Again. "Only the suspects know about the meeting."

"What meeting?" Michael asked.

"I thought you might need some help," Veera said to me.

"How did you find me?" I asked her.

"I saw that sassy security guard lurking upstairs. Then he goes and disappears. I looked everywhere and when I couldn't find him, I figured he had to be down here."

"Bobby." I turned around. There was no trace of him. "Great. Where'd he go?"

I ran to the hallway, Michael at my heels. I shined the light. No sign of anyone.

"What's the meeting about?" Michael asked me.

"I'm gathering the suspects in Big Mac's office at the stroke of midnight."

"What happens at midnight?" Michael wanted to know.

"I uncloak the culprit."

"Just like on those TV detective shows," Veera said.

"You know who it is?" Michael asked.

"I will once they're all together."

"How?"

"I told each one I had information on them. They're going to want to know what I know," I said. "So I figure they'll show up. Unless they're not involved in the murder. Then they'll just think I'm crazy."

The light went back on. We heard Michael gasp. Veera and I turned around. Michael's phone light zeroed in on an object on the cement floor, near the elevator. A black rubber Nike tipped on its side, lay on the ground, a thick, two inch shoe insert in front of it.

"Why would he leave his shoe behind?" Michael said. "Do you think he was abducted?"

Veera clasped her hands in front of her, cutting a glance between us. "Or maybe when a certain someone dove out of the elevator out of sheer terror from the lights going out, she grabbed the first thing she could lay her hands on, which might have been someone's ankle. When the owner of the ankle freed himself and made a run for it, that first someone held on to the shoe, and it might have come off in her hand. That's when I grabbed you." She turned to Michael.

"So you scared him off," I said.

"I knew I shouldn't have taken this elevator," Veera said.

"First, he says he's knocked out by an unknown assailant—"

"This place is crawling with criminals," Veera said.

"And now he's disappeared." I turned to Michael. "Don't you think that's suspicious?"

"Not if she grabbed his shoe and spooked him," Michael said. "I would have run off, too. I haven't known him long, but he seems like a regular guy trying to climb up the security guard ladder, one rung at a time, with one and a half feet, and doing the best he can."

"That's a real nice character analysis," Veera said and looked up at the ceiling. "Even though he did sneak up on me. Hope the lights come back on soon."

"What caused the outage?" Michael said. "The campus has generators."

"If I'd known it'd be like this, I would've worn my glow in the dark sweats." Veera fanned herself with a hand.

I checked my phone. "It's nearly time. How do we get out of here?"

The room lit up with a buzz and a booming sound.

"Good timing," Michael said and turned to Veera. "You go upstairs and wait outside Mac's office. It's on the second floor. You can't miss it. If any suspects arrive, stall them."

The room wasn't the only thing that lit up. Veera did, too. "I can do that." She backed into the elevator and pushed the button. "See you at midnight."

The door closed and Michael turned to me. "I want to show you something before we go up."

"What?"

"While you were fighting off Vader, I was busy, too. I sort of redecorated the sub-basement. I think you'll like it." Michael peered at his phone. "Look at this."

I stared at the phone. The screen was divided into four parts, each displaying a different section of the sub-basement hallways. I regarded Michael with fresh eyes. "You planted cameras. Brilliant, Michael."

He beamed so brightly the dim space took on a warm glow. "Watch the bottom left screen."

Our boy Bobby was spotted shuffling down a corridor. In the next screen he stopped in front of a door, opened it, and hurried through.

"I'm shooting him in the same knee I kicked next time I see him."

"What? Oh, you're kidding, right? You've got a gun? I thought your mom collected your weapons."

"A sub-compact for the sub-basement." I pulled up a pant leg. "Inside my boot. Vader didn't bother checking my shoes. Let's go."

"Wait, you'd better take it slow. I'll do a quick run through and circle back to get you."

"Michael, I am so pumped right now, if I was in the open air and you tied a basket to me, we'd be doing some major hot air ballooning. Now, come on."

I moved down the hall and stopped when we'd reached a passage to our right. The air had grown damp and thick and warm. My clothes clung to me once more, my hair plastered to my head. "Which way?"

Michael studied the phone and pointed to the left. "Follow me."

Minutes later, Michael skidded to a stop. Scattered crates and cardboard boxes blocked the passage. Ahead of us was a familiar metal door punched into a wall.

"There it is." He pressed his fingers around the metal handle and pushed it down. The door swayed open. "Bobby went out this way."

We scrambled through and up the short flight of stairs to reach the double doors. The same doors I'd used for entry earlier that evening. It seemed like a hundred years ago. I pushed them open with my good arm and hurried outside, sucking in the grass-scented air. Automatic sprinklers swished water over the lawn, and the occasional car whizzed by on the street.

"I don't see him anywhere." I looked around. "What a night." I was assaulted and drugged, and still had no clues. "I've failed you, Michael." The side of my head was pounding.

"Are you kidding me? We are closer than ever to the killer. I've just got to hold it together a little longer, and help you find him. Or her."

Michael took me by the hand and led me to a bench. It felt good to sit. He stood behind me and massaged my temples. I closed my eyes.

"The meeting—" I said.

"Let's hang back and review the suspects first. You've got Bobby on your list," he said. "I told you what I think of him. You still think he's got a hand in this?"

"All I know is he's night security. Except he's here twenty-four-seven."

"Hmm." Michael stopped the massage and took a seat next to me. "Maybe he's hell-bent on collecting major overtime. And that's why he's always around."

"Or he's killed Big Mac and hanging around to make sure all clues point away from him."

"What about Loretta?" he asked.

"She confessed she hated Big Mac. Alyce loathes him, too. And so do Ian and Squalley. I still see Ian as the one with the most motive. You remember what he said when he busted us in the closet?"

"That Mac was a rat?"

"That Mac was the only thing standing in his way of getting into LA Tech as a student." I pictured Mac's office. "Hold-it."

"What?"

"Who keeps a pair of shoes by the bookcase?"

"There were more in the closet."

"Exactly. Why would Big Mac keep extra clothes and shoes in the closet, but keep one pair out? He was a neat freak, you said. Yet those Wallabees sat in the open. It's not like there wasn't room in the closet."

"True. And what does that mean, exactly?"

"The answer's right in front of us. We just don't see it. Yet." I checked my phone and stood. "Five minutes to midnight."

"But Corrie—"

"Do you have your knife?"

He patted his back pocket. "Right here."

"How about your resolve?"

"You mean like the carpet cleaner or like I'm going to cut through horse manure and create an incredible fertilizer?"

"The latter, I think. Let's go."

## CHAPTER 38

## AND THEN THERE WERE TWO

"Settle down, everyone."

We stepped into the all too familiar presidential suite where Veera was addressing the occupants.

"Be cool, y'all," she was saying. "Don't make me utilize any of my lethal weapons." She stood on the coffee table in Big Mac's crowded office. Bobby was missing.

Alyce sidled over to me. "I can't possibly imagine what you could know that's worth dragging us here so late."

And yet she'd come to the meeting. "Maybe you've no imagination," I said.

"Don't think I won't report that she broke into this office." Alyce pointed to Veera.

"Big Mac let her in," I said, watching her closely. Her expression remained bland.

"If you were not a top dog…" Loretta marched over to Alyce, "…I would get a few things off my chest right now. Like why you are not capable of responding to students' emails. Returning phone calls a week later is unacceptable."

"She's right about that," Veera chimed in.

"All you do is babble on with the same ridiculous demands," Alyce told Loretta. "Room service in dorms—"

"Students should be regarded as valued customers in a competitive market," Loretta said.

"I was in favor of that idea," Michael said.

"Room service would only be during finals," Loretta added.

"This is not the Ritz Carlton," Alyce told Loretta.

"Our tuition should sustain that service." Loretta stuck her lower lip out.

"Would that mean extra hours for us?" Ian stepped forward, with Squalley bringing in the rear.

"A little overtime would be appreciated," Squalley said.

"Maybe this *is* about overtime," Michael whispered to me.

"I could cook the meals," Squalley continued. "I make a combo lasagna ravioli to die for."

"How about to kill for?" I asked.

Alyce flipped back her hair. "I'm leaving."

"No one's going anywhere." Bobby had joined us. He wore a new pair of black Nikes. "Not until I find out what's going on."

"I say who can come and go," I told him. "You went AWOL."

"You unzip me, the lights go off, and someone steals the shoe offa my foot," Bobby said. "Figured I'd better get out while I could."

He held out my goggles. I snatched them back and turned toward the others. I stole a glance at Veera. She race-walked to the office door and slammed it shut and leaned against it. "I got you all on my radar," she said to the group.

"Everyone around the sofa," I said.

Alyce sauntered toward the couch and stopped. Squalley and Ian sat sprawled along the cushions. They gave up their spots for Alyce. Loretta perched on the armrest.

"Who says chivalry is dead?" Squalley said.

"It's alive because you value your jobs," Alyce said.

Bobby sidled to where the two men stood. "Let's get this over with."

There was a knock on the door. All heads turned toward Veera who opened it. Marty stood at the threshold, hair shaggier than ever, glasses askew.

"Get in here, you," Veera said.

He stepped through and Veera closed the door.

"I took a shortcut through the sprinklers," he said. His oversize t-shirt was splattered with watermarks. He looked around. "I've never been in the president's office. Is this a staff meeting?"

"Forget your questions," Veera said. "What do you know about these people?"

"Um, they either work or go to school here."

"Over by the couch," I said.

"Wait," he said.

All heads turned toward Marty.

"I won't sit near her." He pointed to Loretta.

"Shoot. Get going before I treat you like a hostile witness." Veera shoved his shoulder. "I expected more from you, boy."

"Where's the president?" Squalley asked and looked at me. "What is it that you know about us? You trying to get us into trouble?"

"Yeah," Ian agreed. "We didn't do anything." His eyes shifted around the room. "Did we?"

"I ask the questions," I said and turned to Michael. "Handle the questioning, please." I moved over to the shoes sitting by the bookcase.

Michael straightened his shoulders. "You all know I had a bad day on Friday. I had an argument with Mac and I stormed out afterward. When I came back later, he was…fill in the blank. Loretta, you first. He was…what?"

"A big fat…" Loretta's description of Big Mac was unprintable in its use of excess profanity. Some words I'd never heard and hoped to never hear again. Perhaps they weren't even in the English language. She ended and aimed an evil eye at Alyce. "She is a power hungry witch who ignores student needs."

"Room service is hardly a need," Alyce replied.

"Down with Alyce! Down with Alyce!"

A lively debate ensued. I turned my attention to the Wallabees. The soles looked nearly new. But normal wear and tear appeared on the cushion inside.

"Excuse me!" I yelled over the ruckus. Quiet captured the room. All necks craned toward me. "Does anyone recall seeing Big Mac wear these in the office?"

"No way."

"Those belong on hooves."

"They couldn't hide his ugly feet."

"He has a pair like that at home," Alyce said.

"Do not listen to her," Loretta said. "She does not know anything."

The arguing continued. I returned to my shoe examination. One thing was certain: the soles had never stepped foot outdoors. What was special about them?

"Come on people, settle down," Michael said. "Let's get through this, okay? Just a few simple questions before she…" He pointed back to me, "…takes over and tells you what this is about. Where was I? Oh, yes, when was the last time you saw him in this office?" Michael asked. "Ian, you answer."

"At lunchtime on Friday when I came in to empty the trash. He was standing by the window, hands behind his back."

"Did he say anything?"

Ian nodded. "He said, 'Don't do a half-ass job, you idiot.' That's what he always says to me."

"That is cruel," Veera said.

"Not really," Ian said. "Compared to the other names he's called me, that was actually quite nice."

I came forward. "Tell it to us straight. I know what you've done."

Ian shrugged. "Is this about the missing sticky notes? 'Cause I only took one pad."

"That's not what I'm talking about," I said.

"Oh. You must mean my protesting for animal rights at California Ocean Park. Orcas are not killer whales."

"I hear you on that one," Veera said. "They got a bum rap."

"Did Big Mac say anything else to you?" Michael asked Ian.

"He said I'd be fired if I didn't tell him who took Leo," Ian said. "I'd sooner be fired than give up Leo's secret hiding place."

Cheers erupted from the group. Loretta gave him a standing ovation.

"But I really don't know where Leo is," Ian said.

Michael leaned down and whispered to me, "Does Ian have a criminal record?"

"Just testing the waters," I whispered back.

Bobby moved over to the Wallabees. "That is one homely looking pair," he said to me.

I joined him by the shoes. "Did you dress up as Darth Vader?"

"Wasn't me. Is that really why you undressed me?"

I nodded. "Disappointed?"

"I'll get over it." He shuffled back to the others.

"Your turn, Alyce," Michael said. "When was the last time you saw Mac?"

"Friday morning, early." She lifted her eyes to study the smooth ceiling and dropped them down to Michael. "That's when he told me about your...change in position."

"Was this in or out of bed?" Loretta asked.

"This is getting very uncomfortable," Ian said. He pulled on the collar of his polo shirt with his finger.

"How do you know what goes on in the president's bed?" Veera wanted to know.

"I made an educated guess," Loretta replied.

"Hardly," Alyce said to Loretta. "We talked outside this building."

"I saw you in his car with him that morning," Loretta said.

"So? He gave me a lift to campus. My Prius wasn't charged."

Loretta unleashed more expletives.

"Young lady, I'll have to escort you out if your salty language continues. It's very distracting," Ian said.

"Not to mention there are ladies present," Squalley added.

"The president's car hasn't moved all weekend," Bobby said. "It's been parked in his usual spot. Anyone see him around?"

Heads shook and eyes regarded each other.

"So you didn't see him after that?" Michael asked Alyce.

"That's what I said."

"Then how do you explain this?" I dug into my backpack and whipped out the cigarette butt with the fuchsia lipstick stain at the end. "I picked this out of the wastebasket by the desk. Friday night." I moved to Ian. "The same wastebasket this man claims he emptied after lunch."

"What about it? I had a smoke in my office and came up here to talk to Mac later. He wasn't here, and I threw the cigarette in his trash. That's no crime."

"Actually, it is," I said, stepping forward. "Smoking's been banned in all enclosed work places since 1995."

"So shoot me. I hardly ever light up anymore. I prefer it unlit, dangling between my lips."

"That's messed up," Veera said.

She gave Veera a sidelong stare. "I like being the one in control."

"That's still messed up," Veera said. "If you were in control, you wouldn't need it dangling."

"What can you tell me about those shoes?" I asked Alyce.

"They're hideous."

"Why do they sit next to the bookshelves?"

"Maybe they're special reading shoes," Ian said and broke into laughter, slapping Squalley on the arm.

"Did any of you ever see him wear them?" I asked.

Alyce pushed back her blonde locks. "I never bothered to notice."

"Me neither," Squalley said and Ian agreed.

"Who the ef cares?" Loretta asked.

"Why did you lie about being in here?" Michael asked Alyce. "We saw you leaving the building that night, around nine."

"Alright. I did come back in the evening. To find you." Alyce stood. "So we could talk. I didn't want you to think I had a hand in your demotion. It was all Mac's idea."

I knew then that Alyce was behind Michael's demotion. "Show us the text Big Mac sent you," I said.

Alyce raised her chin and pressed her lips together. She fumbled around in a handbag the size of Rhode Island and pulled out her cell phone. She pressed a few buttons and showed it to Michael. "Happy now?"

Michael read the text on her phone screen. "It says I should act as dean of the department next week. It looks like Mac sent it. It's his number." He turned his gaze to Alyce. "Even if Mac did send this, you couldn't have been happy about it."

Alyce took a spin around the room. "Demoting you was a swell idea. And in my best interest. I took this job because Mac promised me a fast rise to the top. Yes, we engaged in some extracurricular activities. And as my reward, the brute called me Friday morning to say I was next in line for a demotion." She turned to Michael. "He played us both. Because of that stupid dog. He loses Leo, and we get blamed."

I studied the others in the room. My gaze lingered over Ian and Squalley.

"Why are we getting the evil eye?" Squalley caught my stare. "We've been open with you."

"That's true," Ian said. He turned to Alyce. "Mind if I come in a little later tomorrow? I'm going to need my beauty rest."

"Shut up," Alyce said.

Michael moved in toward Bobby. "Did you do it?"

"Do what?" He shuffled back until he stood against the wall. "A guy needs to know what he's being accused of before he denies it. I didn't take Leo if that's what you mean. I been trying to find the dog, and that pig."

"Good luck with finding Archie," Squalley spoke out of the side of mouth.

Ian snickered.

"When was the last time you saw Mac?" Michael asked Bobby.

"Thursday evening. Late. When he left this building."

"Did you exchange words?" I asked.

"Yeah. I said, 'Have a good night' and he said, 'Get out of my way, butt-wipe.'"

"I hate him," Loretta chimed in.

"What's this really about, anyway?" Alyce asked me.

"I'll get to that in a minute. Are these shoes always here?" I returned to the Wallabees.

"They should be fumigated," Loretta said. "They stink. Just like her breath." She threw Alyce a nasty glare. "Can I go now? I have a midterm to study for."

Alyce eyed the shoes. "Alright, here's a news flash. I came in here last week to leave a file on Mac's chair. No one's allowed to leave anything on his desk without his okay. So I dropped it on the seat to avoid trouble." She stared at the chair. "I was almost at the door when I heard noises behind me. Footsteps. Slow and squeaky. I turned around. No one was there."

"And?" I said.

"I left and came back ten seconds later to get something out of the file. Mac stood there." She crossed her arms over her chest and stared at the spot where the shoes rested. "Taking those off. I never saw him come or go."

"Did he say anything?" I asked.

"He barked at me to get out. So I did. That was the only time I saw him in those clodhoppers."

"Those are not clodhoppers. Clodhoppers are not lightweight." Expletives gushed out of Loretta's mouth. "Faculty accuracy is imperative. You are supposed to be a role model to students. But you are not even close."

An argument erupted again. I moved toward the bookshelves, crammed with volume after volume. I retreated a few steps. What was I missing? Skimming the shelves up and down, I removed books and replaced them. I wiped the dust off a marble bust of some old guy. I was so ready to break up this party when I threw a glance toward the top of the shelves. A narrow vertical gap striped one end of the shelf area. A little bigger than the one on the opposite end. I'd seen that kind of gap before, thanks to the secret room behind Mom's pantry. I ran my hands along the shelves and pulled out two books dead center. I pushed them back.

"You re-arranging the library?" Squalley was at my shoulder. "The president's not gonna like that."

"He'll never know, will he?" I said.

"What's that supposed to mean? You're wasting our time. Why not put us out of our misery?"

"Sit down."

"Big Mac's gonna hear about this." Squalley stepped back into the room.

Veera flanked my other side and whispered, "You think one of these books has a clue hidden inside?"

"I think one of these books *is* the clue." I scanned the shelves from top to bottom. "Find something that doesn't fit."

"You mean like a size two pantsuit?"

"Get to work."

Veera turned to the shelves and slapped her hands around the books. My fingers trickled along the spines. Nothing but dreary volume after volume. I moved to the next section and stood on my toes. I ran a hand along the top shelf. A thin film of dust lined my fingers. I progressed to the shelf below. More of the same. Veera mimicked me on her side.

When I came to the edge of the middle shelf, I paused. Three slim books near the gap stuck tightly together. My fingers wedged in the narrow space between the top of the books and the shelf. I pulled. The books tipped forward in unison, revealing a long brass handle. Veera peered over my shoulder.

"That doesn't belong there, does it?" she asked.

I pushed the handle down. There was a clicking sound, and the bookcase moved back. "It's right where it should be."

"What the…?" Loretta ran out of expletives.

I pushed the bookcase and it swung open, like a heavy, jumbo-sized door. I stepped into a small room. Glass shelves loaded with liquor bottles clung to the wall in front of me. Backless bar stools with brown leather seats lined an L-shaped counter. The space reeked of hard liquor. A buzzing sound like a swarm of mosquitoes vibrated across the room. The temperature rivaled that of a meat locker. I heard a cry behind me. I turned toward the far end of the room and sucked in my breath.

## Chapter 39

## The Chase

A boxy cooler on wheels stood in the far corner, blasting chilled air toward a large figure spread-eagle on his back. Bobby bent over the body. I uprooted my boots, forcing them closer. Frozen gel packs were tucked beneath the head, shoulder blades, lower back, and hips. More packs balanced on top of his chest and belly. One brick-size pack rested across his forehead. Michael pushed past me.

"He was here all the time," Michael said.

Big Mac wore a dark blue suit, and a polka dot, batwing bowtie. Wire rimmed glasses tipped sideways across closed eyes; a mop of white hair blew back thanks to the fan. His blue-stocking feet were shoeless. His moustache-free beard belonged on Captain Ahab. Even in death, he looked grumpy.

"That face would stop a subway car," Alyce said.

Loretta marched up to the body and kicked him in the leg. She would have kicked out again if Bobby hadn't pulled her back.

"Get in line," he said.

Michael turned to the onlookers. "Which one of you killed him?"

Squalley stepped forward. "I understand now. Bringing us together was part of the plan."

"What plan?" Michael asked.

"You're pushing the blame on us. But we didn't do this to him. No one here has as much motive," Squalley said, "as you do." He pointed a finger at Michael.

"Me? No, you don't understand. Yes, Mac was arrogant and mean-as-heck, but I—"

"There's his confession," Squalley said to me. "Now we can go."

"No, I'm only saying—" Michael continued.

"Take him away, Veera," I said.

"Who?" Veera asked. "The Mafia guy?"

"I won't put up with your racial profiling, young lady," Squalley said.

"Take Michael away," I said.

"What?" Michael's voice went up an octave. "You can't mean me."

"Yes, I can. Veera," I said. "Now." I moved to the entry. "Cuff him to Mac's desk."

"I thought we don't have any…" Veera started.

"You heard me."

Veera took Michael's arm. "I'm not gonna say it, but this is not the right move, C."

I followed them and whispered to Veera, "Call the police." I looked at Michael. "Can you retrieve deleted emails from Big Mac's computer?"

Michael nodded. "I already went through his deleted emails."

"You went through what was *in* there, but not what wasn't."

Michael leaned close to me. "I'm not going to get cuffed to the desk? What do you want me to do? His trash is emptied daily. But…" He snapped his fingers. "I can go through his backup."

"Good. Find out if Big Mac received any threats." I cocked my head toward the others. "From someone in there." I tossed my head toward the suspects.

"Why didn't I think of that?" Michael's palm slapped his forehead. "That's radical. I'll get on it."

"This must have been a safe room during Prohibition," Ian was saying when I rejoined them. He was touching the walls. "This looks like original plaster."

"Pour me a whiskey, will you?" Alyce said.

"I'm not a bartender," Ian replied. "Although I do buttle on occasion."

"Boozer," Loretta said to her.

"My nose is frozen. A-choo! Brrrrrr." Squalley rubbed his shoulders.

"A-choo!" It was Bobby's turn to sneeze. He faced Squalley. "You're spreading germs." To prove it, he sneezed again. "I gotta get outta here."

"The cops will be here in a few minutes," I said.

"How do we know the former associate dean won't try to kill us before the police arrive?" Marty wanted to know.

"Co-associate dean," Alyce said.

"I ask the questions, pal," I told Marty.

"I'm not staying another minute," Alyce said.

"I'm with her," Squalley said.

"I go where he goes," Ian said.

They advanced toward me.

"No one leaves until I say so." I pulled out my pistol. The pain in my head and arm cranked up a notch.

"That's a little drastic," Alyce said.

"So is that." I waved the gun at the body. I stared at Big Mac and gasped. "Did he just move?"

All eyes turned to the body. But only one person in the room lunged toward Big Mac and leaned over him, squinting.

"I knew it," I told Loretta. "You killed him."

"I would not—"

"—graduate if he had his way." Michael stood behind me. He held a sheet of paper in his hand. "I found eight emails from Loretta threatening Mac. He was about to flunk her out of school." He turned to Loretta. "You were on probation this semester."

"Are you turning on me?" Loretta's lower lip stuck out again. "I thought you were the smart one on the faculty. You, of all people, should understand. I did not deserve to be expelled. Do you know why?"

Michael shook his head.

"I have a 3.75 GPA!"

"A 3.7 didn't put you on probation," Alyce said.

"See what I mean?" Loretta said. "She is an idiot. It is three point seven *five*. My academic record was doctored. MacTavish did it. He gave me a…" she whimpered, "…C minus average." Loretta's face looked like it had been splashed by beet juice. "Do you know how humiliating that was?" She moved closer to Michael and stared up into his face. "You did not deserve the demotion. I did not deserve the C minus. It was not fair." She stamped a heel. "I was asked to step down from being student body president. Just like you. He was angry with my grandfather for not donating to the college this year. My family is very well connected. I told MacTavish it was not my fault. He laughed in my face. He called me stupid!" She pointed a finger at the lump in the room. "He deserved to die."

"You stabbed him?" Veera wanted to know.

"With my favorite carving knife. After I hit him in his fat head with that ugly orange lamp in his office. If that fake detective…" Loretta said and tossed me a glare, "…had not snooped around, he would never have been found. My plan was perfect." Loretta's glare turned to Alyce. "I sent you the text, promoting Dean Parris like he should have been. MacTavish could not send it because he was dead." Loretta threw back her head, squeezed her eyes shut, her breath chopped into a series of cackles that would have made Machiavelli proud. She focused her squint back on Alyce. "You slept with him to get what you wanted. I would never stoop to such primitive tactics. I have standards."

"Homicidal standards," I said, stepping forward. "So instead, you killed him."

"Grandfather got into a fight with MacTavish over how the money would be used. Grandfather refused to make his annual donation and MacTavish retaliated by putting me on probation. That was the wrong move." Loretta slunk over to Michael. "I never meant for you to get involved. That is why I took your resignation letter and burned it."

"You did?" Michael asked.

"Yes, when I went in to hide the body. I cleaned up the mess you made so no one would suspect you. MacTavish was going to be moved tonight. I stole the map off that creepy security guard to find the tunnel leading to the L.A. River so we could dump MacTavish after we tied him to a block of cement."

"I called that one," Veera said. "I knew cement was involved somehow."

"Hold up," I said. "Did you say 'we'?"

Loretta nodded. "Me and him." She pointed to the back of the room. "He is gone."

Bobby, Ian, and Squalley were missing.

# CHAPTER 40

## KILLER GONE MISSING

"I was the brains. He was the muscle," Loretta said.

"Who? Who was the muscle?" Michael asked.

"No more talking unless someone cuts me a deal," Loretta said.

"No one's cutting you anything," I told her.

Loretta crossed the room to where the body lay, planted one heel on top of Mac's belly, and turned to face us. "If no one cuts me a deal, I will say he helped me." She pointed at Michael.

"Loretta," Michael said. "I thought we were friends."

"After I invited you to my house and you questioned my sighting?"

"You lied to me about seeing Mac on campus," Michael said.

Loretta crossed her arms across her chest. "I spread the rumors about him being alive so I could get him out of here. That is why I caused the power outage...to get in and out without being seen. See how powerful I am? I saw the security guard talking to you." She turned her crooked lips toward me. "And I followed him."

"I'm glad you didn't follow me," I said.

"Why would I? You are just a stupid pretend detective."

"Private investigator." My hand reached for the Taser. "You stole the ice cream truck?"

"I borrowed it. For a small sum. And threw away all that junk. I hauled in the ice packs from my family's medical supply company. It was brilliant of me. I did not want MacTavish to stink before we got him out. He smelled enough when he was alive. I cannot imagine the stench once he was dead. He wore those hideous Wallabees in this room only. He insisted everyone go shoeless in this bar, so it would stay clean. Except him."

"You'd been in here before?" I asked.

"Not me. Grandfather. He told me about it." Loretta squinted toward Michael. "After all I did for you, you turned on me, an innocent student standing up for her rights."

"Innocent?" Michael asked. "You killed a man."

"He asked for it. He did not appreciate how smart I am."

In two quick moves, I pulled out the Taser and pressed it to her shoulder. She opened her mouth and squealed before crumpling on top of Big Mac.

Michael moved to my side. "Isn't that illegal?"

"Only if the stun gun was used as an assault weapon. This was self-defense. I couldn't handle any more of her talking."

"You know, for the first time, I don't mind being in the same room as Loretta," Veera said.

"Turned out to be a red letter night," Alyce said. "Glad I hung around." She rummaged around her handbag and extracted a cigarette. She stuck it between her lips and let it dangle. "What are you staring at?" She landed her steely gaze on me.

"What was that noise? Sounded like a growl."

"It was probably him." Her gaze dipped to the body.

"Michael," I said, "you wait here for the police."

"Where are you going?"

"After the guys."

"Not without me," Michael said.

"I'll watch over this place." Veera held up a long, shiny piece of polka dot material. "Lookie what I found."

I turned toward Big Mac's body. His bowtie was MIA.

"It'll look better on her, don't you think?" Veera asked. She tied Loretta's hands behind her.

Loretta stirred and lifted her head. The profane outpouring was as thick as week-old porridge. Veera stuck a wad of red cocktail napkins in her mouth.

"Red complements your hair," Veera said over Loretta's grunting.

"I have a question for her," I said, looking down at Loretta. "Why were you toeing the dirt beneath the president's window?"

She grunted. Veera pulled out the wad of napkins.

"Because I climbed out after I killed him and broke my bracelet."

"Gold or silver?"

"Neither. It's organic, from the Amazon in Peru."

"That little cocoa puff bead I found…" The bead belonged to Loretta.

"Not beads! Acai berry seeds I strung with my own hands, you freaking…" And the profanity poured out again until Veera stuffed the red wad back in her mouth.

"Send the cops to the sub-basement after they're done here," I said to Veera and turned to Michael. "Let's go."

"What makes you think Bobby or Squalley and Ian are still around?" Michael asked once we landed in the sub-basement. "They could be on their way to Mexico."

"Why Mexico?"

"That's where Bogart headed in *The Petrified Forest*."

This was why I loved the guy. Only another Bogart fan would come up with such a logical explanation. "I'm with you on that one. But they won't leave until they retrieve items they've hidden in the sub-basement. Ian and Squalley spent a lot of time down here. They're very proud of their handiwork."

"Really? Couldn't they have just been cleaning up the place?"

"Does it look the least bit clean?"

We headed down the corridor.

"I see what you mean. But I'm glad Squalley kept his impressive supply of beer down here. It came in handy. Your cheek's not as swollen anymore." Michael checked his phone cam. "I don't believe it. They're on to me. The cameras I installed aren't working."

I stared down at his phone. The lens focused on a glop. "They've smeared petroleum jelly or something goopy on the lens. It's okay. We can do this. We've got two older dudes in not the best shape. They can't be far ahead."

The dank corridor was ripe with the scent of thick steam. I raced forward. We passed closed doors, scattered debris, and finally reached the fork in the road.

"You continue straight," I said. "This is where I turn."

I started to run.

"Corrie."

I stopped and turned to Michael. He hurried over to me.

"I need to tell you something."

"Now? Can you hold on a bit?"

"Thank you for everything. For believing in me. For being my best friend. For helping whenever I need help. You've been a great pal—"

"A *pal*?" I wanted to shake him by the shoulders. "Really, Michael?"

"Is that not a good thing?"

"I love you. What do you think of that?"

He gave his head a brief shake. "Did you just say you love me? Just double-checking, 'cause it's kind of noisy down here and it would be really weird if all you said was 'we're cool' and I said I—"

A small sonic boom exploded in the hallway behind us. Michael's eyes rolled upward and his knees buckled. I grabbed him just before he folded. He was heavy in my arms. I braced my body against the wall and eased him to the ground.

"Michael."

"I've...been hit." His hazel eyes blinked and focused on me. "I..."

Another shot shattered the quiet, and I ducked. I reached for my boot and pulled out the pistol. I fired twice down the hallway where the boom sounded. I rose to all fours and crawled to the nearest door. I lay on my back and kicked out hard with both feet, aiming below the doorknob with my heels. Just like Miss Trudy showed us. Two small dents marred the wood surface. I fired my pistol and kicked out again. Splinters wounded the doorframe. I kicked again and again until the door keeled over with a crash. I turned to Michael. He slumped against the wall, pressing down on his shoulder with the opposite hand. Blood dripped down his arm. The hallway sat quiet except for the hiss of the pipe running along the ceiling. Pistol in hand, I grabbed Michael's good arm. We crawled our way into the compact room.

I pressed my fingers lightly around his shoulder. "Does it hurt a lot?"

"Not much. Kinda like there's a hot coal pressed against my bare skin. Argh!" He clenched his teeth.

"It's a graze. A scrape really."

"Are you sure? I heard a bunch of shots."

"That was me firing back." I unzipped my boots and took off my socks. "Keep these pressed against your shoulder. You'll be safe here." I slipped my boots back on.

His fingers curled around my wrist. "Wait. You're not...I'm coming with—"

"*This* is coming with." I held up my pistol. I stood. "I've got a job to finish."

I peered down the hall, inhaled deeply, and took off like a shot.

## CHAPTER 41

### NON-LETHAL WEAPON

I charged down the hallway toward the direction of the shooter. I'd barely made headway when I heard a racket behind me. I pressed my back against the wall, gun barrel along my chest.

Moments later, a metal utility cart rattled around the corner, pushed by a stocky guy with slicked back hair, wearing an umpire's mask and a heavy vest, Kevlar at a glance. I recognized the dragging sole and stepped onto his path, gun pointed.

"I like to start by shooting low." I'd never shot any one before. But he didn't know that. "Your vest won't save your knees."

"Hey," Bobby said, hands in the air, wheels rolling to a crooked stop in front of him. A towel covered the top half of the cart. A dented cardboard box huddled in the bottom tray. He brought down a hand to push up the mask. "What are you pointing that at me for? I'm here to take down the maintenance men. Just like you."

"Manila folders don't cut it as a weapon." I waved the gun at the box.

"They're my bargaining chip. MacTavish stole these files from Ian and Squalley. They've been trying to get them back."

"How do you know?"

"Ian told me. He asked me to keep an eye out for the files. I looked everywhere. I figured if MacTavish took them, they'd be in his car. His car's in the lot, so I opened his trunk tonight. That's where they were."

"What are you going to do with the files?"

"I'm not saying 'til you lower your gun."

"Since when do criminals have the right to bargain?"

"I'm no criminal."

"You broke into Big Mac's trunk."

"He's the one that stole stuff and bullied the staff and employees. I've been cooperating with you the whole time and you know it."

I lowered the pistol.

"Your friend's job isn't the only one at stake here," Bobby said. "Who do you think's gonna get blamed for not knowing the president was dead?"

"What's your plan?" I nodded toward the cart.

"I turn over the files to Ian and Squalley. They turn themselves in, testify against Loretta, she admits she's the mastermind, which shouldn't be hard to get her to do, and we're all good."

"And if they don't turn themselves in?"

With one quick hand flick, the towel was whisked away. The front of the cart was fitted with a row of nails, sharp ends pointed outward. "I ram them 'til they do."

The campus was swarming with wannabe inventors. "That's very…medieval." I fastened my gaze on him. "How do I know you're not the guy that helped Loretta stab Big Mac?"

"Why would I help her?"

"I heard she pays well."

"Ever think of leaving your piece at home?" a voice spoke behind me.

I pivoted around, gun pointed. My head snapped back and forth between Bobby and the new arrival. "I have separation anxiety. I expected you a long time ago," I told James.

"I had a promise to keep." He semi-circled around me and stopped next to Bobby, eyeing my gun-toting arm.

"How'd you find me?" I asked.

"Michael called. Said you might need a hand."

I eyed the hyper-masculine specimen standing in front of me all toughened up in a black leather motorcycle jacket and hip hugging jeans. My stomach growled long and loud, reminding me I hadn't eaten in a while. An empty stomach could send me over the edge. It wouldn't be the first time. We were motionless, except for the twitch of my index finger, but that's what trigger fingers did.

"We'll do this my way this time," James said. "Follow my instructions, without deviation, and we'll wrap this up in thirty minutes. I've got something you're going to want to see. Afterwards."

"Are you trying to bribe me? That's not going to work. I'm calling the shots. You." I motioned toward Bobby. "Go back down the corridor about ten yards to where there's the fork. You'll find Michael in a room nearby. He's okay, but he'll need patching up."

"Alright," Bobby backed off. "Here." He pushed the cart toward me. "In case you need it." He turned and hobbled down the hallway.

"That was really nice. Thank you." I meant it. He'd been trying to help all along, and I'd not given him a chance. Which is what I could say about the man standing in front of me as well. I turned to James. If I was able to squeeze out an apology, I was just as able to team up with him to help Michael. "Okay, there's another fork ahead. You go straight. I'll take the left."

"Did anyone call the cops?"

"They should be upstairs by now, taking care of Loretta."

"Finally. Let's finish this job."

I led the way down the corridor. No sign of Ian or Squalley. No sign of anything other than a mouse pausing on its hind legs to contemplate our presence. I careened to the old section of the sub-basement with the leaky walls and sticky air. The temperature grew dizzyingly warm.

I stopped to survey the environment. I hadn't trekked this way before. I peered down the gnarly passage on my right. "This is where we part ways," I told James.

"We'll do this together," he said.

"It'll take longer. They could escape." I checked my phone. I un-muted it and turned to James. "Text me if you find anything. And I'll do the same."

I hung a right down the narrow corridor. The air grew light and cooler; the smell of chlorine stung my nostrils. I passed doors on both sides, civilized looking doors with paint and plaques that read *X-ray Lab* and *Archives*. I tried every knob. Each one was locked. I'd reached a dead end. "I'm so tired of this," I said. My arm hurt, my body ached, my head throbbed. I was tired of chasing, tired of running, just plain tired.

*You can't be tired, angel. You have enough energy in your body to light up the city of Chicago for three days. Remember?*

There was the voice of a mostly absent father who'd cared more for his investigative work than he did for his wife and daughter.

"I can't hear you," I said, and clapped my hands over my ears.

I leaned against the wall and blew back wisps of hair dangling over my eyes. I pulled out my phone to text James and noticed a part of the floor glowed, filtering light out from a gap beneath a door. I moved in closer. The sign on the door read *Glass Blowing Lab*. I pressed an ear to the wood. Voices droned over the whirr of a fan. Familiar voices. Belonging to Ian and Squalley. I turned the knob and gritted my teeth. Locked.

I examined the knob. It was a knob lock, old like the door, which meant low security. I had just the tool. I rummaged around my backpack and found my wallet. The voices inside grew louder. They were arguing. I pulled out a credit card and inserted it between the frame and the lock. I slid it down and heard a click. I turned the knob and edged in, gun drawn. Ian was tied to a wooden chair at the opposite end. Before I could budge, I was tackled and knocked back against the wall. I slipped to the floor.

"Ow!" On a scale of one to ten, my back pain broke the scale.

"Inside voices." Squalley leaned over me. He carried a black briefcase and gripped a revolver over my head. A revolver that was about to smack my crown.

I rolled aside. His hand banged against the wall. It was his turn to yell. I leapt to my feet. My gun lay behind Squalley. "What's in the case?"

Squalley was panting, an odd smile pasted to his thin lips. "All I need to become a rich man. My patents."

"What about me, bucko?" Ian shouted from his corner of the sterile room. His ankles were tied to the chair legs and his arms pushed behind him through the slats. He was trying to stand with the chair on his back. "We were partners on some of those."

"You're more of a liability than an asset to me now, big buddy. I'm going to Mexico by myself."

"Mexico?" I asked. Michael and I had been right.

"Yeah, I've been after Ian for months to get his passport in order, but he didn't, so I'm going alone. Love the guy like a brother, but he's a slacker. " He turned back to Ian. "Be happy I didn't kill you." Squalley turned back to me, gun raised. "Like I'm gonna kill her."

## Chapter 42

### Holy Intervention

Squalley raised his gun. Could I tackle him before he pulled the trigger?

"You're crashing my party for the last time." His lips curled in a wicked grin. "Any final wishes?"

"Why do you ask?"

"I'm not heartless, you know. I'm just a pragmatist. And it would not be practical if you roamed freely while I made my escape." He circled the gun around. "You got anything you want me to say to anybody? After you're gone?"

"That is so thoughtful of you." Stalling was the name of the game. "I've never had anyone who's pointed a gun at my chest ask me that before."

"That's what they do with firing squads. I'm kinda like a one man firing squad here."

"Don't, Squalley!" Ian said and fixed his gaze on me. "He wouldn't have done it if that loud mouth girl didn't keep throwing money at him."

"Did you say something, Ian?" Squalley cupped his ear with his free hand. "I can't hear you." He turned back to me. "He don't know anything. He's been waiting years to get into LA Tech as a student. And where is he now? Still the lowly worm chewing his way through this crab apple." Squalley squarely pointed the gun at my head. "Meanwhile, who's got the patents? I do."

"Bobby's outside with the rest of your patents," I said.

"I got what I need. You got thirty seconds."

"You're timing me? That's so insensitive. You grant me a last wish and then tell me to hurry? No firing squad would behave in such an unholy fashion."

"Twenty-two seconds."

"You were Darth Vader."

"Love that guy. He's so vibrant and compelling."

"And somewhat misunderstood," Ian added.

"Fifteen seconds," Squalley said to me.

"Can you press the pause button for a moment?" I asked. "I've got more questions."

Squalley's tongue circled his cheek. "Okay, I'll grant you one minute."

"How did you know I was in the sub-basement?"

"You underestimated me, kiddo. That's everyone's mistake." He waved his gun at the ceiling. "Any time an exterior door opens, I hear a beep on this thing." He reached into a pocket and pulled out a small black device resembling a pager. "I rigged the doors myself. And, I have another one that works any time anyone comes down the elevator. I saw you go into the room. Who'd you think setup that laptop? I own this sub-basement. Nothing gets past me. I know all the shortcuts too. That's how I shot Michael Parris tonight and got back here in no time flat. Figured it would hold you back, but it didn't. Not too smart of you to track me down, was it?"

"And let you get away? I don't think so."

"Uh, who's holding the gun here?"

"Why didn't you shoot me instead of Michael?"

"Figured you'd shoot back. This way he distracted you. Fifteen seconds."

"Did you and Loretta plan this whole thing?"

"She came to me with a proposal. She was after my knowledge of the inner workings of this campus. And my brute strength to move and store the lug. Which I did not give away freely. I needed the dough."

"She was behind it all. That means you could get off easy."

"Then what? Return to my old job? I'm done here and so are you."

"Okay." I took a deep breath. "About Michael…"

A figure stood in the shadows behind Squalley. Just outside the doorframe. A dark figure with a gun pointed at Squalley's back. James had found me.

"Tell him that I…"

The figure stepped out of the shadows, arms stretched out, hands clutching a long nosed pistol. My heart skipped a beat. It wasn't James. It was—

An angry puff of powerful air blasted Squalley between the shoulders. It wasn't the air-splitting crack from a regular pistol. Squalley arched his back and swayed. The shooter scrambled up to him and crashed the butt of his gun over Squalley's skull.

"Ow." Squalley rubbed his crown. "That hurt like the dickens."

I hurried forward, grabbed the gun, and slammed Squalley harder on top of his head. He groaned and crumpled onto his stomach. His pistol hit the ground. I looked up at the gunman. "Michael 2.0."

A wide grin filled the lower half of his face. "All this time I've avoided carrying a gun because of the terrible, possible side-effects, like shooting someone, or myself. But I don't mind using that." He pointed to the gun in my hand.

I examined Michael's weapon. "What kind of—"

"A tranquilizer gun. I found it on eBay. In case you needed backup. Not that you do…"

"I would have been toast if you hadn't arrived."

"You would have figured a way out of this jam, like you always do. But I hurried things along, didn't I?" He wiped his forehead with the back of his hand.

"Is he dead?" Ian asked.

"No," Michael and I said simultaneously.

"That's a relief. He owes me fifty bucks."

My fingertips touched Michael's shoulder. Gray duct tape secured a large piece of gauze against the top. "That's some fancy first aid."

"Bobby got me the duct tape. I patched myself up. Rambo style. Almost." Michael turned sideways. "Luckily, it's my left arm."

A low moan seeped out of Squalley.

"We'd better cuff him," Michael said.

I reached into my backpack and withdrew an empty hand. "I'm fresh out of cuffs."

"I'll go back for the tape."

"Hey, guys," Ian said. "Did you say something about cuffs?"

We peered at Ian.

Ian tilted the chair to show the hands secured behind him. "Jack has the key." He flicked his chin to a spot behind us.

Michael and I flipped around. Wall slots held dozens of glass tubes in all sizes. A long table rested near the back wall with drawers like those found in a library card catalog. A white skull tipped its head back in one corner of the table. Between the teeth sat a small key. I reached in and grabbed it.

"Why should we trust you?" I asked Ian.

"Because I'm not like Squalley. Or Loretta."

"Since when?"

"Since the beginning. Well, almost the beginning, but especially since I found Squalley dressed up as Darth Vader. He could have killed you. I convinced him not to. Big Mac wasn't supposed to die. He was supposed to be kidnapped and maybe slapped around a little. He deserved it, you know. All we wanted were our patents. He'd convinced us he was keeping them safe. When we asked to get them back, he laughed. He said they belonged to the school. But you gotta believe me, murder was not an option. I'll testify against Squalley. I'll testify against Loretta too."

Michael moved toward Ian. "I want to believe you."

"Maybe you'll believe him." Ian's eyes flew past us.

We turned. Squalley stood in the doorway, gun aimed my way.

"Oh boy," I said. Sleep deprivation and pain made me forget to grab his gun.

"This is getting old. Now I've got a massive headache, thanks to you two," he said. "No more interference."

Michael jumped in front of me. "You'll have to shoot me first."

"I shoot you, I shoot her, go out for a late snack, I'm thinking a couple of soft pretzels, and head down to Mexico. *Ciao*."

"MacTavish!" I pointed to the entryway.

"I'm not falling for that crap," Squalley said.

"I thought he was dead." Ian's mouth dropped open, his small eyes popped toward the doorway.

Squalley turned, and I lunged past Michael. I wrapped my arms around Squalley's waist, body slamming him to the ground. All air left my lungs. Squalley hit the floor hard, his gun clanging to the ground. Michael grabbed the gun and emptied the barrel. Bullets clattered to the floor. I jumped to my feet.

Squalley, panting heavily, rose to his knees. "What do you people take me for? A twenty-five-year old? Jesus H. Christ. I'm pushing sixty." He turned and sat on his rear. "I knew I should have taken early retirement. You." Squalley pointed to Ian. "You turned on me."

"Tell them, Squalley," Ian said. "Tell them I had nothing to do with killing Big Mac."

"Okay." Squalley grabbed the table and hoisted himself to his feet. "He's on the up and up. He tried to convince me not to go after the president, but what can I say? I gotta mind of my own. He's a good man. Ian, you're the kind of guy I'd want my daughter to bring home, if you were Italian, had clean fingernails, and I had a daughter." He flailed his arms and charged forward. I pushed Michael off to the side and dove out of the way. Squalley crashed into Ian, knocking him to the floor. The wooden chair holding Ian cracked in two. The ropes gave way and Ian stood, hands still cuffed behind him. He took a swing at Squalley with a chair leg. Ian's aim was true. Squalley hit the floor, pinned down by Ian's knee.

"You should never have listened to that foul-mouthed school girl," Ian said.

"You kidding me? Her sixty G's are gonna hold me over 'til I sell these patents. Let me up."

"No."

"Come on, Ian. You know I'll cut you in."

"He knows you won't," I said. I threw a look at Ian. "Did you help them drag Big Mac to the secret room?"

"Wasn't me," Ian said. "That's the truth, cross my heart and hope not to die."

"No one will believe you. And you'll still get in trouble for transporting Archie to the sanctuary," Squalley said to him. "You're better off coming to Mexico with me."

"I only learned she stabbed Big Mac after I caught Squalley shooting you with truth serum." He pushed his knee down harder. "Tell them, Squalley."

Squalley moaned and squeezed out: "Lawyer."

Ian looked at us. "You can help me, right?"

Men in black burst into the room followed by James and Bobby.

"You missed the fireworks," I said to James.

"I can see that." He turned to Michael. "You okay, bro?"

Michael nodded. "I'm great. Greater than great. I've only got a flesh wound, I didn't kill anyone, and we solved Mac's murder."

"Sounds like the close of a perfect weekend." James grinned and moved over to the cops circling Ian and Squalley.

Michael inched closer to me. "About before. I wasn't sure if, well, if you really meant, or if you were just—"

"Later, Michael. Neither of us was thinking clearly." That part was true, but the next part wasn't. "I can't even remember past two minutes ago."

Michael lifted his arm and turned stiff as a surfboard. "Ouch. I have a very low threshold for pain. But you already know that." He reached his good arm over and flung it around my shoulders. "And just about anything else there is to know about me. Maybe I can help you remember what you said."

Out of the corner of my eye, I spied James leaning against the wall. He was listening to the cops, but watching us. An officer walked up to Michael.

"Let's get your shoulder looked at," he said. "Step outside, please." He turned to me. "You too, miss."

We followed him into the hallway.

"A paramedic'll be here shortly," he said and returned to the room.

"Thanks," Michael called after him and turned to me. "You should know—"

"Michael." A voice that belonged to a camel waltzed between us, heavy, lumbering and breathy. Alyce pinned Michael beneath her smudgy eyes. The usual cigarette dangled between her lips.

"What are you doing here?" I asked her.

"I'm the only senior faculty member on campus. They need me to oversee this emergency situation." She turned to Michael. "Now that Mac's dead, I'll make sure you're promoted to associate dean."

"You mean co-associate dean, don't you?" Michael asked.

"No, I don't. Turns out the department dean is going out on paternity leave. Loretta got that part right, anyway. I'm the only logical choice to be interim dean. I wasn't formally demoted, but you were. I'll be taking over. You'll back me, of course."

"Of course." I stepped up. "He won't."

She settled her withering gaze on me. "I don't know who you really are, but I do know you're no student."

"Took you long enough," I said.

"Why would I back you?" Michael asked her.

"Because if you don't, your demotion goes forward. I will personally oversee your transition to junior faculty advisor. And once you're there, you'll be stuck. You'll find mud is a lot thicker than water."

"In one weekend, I was demoted, found the body of my very dead boss before it disappeared, and was wounded while tailing a killer." Michael's hands balled into fists. "You think I'm going to stand by and let you intimidate me into submission? Just like that?"

"I do."

My eyes rolled over the lanky Alyce and stopped at the hem of her pants. "I have a question." The police had Squalley handcuffed and were questioning Ian. But there was still a missing piece of the puzzle. "Where's Leo, Alyce?"

"How would I know?"

"Because you have him," I said.

"I have no interest in that creature."

"You kidnapped him to use as leverage against Michael."

"She did?" Michael faced Alyce.

"You were behind the demotion. You led Big Mac to believe Michael took Leo when it was you," I said. "It paved the way for you to be sole associate dean and under consideration for a higher position. Big Mac blamed Michael for Leo's disappearance. Which was exactly what you wanted."

"I'm not interested in your vivid imagination."

"I'm not imagining the dog hair on your slacks."

James had moved in and knelt close to Alyce. "Michael, can you ID this fur?"

Michael knelt next to him. "I'd recognize that corkscrew hair anywhere. It belongs on Leo."

"Shemway," James yelled over to Bobby. "Get over here."

Bobby left the cops and shuffled over. "What now?"

"She's got the missing mutt."

"I do not." Alyce lifted her chin.

Bobby pulled out his baton. "She's got a face that belongs in a line-up."

"I should have fired your butt ages ago." Alyce turned to leave. James blocked the hallway.

Bobby tapped the end of the baton onto his palm. "I may finally have a chance to use this thing. Come with me."

"I'm not going anywhere. You've no proof other than a few strands on my pants, left over from my playing with Leo a few days ago."

"She's right, we don't," Michael said, shoulders drooping.

"You're finally talking sense, Michael." She turned her horsey face to him. "But it's too late. I gave you a chance, and you refused it. I also showed you who the smarter of us is. Your demotion is still on."

And yet, she'd left dog hair stuck to her pants. "Wait," I said.

Alyce turned to face me. "This show is over." She flipped back a stray blonde lock with a red fingernail. "Ta ta."

"I forgot something." I had one final trick left in my almost empty pockets.

Alyce flashed me a sharp look. "No more juvenile delinquent games."

"I forgot to compliment you." I was willing to bet she couldn't pass by a compliment.

She stopped and pivoted to face me. "Okay, I'll take the bait."

"That is a fabulous purse you're carrying."

Her eyes dropped to the oversize handbag at her shoulder. "Thanks."

"It's so elegant and…roomy," I said. "Perfect for sneaking snacks into movies—"

"More like a propane grill and five pounds of burger meat," Bobby said.

"You could even carry a few pairs of shoes in there…" I edged closer, "…and a small animal."

Together with Michael, James, and Bobby, we formed a loose circle around the woman. She clutched her oversized handbag.

"What have you got in there?" I asked.

"Move aside." Alyce barely took a step when we heard a low growl. She froze.

"What was that?" Michael asked.

"That's what I heard in Big Mac's secret room," I said.

Alyce plunged past Bobby and made a run for it. She collided with Veera who stood in the hallway. Veera held her ground. Alyce landed on her butt.

"Watch where you're going," Veera said.

"Idiot!" Alyce's purse had dropped to the floor.

All eyes were glued to a large lump moving inside the handbag. Out scampered a small, white, furry creature on four wobbly legs. Big brown eyes stared up at me through a mass of short, curly hair.

"She did have him," Bobby said.

The round black nose sniffed the air, before swaying toward Alyce. He gave out a high-pitched bark.

"What's that, boy?" Michael crouched next to Leo. "This big bad lady took you from the president's office, hid you in her purse, and pinned the blame on me?"

"Grand theft canine," James said. "Get rid of her, Shemway."

"You mean like tie her up and throw her into a dark alley or give her to the police?" asked Bobby.

"What do you think?" James asked.

"I did what was best for this school. And Leo. I kept the dog sedated and with me all the time. To protect him and make sure he was safe. Just temporarily until I had things squared away. Mac was no more fit for running this college than he was of taking care of a dog." Alyce shoved a hand on her hip. She turned to Michael. "You know that's true."

"No, Alyce, I don't." Michael took a step toward her. "I do know that I need to go home and get my rest since I'll have a busy week ahead of me. And you'll be where? In custody at county jail."

"This way." Bobby took her arm.

"Don't think I'm going quietly. I'll be the head of the department. You'll see."

"Not if Leo and I have anything to say about it," Michael shouted after her.

"I'll make sure Leo's taken care of." Veera picked him up. "Animal lover that I am." She scooped him up.

"I'll let the cops know," James said and returned to the room.

Michael turned to me. "This has been the most amazing night. I helped you capture a killer with my own weapon, even if it was a tranq gun, and avoided getting myself arrested for murder and getting my best friends arrested as accessories after tampering with a crime scene. Ouch." He held his arm. "Who'd have thought?"

"Isn't that what weekends are for?" I asked.

Nearly two hours later, Michael was formally treated for the abrasion on his arm, patched up properly, and released. I was given a strong dose of aspirin for my aches and pains, and a hefty dose of back patting. We gave our statements and were ready to finally leave LA Tech and head home.

"Gee, Corrie, I can't believe this nightmare is over," Michael said after we stepped into the fresh air. He ran a hand through his hair. "I'm dripping with sweat, but mostly with gratitude. If it weren't for you and James and Veera, I'd be the one arrested for murder."

"Never would have happened."

"Involuntary manslaughter?"

"You didn't lay a hand on him."

"But I threw my resignation letter at him. Is it assault when you throw paper at a guy you didn't know was dead?"

"Glad it's all behind us."

"But, there is something else." Michael stopped and took my hand. "What you said before...I want to say...I've seen the way you look at him, and if that's what you want—"

"Look at who?"

"Wait up." James jogged behind us. "I want to show you something." He lifted his phone screen toward me. Michael peered over my shoulder.

"What's this?" I asked.

A gray hued video played against the street noise of car engines and horns. The camera aimed downward across a portion of an asphalt parking lot. A single story building with white stucco and a blue awning was the target. Yoko's lab. Seconds later, the silhouette of a man poked through the gray. He stepped from around the corner of the structure and took long strides toward the entry. The slight stoop of his shoulders made me catch my breath. He hunched over and played with the doorknob. In seconds, he'd slipped inside, and shut the door behind him.

"Is that—" My heartbeat quickened. I wanted to say I recognized him, but did I? There wasn't much to recognize. The guy wore a black beanie, bomber jacket, and jeans.

"Thought you'd want to know," James said. "Could be anyone."

"Your dad never dressed like that," Michael said. "And this guy wasn't wearing glasses."

Dad never left home without his wire rimmed spectacles and white leather jacket.

"Unless he thought he was being watched," I said.

"I placed the camera in a tree at the edge of the parking lot a few hours ago," James said. "He wouldn't have expected it."

"You did that for me?" My mouth went dry.

"I said I would."

"Maybe," I said, forcing saliva down my throat, "now that everyone thinks he's dead, he's become a master of disguise."

"I'm showing you to prove it's not him."

"You don't know that." My pulse quickened. "Who else could break into a facility so quickly?"

"How do you know he didn't use a key?"

I didn't.

"Watch the hand gestures." James replayed the tape. "He stuck a key in the door."

"Maybe the lab gave him a key."

"Now watch this." James forwarded the tape. The man stepped out, closed the door, paused to tie a black sneaker, and disappeared around the corner. "What does this tell you?"

"That he's familiar with the lab, felt comfortable going in the middle of the night, was in no rush, and dressed in head-to-toe black so I couldn't ID his hair." Dad's longish, silvery hair would be obvious, even at night.

"Maybe it's just an employee," Michael offered. "Or Yoko's dad."

I shifted my weight to my other foot. My brain ticked so slowly, it was about to stop completely. I blew out a sigh. "You're right. There's nothing there to make me believe it's him."

"The lab tech lied to you," James said. "Just like we thought."

I turned to James. "Must be my karma. Lying to a liar." I took a step closer. "James...I want to say...thank you. And also...I need to say this again...I'm sorry. Sorry for tripping you up when all you've been doing was trying to help."

His stony green stare softened. "You're welcome."

"I couldn't have asked for a better ending," Michael said to me and turned to James. "Thanks again, bro. I'd do anything for you. You know it."

Michael and James shared a homie handshake and leaned in for a quick, back-pat-hug. James retreated back into the building with the cops. Michael guided me down the walkway.

"Corrie, I see our future and it's bright. Dazzling, in fact. We'll need to wear shades most of the time."

"I've got a sweet pair of Ray-Bans."

"All paths are open," Michael said. "We'll take this one for starters."

We turned onto a concrete path that led to the parking lot. The cool air put a spring in our steps. I filled my lungs with the sweet scent of jasmine.

"We'll make a fresh start," Michael said. "A clean slate."

"You mean like we've never met?"

"Well, not like total strangers."

"We'll get to know each other all over again."

"That's it. We'll get to know each other, but in a whole different way. You've been trying to shed this PI work for way too long. Then there I go with a missing body. Poor Mac."

"If you hadn't found him, Loretta could have escaped."

"I didn't think of that. Not that I'm able to think much of anything lately. Except this." He stopped and faced me. "Starting now, I'm going to help you kick the habit for keeps," Michael told me. "No more breaking and entering. Except at your mom's. She wouldn't have you arrested, would she?"

"She's never actually pressed charges."

"No more questioning suspects or hiding in bushes. No more weapons unless there's a zombie apocalypse. And if that should happen, I've got a cordless chainsaw you can borrow. Ouch." Michael withdrew his arm.

"I can't imagine life without cases to crack. That sounds...peaceful. Think of all the spare time I'll have. Maybe I'll take up fly fishing."

"That's the spirit. And if it gets too peaceful—"

"Oh, it'll never get too peaceful for me." I slowed my steps, my breath, my thoughts. I was in no rush to go anywhere. Yes, life would be different. And Michael and me? Like Michael said. All paths were open.

"Corrie, what I was trying to say before—"

"Bunny ears!" I put on the brakes.

"Rabbits? Around here?"

"He tied his shoes by making bunny ears. I knew it. Come on." I raced across campus, Michael at my heels.

"The rabbits wore shoes? This is worse than I thought."

"Hurry." I scrambled toward my car.

"Is this part of being peaceful?"

I stopped. "Dad made two bunny ears whenever he tied his shoes. Most men don't do that."

"Uh, I tie my shoes the same way."

"It was him, I know it. You up for a new case?"

He checked his watch. "I guess four minutes of peace was long enough. I'm ready."

"I knew you would be."

⚜ ⚜ ⚜

## ACKNOWLEDGEMENTS

With tremendous gratitude to each of the four talented points of my compass:

North:  Alicia Dean
South:  Kim Pendleton
East:  Ramona DeFelice Long
West:  The brilliant editing team of Verena Rose and Shawn Reilly Simmons.

More heavy-duty gratitude to:

- All the kind librarians, booksellers, and fellow writers I've had the pleasure to meet;
- The incredibly supportive Santa Barbara legal community. Too many to possibly name, but special mention goes to Marilyn and Naomi;
- All my wonderful friends, readers and reviewers; and
- The very supportive Parsa posse, the three extraordinary men in my life and my almost twin sister.

**Lida Sideris** is an author, lawyer and all around book enthusiast. She was one of two national recipients of the Helen McCloy Mystery Writers of America scholarship for her first novel, *Murder and Other Unnatural Disasters*. Like her heroine, Lida worked as an entertainment attorney in a movie studio. Unlike her heroine, she keeps her distance from homicides. To learn more about Lida, please visit her website: www.LidaSideris.com